MAN OUT OF TIME

MICHAEL HOGAN

MAN OUT OF TIME

DELTA TRADE PAPERBACKS

MAN OUT OF TIME
A Delta Book

PUBLISHING HISTORY
Delta trade paperback edition / October 2003

Published by
Bantam Dell
A Division of Random House, Inc.
New York, New York

Library of Congress Cataloging in Publication Data

Hogan, Michael, 1950–
Man out of time / Michael Hogan
p. cm.
ISBN 0-385-33693-4
I. Title.
PS3608.O4826M36 2003
813'.6—dc21
2003043557

Manufactured in the United States of America
Published simultaneously in Canada

RRH   10   9   8   7   6   5   4   3   2   1

To Lisa

MAN OUT OF TIME

MAO-KID

Mary's supposed to meet Eddy and me at the bar by seven o'clock, so when I see her come through the door I know it's her even though she's changed her hair again. She's with her friend Jeanne from the West Side who wears ankle-length dresses and thinks she's some kind of Earth Mother type. Jeanne's always talking about women and their rights and the Wicca cult she belongs to somewhere north of Westchester, and I figure Jeanne must have heavy legs because I've seen a lot of women go "Earth Mother" because of their legs. Mary's told me that Jeanne is a rare and special person, a "diamond in the rough," a font of wisdom and arcane information, untainted by anything as pedestrian as attending school or gaining professional certification. Mary doesn't come right out and say it, but she's taken up Jeanne because a small part of Mary reserves room for the exotic, and a large part of Mary patrols the outer borders of herself through the lives of those who appear to live there.

"We did it," Mary says, making her way through the happy-hour crowd, snapping her fingers over her head with a move that is vaguely Continental and somewhat out of place. I'm not sure what she means when she says, "We did it," though after she starts in on Eddy about the tax question on Tuesday (which I didn't even know was a tax question), it's clear she's talking about law school and graduation and how we, meaning Mary, Eddy, and I, had somehow gotten through the bar exam.

"You can't deduct those items on a state return," Eddy says, his voice loud with intent but thin with uncertainty, the two of them facing off on something ridiculous about credits and estates, while Jeanne just stands there trying to look enigmatic and poised and peaceful all at the same time. "And that's got nothing to do with the 'Rule Against Perpetuities,'" Mary says, and I wonder what it is about law students that compels them to test one another in their relentless quest for the simple certitude of being right.

Behind Jeanne, a few stools down the bar, there's a kid with a Mao hat with a red star above the bill. He's been on a jag for hours, saying he's one of the chosen few because he goes to Harvard, preaching to no one in particular about the proletariat and the working man and Labor's failure to give Management what it really deserves. He looks around for somebody to bother and I give him a don't-even-try-it look, but before I can ask Jeanne about the summer solstice and what really happens on the shortest night of the year, the Mao-kid's got his face over her shoulder and he's complaining about lawyers and how they're completely fucked, with their money and the way they screw society. I figure I might have to do something about this, nothing chivalrous, just the normal mind-your-own-business stuff, but Jeanne just stands there and listens to him as if she's not put off by it, all the time smiling her hippie-bliss smile as if the Mao-kid were some kind of noble and savage entertainment.

Later, after Eddy has the good sense to get us to the back room where we can sit in overstuffed leather booths and order from walk-about waitresses, Jeanne says people like the Mao-kid are just "young souls" who haven't been reincarnated more than a few times and that "old souls," meaning herself, of course, have a responsibility to lead them gently through experience. It's all such a crock that I look at Eddy with my eyes doing the 180-roll-around-the-ceiling thing, but Eddy likes this stuff about old souls and young souls, and he and Mary ask Jeanne what they are, and I wonder what's the big deal about having been around the block a couple of thousand times.

Mary orders another drink and doesn't hesitate or debate the big "yes" or "no," or whether she's going to have some sugar-laden, syrupy, doesn't-taste-like-liquor drink. Mary just orders gin straight up and straight out, because Mary always knows what she wants, whether it's a drink or something big, as in the "big picture," which for Mary is a very big picture, and which, at present, has little to do with men, since she's slotted a man for herself somewhere down the road, having carefully plotted exactly how she intends to proceed successfully along the treacherous path of life among adults.

Mary's going to work downtown in a big firm. That's what she's wanted to do forever because that's what her father does, and there's something in those muscular, hard-featured WASP girls that makes them want to be like their fathers. Mary says she'll gladly endure the forced camaraderie of late nights with bleary-eyed associates, driven by caffeine and ambition, for the prestige of being a young lion on the street—not to mention the perks of young boys who'll pick up and deliver her photocopies and bring around fresh coffee and sweets in the late afternoon. "Those are just some of the accoutrements," Mary says, and Mary wants all kinds of accoutrements, and being brilliant and having been raised the way she was raised, she'll probably get all of it and not give a damn about what the less-than-brilliant students used to say about her. They were the ones who called her hard and shallow because she made no excuses for her ambition, but just went her own way, distinguishing herself from the others, who, despite themselves, didn't know what they wanted, but out of fear, or insecurity, or some blind passion for growing up on time, acted cocksure and arrogant so as not to acknowledge their own insecurities concerning the prospects for their own driven futures. There were a lot of students like that in school. I'd say there was a floating constant of idiots, myself included, who were intermittently struck dumb by the chronic arrogance of apparent control—the constant itself comprising different people from time to time, particularly at semester's end when the number grades had the deleterious effect of knocking the underpinnings out from under many, who then, humbled and chastened, rationalized away the importance of professional success in favor of the "more important" things in life—things like an appreciation for art or nature or loved ones—pretending to be deep, even eccentric, because they'd been marginalized, driven to the outer rim of credibility, to the arena of quiet reflection, having slipped so badly along the fault line of uncertainty where existentialism and bad grades meet.

We order more drinks and listen to the Bobby Short look-alike try to sound like Nat King Cole, while Jeanne tells us about the power of the gems she carries in a small velvet pouch. Mary listens with the same unaffected interest she shows everybody, and I imagine Mary at work on her first day and how she'll know what to say when she greets lawyers and bosses in corridors filled with semi-important people.

Mary and I both made the *Law Review*. Everyone expected her to make it, and nobody expected me to make it. In fact, the gang I ran with the first year acted like I'd somehow betrayed them when I made it and they didn't. At first I was embarrassed by it, but then one day in the beginning of second year Professor Kohler, this nondescript little guy with huge glasses, called on me to brief some case I'd never seen before, and I fumbled over words that made no sense until I admitted that I was unprepared. Then Bob Bradley, who sat behind me, and who'd been a Green Beret, leaned over his desk and said something about "the kid on *Law Review*" not knowing his cases, clicking his tongue with that "tut-tut-tut" thing kids do when they're being real assholes. I just turned around and told him to fuck off. I said, "Fuck off, Bob Bradley," and Kohler heard me and looked at me, and I didn't even feel bad about it because I'd had enough of Bob Bradley's envy. It was about that time that Mary and I became friends. She said: "Don't let the bastards get you down," which is one of those WASP things WASPS say when they're calling on that stiff-upper-lip stuff.

Jeanne continues to tell us what her gems can do. She says that thousands of people are using them to change the world for the better. Eddy fingers a stone, and when the waitress comes by I ask her if she's heard about how people are going to change the world by using stones. The waitress looks at me like I'm crazy. She thinks I'm just another jerk customer who's drinking and saying stupid things. I want to tell her I wasn't kidding, that the girl with the round face and the Oriental dress is the one who's really crazy. But it's over so quickly with the waitress putting the glasses down and fingering the money that I can't explain myself, and I watch her walk away with her muscular legs and small body and Dutch-boy haircut. Then Eddy asks, "How do these gems do all this good stuff?" and Jeanne starts in on magnetic poles and higher consciousness and the secrets of the pyramids, and Mary just looks at me and whispers, "Isn't she a kick?"

Outside, in a foyer with a spiral staircase, kids no older than ourselves, dressed in tuxedos and gowns, climb the staircase to a ballroom from where I can hear the first sounds of music in the bass that rumbles over the ceiling and down the walls.

"Where are they going?" I ask, and Eddy tells me about

the private club the owners run upstairs for people with money and old names.

"Money," I say.

"New money," he says. "Only the names have to be old," and he places the gem he's holding in the small velvet pouch that's open on the table.

Eddy's a strange guy, but he's a good-looking guy, too. People say he looks like Fred Astaire, all pressed and clean, distinguished, a little older than his years, everything about him having been compacted, smoothed, and polished, if not by the passage of time, then by that kind of experience usu-ally reserved for the wealthy which makes them shine and cut figures as they age toward some imperishable beauty of self-justification. But there's a lot more to Eddy than the me-chanics of manners or style. He's a kind person, and he's not even rich. He's just a middle-class kid from New Jersey who wants to be a priest, and in two weeks he leaves for a semi-nary somewhere in Upstate New York where he'll live in an old Jesuit mansion with about thirty other men and do what-ever priests do when they live together. When I first met him, I asked him what he planned to do after graduation. I figured he'd work in some small family firm and handle the minor problems of wealthy widows with blue hair and black topcoats. But then he told me what he was going to do, and I coughed a few times and said, "Oh, yeah. Jesuits. I've heard of them." I didn't let on that I thought it was an unusual ca-reer move. Later he told me that I was the only person he'd told outside of his parents and his single old aunt who gave him money to enjoy himself. I asked him why he'd confided in me, and he said he'd done it because he wanted to get to know me. I said, "Well, then, let's get drunk," which we did that very day and most days since, he drinking his Manhattans and I drinking my Scotch; he never getting looped and I al-ways getting looped.

Eddy's a loner, although he used to hang around with a group who looked like the guys with precise diction and soft bodies who sang in their college glee club. He says he liked them, but not really, because they got together more for self-protection than for reasons of friendship, and that underneath their talk about opera and bridge there was a cynicism and a deep unhappiness. Eddy figured I was a loner, too, which is true as far as it goes, though not altogether true, since I've always wanted to belong to a group of friends in the same way that kids in high school want to belong to a clique. "Clicks and circles," I'd say, and it was the phonetic shorthand I used for the mitochondrial activity of social cells about which I and a few others floated freely, though not wholly free, our movements and sometimes our perceptions being necessarily affected in the shadows of envy of what others did without us.

The waitress comes again and, except for Jeanne, we order without any thought for the amount we're drinking. Jeanne has switched to tonic water, and she just sits there trying very hard not to look like some kind of personified indictment.

"I can't believe she didn't invite you," Mary says, and she's talking about Nicole Caravaggio's party, to which she and Eddy and just about everybody else had been invited, and which I crashed with a flourish of bad judgment.

"She was pissed," I say. "I figured it had to be some kind of oversight," and I say all of this knowing that popularity meant less to me than getting drunk.

"It was a terrible party," Mary says.

"Eddy ran me drinks out to the car on the half-hour," I say, because I left the party very soon after Nicole asked me to leave, a request to which I responded with some Scripture about the stone the builders rejected becoming the cornerstone. Bob Bradley, the former Green Beret, who'd never forgiven himself for not making the *Law Review*, helped Nicole get me out of her house, which wasn't a difficult thing to do since I didn't want a scene in which I'd end up looking worse than everybody else.

"We used to say he'd be the next senator from Missouri," Mary says about Bob Bradley, because Bob Bradley was older and from St. Louis and had that take-charge look of competence one imagines in Green Berets and senators.

"Well, there was no reason for Nicole to snub you," Mary says, though I knew there were reasons, because I'd said some things, and they were unkind things, and having said them I was an easy person for Nicole to hate.

By the spiral staircase, the Mao-kid's saying things to the fancy crowd ascending the steps to the ballroom upstairs. The maître d', who's just another one of those men in their fifties who grew up being told he looks like Humphrey Bogart, tries to usher the Mao-kid from the stairs, where the women look down on him as they continue to move with the economy of disdain, their hair shining perfectly under the light of the chandelier. The Mao-kid says something about the bastards who've screwed people all over the world so that other useless bastards can enjoy themselves in ballrooms, and I watch him, and I don't hate him as much as I hated him when he was bothering us. The maître d' motions for two bouncers to come and take him away, and two bullet-headed, cloudy-eyed musclemen knock off the Mao-kid's hat and start to toss him out. One says something about his uncle dying "in country" for the "likes of an asshole" like the Mao-kid. Then a handsome swell in a tux, escorting two perfect ladies, the three of them forming a triptych in homage to the fashion-god, recognizes the Mao-kid, vouches for him, and negotiates a departure that is better than the departure the Mao-kid had drawn for himself. The Mao-kid gets his hat back and leaves with some dignity. The bouncers pass by our booth on the way to the bar. One says, "Fuck Harvard," and the maître d' resumes his place, and the night continues on with the sound of the bass pounding recycled hits along the dance floor overhead.

Eddy says, "Here's to reality," meaning here's to what we've got to do no matter how hard we try to avoid it; and Mary says, "Here's to work," and Jeanne just smiles her wisdom smile, as if there's infinitely more to reality than what we've been talking about, and for the first time all night I think I agree with what I think she's thinking, and without saying a thing I just drink my drink like it's some kind of potion.

LABOR DAY

I'm lying in a hammock strung between two pine trees that shade the beach where Jeanne is waving to Mary on the raft in the water of the Sound about thirty yards offshore. Jeanne's saying something about the fire; it's a message from Mary's dad who can't find the lighter fluid. I turn a few inches to see over the hemp and canvas, and I watch the old man flap around the cookout utensils, overturning paper bags, lifting the benches and the picnic table. He's in a fury looking for that lighter fluid, and it's clear he's the type of person who's used to getting his way. Jeanne probably figured she could handle him, but Mary's the only person who can handle him, and after she cups her ear to hear what Jeanne has to say, she sees the old man and dives in the water for the swim back to land where she calms him down by producing the lighter fluid, which had been sitting under plates in the cooler. Jeanne walks over to the hammock and draws her hand over her hair as if to say she's just dodged a bullet with Mary's crazy father. I say that lawyers can be highstrung, and she takes her cool hand and wipes my forehead. I look at her in her bathing suit, and I see that she's not as large as I'd once suspected and that it doesn't matter because there's something about her, particularly in the way she cares for me when I'm hungover.

"How are you feeling?" she asks.

"Better," I say, and I ask her about William, who calls himself "B.J." on the weekends, and who seems out of place because he just met Mary at the firm where they started. It's clear William's not used to life at the beach, and Mary's family has made him so uneasy that he moves and talks with a microsecond delay of self-conscious hesitation, always assessing and correcting his behavior as if he were possessed of some internal gyroscope designed and implanted for the socially inept.

"He's news to me," Jeanne says as she waves her arm across the water. "I thought you were a swimmer."

"I was in high school."

"I hated high school," she says, and frowns as if she'd just recalled something unpleasant from her teenage years.

Jeanne works for a record company on the West Side. She started there during her third year at a Catholic girls' college in New Rochelle. She never finished college. The music business was too hot, and she went from being a receptionist to a producer's first assistant. I met her again one Friday night at the Blue Blazer on the East Side. She remembered me from the night with the Mao-kid. We talked, and she laughed at my jokes, and she wore large round wire-rim glasses that made her look Swedish. That night she invited me to her apartment, which she shared with a model from France who spent the summer in the Hamptons. The walls of her apartment were covered with record jackets. She made me tea, and we talked about everything, and I told her that I didn't want to be a lawyer, that I'd done it for all the wrong reasons, and that when I thought about spending years of my life in an office with other lawyers it made me sick inside. She didn't say anything, and I stayed at her place. I didn't sleep with her, though, and in the morning we went for breakfast, and there wasn't the heaviness that sometimes hangs over couples who want a divorce before the coffee comes with their toast and eggs.

Mrs. Bain walks down from the house they call "the Cabin," which is larger than most mansions in Westchester. She carries a pitcher of her iced tea, which is supposed to be famous. Mary's sister, Jennifer, had begged her mother to make it for the cookout, and when she begged it was with the phony, eyebrow-furrowed tone of the middle child invoking the call of mock duty, as if her mother's iced tea, made from a secret recipe of lemons and sugar, was one of the few truly important things left in the Western world. At first Mrs. Bain declined, saying, "No one really cares about my iced tea." But Jennifer kept at her, coaxing and pleading until the compliment was clear and sufficient. Then Mrs. Bain, with a tired, grudging tone, said she'd do it because there was just nothing else to be done, and Jennifer applauded, pretending to be relieved.

"They can be so ridiculous," Mary whispered as we watched her sister and her mother go through the elaborate dance; but I kept still, neither agreeing nor disagreeing, having learned from other experience that criticizing one's family is primarily a question of personal jurisdiction.

Mr. Bain lights the fire and circles the grill from time to time as if the wind, which had blown off the ocean all day, was about to change direction and whiten the other side of the small pyramid of briquettes sitting in the well of the Weber. William-call-me-B.J. stands nearby and says, "It's a good fire," and Mr. Bain, with his brown, wiry legs stuck in his oversize Docksiders, ignores him as he works furiously, moving back and forth, his skinny, muscular arms snapping one of his son's album covers across the briquettes to counteract the wind from the ocean. Then he replaces the top of the grill and the smoke curls upward in three delicate funnels. He checks the utensils again and looks at William as if he's seeing him for the first time. Mrs. Bain joins them and there's talk about Robert and Billy and their girlfriends sitting in the living room with the stereo blaring and how she wishes everyone would join in and help out.

"Mary, get your brothers down here," Mr. Bain says, and Mary, who knows how to ignore her father without upsetting him, says, "Sure, Dad," and joins us on the hammock.

"So what did Eddy's letter say?" she asks, and I pull it from my back pocket and hold it against the sun, causing a square of shade over my right eye.

"He says they made him some kind of 'prefect' or something because he's a little older than the others. He talks about the routine and what they do each day. It sounds pretty good. They do some classes, some meetings. Eddy spends a few hours each week at a nursing home."

"They don't just sit around and pray?" Mary asks, but she's not looking for an answer. She only asked the question to express her willful ignorance about things like Catholics and their seminaries. Mary's upset over what Eddy's done, and she's been uncharacteristically harsh about it. Last week she even said he was a "fool," and then wouldn't talk about it.

"I just never dreamed Eddy for that," she says, and she looks at me with a curious smile. "Maybe you," she says, "but not Eddy."

"Why me?" I ask.

"Because you like going to extremes."

"Everybody's got to find their own way," Jeanne says, and the comment is offered less for its wisdom than as an attempt to close a sticky subject.

"How come he didn't tell anybody?" Mary asks.

"He told me."

"Besides you."

"I don't know. I guess he just considered it a private thing."

Mr. Bain calls Mary again and she saunters off, moving slowly, her long legs shaking with each step, the shape of her large head against the sky outlined perfectly under the weight of her wet hair; and for a moment I see her clearly and how she will look when she is old.

"It is a little strange," Jeanne says.

"We all do strange things. It's just that what Eddy's done kind of scares people, too."

"Maybe," she says, and the smell of the burgers on the grill fills the air as Mr. Bain orders his sons to do something with the chaos of boxes sprawled about the picnic table. William sits off to the side and strums his guitar, and I close my eyes as another wave of nausea starts again and rises and settles over my forehead in a band of sweat and dull pain.

"Is he going to play that thing?" Jeanne asks.

"I guess," I say without opening my eyes.

"Now that's scary," she says, and I remember how Mary had introduced William-call-me-B.J. as the best folksinger since Bob Dylan. William just stood there with his guitar, and we shook hands, and he was tall and thin and bone white, and his eyes doubled themselves and were made small and hard behind his glasses.

"How long you been playing?" I asked him, and he said since college, and I looked at the guitar case, which looked brand-new except for the stickers he'd placed there and a scrape or two he'd inflicted to make it look real or old or authentic.

Mary's sister, Jennifer, skips across the flat stones that make a path from the boathouse to the cookout area. She walks quickly. Her smile is broad and forced, but her eyes are flat and communicate nothing. It seems to be her job to appear as if everything is light and fun and perfect in the Bain family. But everything's not perfect in the Bain family. Mary's told me that. Mr. Bain is a hard man, a lunatic when he's upset, and at the moment, the fire under the grill is enough to set him off again, so that when he speaks to Mrs. Bain, who lives in a cloud of matronly respectability, his voice is hard and cutting.

Jennifer stands next to her mother and furrows her eyebrows again. She says, "Oh, Daddy. You know you're the only one who can handle that old grill," and it's the petulant, almost Southern voice that flatters and cajoles, only to disarm the threat of her father's anger.

Mary pushes her father aside and tells him to drink some iced tea as she flips the burgers. The sound of the fire glazing the patties of red meat is lost in the rustling of the leaves brushed by the wind off the ocean. The light has changed and the shadows are deeper and darker than the shadows of summer. September is one day old, and autumn has begun in the subtle changes of light and air as the sun moves in a lowered arc over the tops of the fir trees beyond the Cabin. My hangover recedes again, and soon I'll drink a beer and try to calm that other pain that comes with the anxiety I feel anticipating my first day at Westphall, Sellars & Jaynes.

"Look at this," Jeanne says, waving her arm across the area. "In ten years, after you become a partner and make a million dollars a year, you can have a place just like this, and won't that be nice."

The night is cool, and Jennifer has gone to the Cabin to get sweaters for herself and her mother. I've had three beers and the obligatory cup of Mrs. Bain's oversweetened iced tea. I complimented Mrs. Bain profusely and made sure that Mr. Bain heard the compliment. The two Bain boys have taken their girlfriends to a bar in the town five miles away. The boys are too wild for any of the other Bains to handle. Mr. Bain sits by himself on the overturned trunk of a huge tree overlooking the beach, where the water laps under the sound of the wind, and I wonder if he's feeling some disappointment that he can articulate only to himself.

"He does that every cookout," Mary says. "Sits there by himself, staring out at the ocean."

"Wonder what he's thinking?" I say.

"Law," Mary says. "That's all he ever thinks about. His firm and whatever's happening. Later he'll go in and stay up till two writing something on his legal pads."

"I couldn't do that," I say, and I feel a little inadequate for not wanting to do what has made Mr. Bain so successful.

Jennifer returns with her mother's sweater, and I notice that Mrs. Bain isn't sipping her iced tea but has discreetly poured some vodka in her plastic cup. I crack open another beer and watch William with his guitar as he spies a location near the fire and waits for everyone to join him and listen to the best folksinger since Bob Dylan. Then he begins to sing, and his voice is surprisingly strong and it fills the campsite with untrained volume. There are a few passages he does very well—melodies that fall on an expulsion of breath like a sigh sung against the backdrop of a minor chord. He knows he sings this well, and every one of his songs contains the passage or some variation of it. After his first song Mrs. Bain says, "Oh, isn't he good," and Mary says, "I told you, Mother," but by the third song the novelty has worn a little thin, and Jennifer asks him to play some songs everyone knows so that the entire group can sing along. Mary's just about had it with her sister, and from across the campsite, shaped by an octagon of logs placed end to end about a clear area of ash raked clean, William sings another song about something tragic that happened to him in the not-too-distant past.

Mr. Bain sits by the water looking out into the darkness as the night sky reveals stars overhead. After a while he gets up and passes us without a word and returns to the Cabin. He's gone to do his work for tomorrow morning, and I think how growing up means that some people still have homework.

I drink another beer, and it goes down easily and calms my nerves, which wrangled all day as I lay in the hammock like a zombie. It's only when I think about tomorrow morning, and how I'll have to wake up early, and how I'll probably be tired and still have to prepare a face of great enthusiasm, that I feel something like an electrified wire searching out and probing the tissue over my stomach.

I think: Perhaps if I had papers to review or files to organize, or memos to draft, perhaps if I had a briefcase containing documents pertaining to some project or assignment in which I was engaged and fluent, perhaps if I had some "homework" to do, then the anticipation of a job I don't feel up to wouldn't worry me so. But it's Labor Day, and there's nothing to do except to wait, to drink a few beers, to proceed through an evening of original folk songs and the sound of the ocean mild against the shore of the Sound.

I watch Mary sitting next to William. I listen to his voice break just so in every song. I take Jeanne's hand as she moves closer to me in the dark, perhaps wanting more affection than I'm willing to offer; and from time to time, I look past Jennifer and Mrs. Bain, and I search out the light in the window of the Cabin where Mr. Bain, with an alien and dry effort, does the rigorous work of details, which, like the mechanics of mathematics, can afford the beneficial effect of calming some very troubled minds.

RAY

R ay's my friend. At least that's what I tell myself when I have doubts about it, and I do have doubts about it. We hang around together. Some people say we look alike. We even wear the same kind of clothes, though I'm more certain about what's right to wear than he is, and he, being less certain, spends a lot of his time watching what I wear, because he's got it in his mind that I'm not the kind of person to make a big mistake in the fashion department. Somewhere along the line Ray must have made a big mistake in the fashion department and suffered some big embarrassment for making it because he's got an absolute fetish, not so much about wearing the right thing, as about not wearing the wrong thing. Ray is not a sensitive guy, but he is oversensitive to the notion that in New York City not making a big mistake is much more important than making some kind of big statement.

Ray, Mary, Eddy, and I all went to the same law school, but Ray graduated with honors one year ahead of us. Ray's a pretty smart guy. He's almost as smart as Mary, but he didn't go to Yale like Mary, and he's pissed because he got his B.A. at some small college outside of Syracuse that nobody's ever heard of. He's also pissed because he's insecure, and because he thinks that no matter where he goes or what he does he's going to be judged for the college he went to. I've even heard him lie about it, saying he went to Dartmouth when he figured the person he was talking to cared about things like schools and pedigree.

Ray's from Brooklyn, but he wants to be a snob. He wants to be one of those spoiled people with family money, because that'd mean his blood is somehow special, in the way that aristocrats deem unearned status to be superior to earned status because it hearkens all the way back to notions of royalty and the divine right of kings. It'd be easy to dismiss Ray as a complete phony, but I don't do that because I like him, and I like him because even though I hate to admit it, I think about things pretty much the same way he does. I might not want it as badly as he does, but I'm aware of wanting it, so that at the level of self-promotion where boys from the outside want to become boys on the inside, Ray and I know we see eye to eye. We just don't talk about it, because being shallow is not the flattering kind of thing we like to talk about.

Mary doesn't like Ray. She thinks he's obvious and a loser, and that I'd be better off not hanging around with him. But Mary's got funny tastes when it comes to guys. All I've got to do is look at William-call-me-B.J., and I know that.

Mary might not like what Eddy's done, running off to a Jesuit novitiate without a friendly good-bye, but she knows Eddy was a good influence on me, and she thinks Ray is a bad influence on me. I don't look at it that way, because neither one influences me in that I copy their conduct. They just provide different thresholds for the type of behavior they'll accept from me. With Eddy I can go out and get loaded and it'll never turn into a horror show, because he'll either stem the tide or get me off to a safe place. But with Ray it's different. Ray will just stand back and let the whole thing go, which is why, at times, I question whether he's a friend or not. Sometimes I think he eggs me on to do something stupid or silly so he'll have something to talk about, frothing up all this "living-legend" garbage about how wild I am, so that he'll look normal and stable by contrast. I never know where I stand with Ray. Most of the time I stand off to the side, and sometimes I stand right in the center. But I do know one thing from hanging around with him: Girls don't go for living legends; they go for the guys who hang around with living legends.

After the long ride in from Oyster Bay with the Labor Day traffic, Jeanne drops me at my apartment, and the last person I expect to meet is Ray; but there he is, walking out the front door of my apartment building. It's a quarter past midnight, and I duck to miss him, but it's too late because he sees us, and he puts on that wild grin of his, which means he's been out all day. He comes over to the car and puts his face right up to the window. He says he's been looking for me. Then he sees Jeanne, and although he's never met her, he knows who she is, and he's taken aback that I'm hanging out with a witch.

"You missed the party," he says, and I don't know what party he's talking about, even though it's not beyond him to talk about a party that never happened just so it doesn't look like he stayed home and did nothing on Labor Day. He gets in the back of the car and introduces himself to Jeanne, who wants him out of the car. I finesse the whole thing. I remind Jeanne about some appointment she has early in the morning and give her an excuse to leave. Then I get out and Ray gets out and I thank Jeanne for the great day we spent together. I don't mention Mary's party, because I know Ray would've wanted to go, and he'd be real upset if he knew for certain that Mary didn't want him there.

Jeanne starts the car, and Ray says something about the witch, and I don't answer because Jeanne's off, and we start down the street to the Mad Hatter, where everyone from Ray's imaginary party is ringing in the school year with drinks until closing.

I know I have to get up in the morning; I know going out at half past midnight before the first day of work is a stupid thing to do. I know I'm breaking all the rules about preparation and rest and all of that, but when it comes to Ray telling me about something happening someplace, there's nothing I can do. I've always worried about missing parties. I worry about missing things in general, and even when I know deep down nothing's going to happen, I convince myself that on any given night something good could happen. So when I walk into the Mad Hatter and see nobody except for a group of girls standing by themselves, I kid myself that the Scotch won't hurt because I'm doing what a young man prowling the town in the flush of his youth is supposed to do, is even expected to do, on the last night before he starts the first real job of his adult life.

"They'll be here in a minute," Ray says, stretching his neck, looking without appearing to look, checking the bar, checking the front door.

I ask him about his work, and it's a real question because he's been doing it for a year. He says it's a piece of cake once you learn the rules, which have nothing to do with practicing law and have everything to do with the way you look and the way you impress and all of that.

The girls at the end of the bar gather like birds, their heads bobbing back and forth as they stand in a small circle focusing their attention on the blonde who catches Ray's eye. Ray sees it, and he's hooked, and he knows the blonde's going to make her way down the bar to get his attention. I watch all of it, all the time keeping up the useless conversation, spoken in earnest, while neither Ray nor I acknowledge what's really going on. I catch another quick look at the girls and notice that not one of them is looking at me, except to look once and then to look at Ray. I blame it on my hair, which is growing thin in the back, while noting Ray's head of thick black hair. All the while I keep talking nonsense about money and law firms and girls we don't know, when Ray says: "The one thing you gotta make sure is you don't piss off some asshole who can hurt you," and he gives me this halfhearted advice about surviving in law firms as his eyes dart to the right and then back again.

I order another drink and step aside as the blonde who's been looking at Ray stands next to me. She's making her way to where Ray's standing, and Ray, who makes a fortune at White & Case, waits for me to buy him a drink. I order his drink, and the blonde looks over her shoulder and catches his eye. I feel myself tense up because I'm jealous, and the bartender knows her, or acts as if he knows her, and he treats me like shit even though I spend a fortune in the place; and in one of those subtle tectonic shifts of status that mark the ups and downs of the respective trajectories of young professionals who search the Upper East Side for something good in a city of large statements, I feel a faraway grinding along the edges of change.

I hand Ray his drink and the girl turns toward him. They speak for the first time, cutting me off, disregarding me, though I stand there as if I'm a part of it, as if I'm the one she wants to meet, the one to whom she'd like to introduce her friends. They continue their conversation, listing the essentials, establishing common ground, and I wait to hear Ray lie about his education. But the conversation turns away from that, and Ray continues to ignore me as if the person he'd waited for after a party that never happened is now the person he never should've waited for, and I'm like one of those rockets that fall off the space shuttle after it does its business, which is to get a huge bulky piece of metal past gravity so it can fly on its own.

I listen to them laugh about a person at White & Case. Ray says he knows him well. He says the person's famous for the night when he threw corncobs off a balcony of an apartment on the Upper West Side. She knows the story and they laugh, not because they've said anything funny, but because they've decided to like each other. After that everything is easy for Ray; the conversation is a cakewalk. I stand there like the invisible man with no voice, and I laugh along with the next thing they talk about, which isn't funny. But I laugh because laughter from the perimeter is the last refuge in the charade of contact, and I can hear my voice, and it's as dry and thin as paper in a dust storm. I know they want me to move on, but I don't have it in me to leave. I can't afford to let them know how desperate I feel, hanging on to the whole thing by the tenuous and febrile sound of forced laughter. I can't afford to think that Ray's a user who's used me for an entrée into a social scene he once thought was beyond him. Tonight Ray's out there on his own, and I want to disappear in a way that admits nothing, so I start to float above them like in those stories of people who die and float around the world and watch their dry empty bodies that look like clothes rolled up under covers. I float over the bar, looking down on the girls at the end of the bar, seeing each of them with the clarity of distance, noticing how their friend is the only good-looking one, and that they are the obligatory phalanx of almost-good-looking girls who, like pilot fish, hook themselves to truly good-looking girls so everyone will think by some power of association that they're just as good-looking as their friend. And they stand there, the lot of them, their tan faces frozen in the belief of the observable truth that good-looking people tend to hang around with good-looking people. And they like Ray, because it's OK to like Ray, and they ignore me, because it's OK to ignore me, knowing that to do otherwise would be a fatal step down the scale of their own measure, an admission to the world that they are just average girls and somehow mad with envy about it.

So I fly up through the ceiling and the stories overhead, where some Chinese guys are playing cards. I fly up through the third floor where two boys are sleeping together, and farther up, moving more quickly now, through a dark room where I can't see anything but hear the muffled moan of a woman turning in bed. Then I break through the roof, and despite the floors and the ceilings between me and the place where my lifeless body still stands, I can see myself standing there, not moving, not talking, almost paralyzed, emitting from time to time a small laugh, barely a sound, a squirrel's sound. Then, with the sound of Ray's hard, almost genuine laughter as he and the blonde with the eyes, wide-spaced and blue, leave the bar, I rise like a ghost all the way above Manhattan. I see its shape outlined in the millions of lights below, and I see how it looks exactly like the maps of Manhattan, and I think about the great cartographers of the Renaissance, and I wonder what it would be like to have some sense of perspective. Soon I'm above the five boroughs and Long Island Sound, and I can see where Mary is sleeping in a dot of light that is her window in the Cabin on the North Shore. Then I'm over the horizon like Alan Shepard looking down the Atlantic to Africa, where bits of low pressure peel off the Ivory Coast like great gobs of cotton over water, forming tropical waves that move westward over the ocean until they spin themselves into storms, whirling counterclockwise, hurricanes with the names of women, threatening the homes of simple people in lands many miles away. The stars begin to brush by my ears as if someone had decided to touch me. There is affection in the emptiness of space, and the darkness is warm, and I wonder why astronauts need the clothes they wear, and the laughter is rich and loving and large enough to make me wonder about nothing at all.

This happened when you were a kid:

You went to bed that night, but you couldn't sleep with the excitement you felt because the hurricane was headed for your house. The weatherman from the Hartford station had said that if the hurricane continued to go the way it was going it'd cross Long Island and Connecticut by midday the next day, and you knew there'd be a lot to do in the morning with your father, who had to get up for hurricanes and snowstorms.

The next morning you weren't certain whether it was the sound of your father in the bathroom, or the light from the hallway, or the sound of the wind banging the house that woke you, but when you woke up you heard and saw all of these things and you followed your father downstairs to the kitchen, where he'd placed his folders with bar graphs and typewritten pages and a clean pad and three sharp pencils on the kitchen table.

The phone rang and your father answered it. "It looks pretty bad," he said. "That's what the Waterbury station said. Doesn't look like it'll go out to sea now. Right, Jim. Litchfield's closed. Barkhamstead. Goshen. The others are just coming in. I guess we better close, too. Right, Jim. Right."

Then he hung up the phone and turned up the volume on the radio.

"Are you going to call off school?" you asked, and he

said that he was. He said it looked pretty bad, and schools were closing all over the state.

You listened to the radio. Mr. Walt was the morning DJ. He was an old guy, and the housewives loved him because he was funny and comfortable and gave the news without upsetting anybody. Mr. Walt started down the list of towns where they'd already shut down the schools. He repeated the names that your father had mentioned on the phone. All over the state there were other men who had the same job as your father, and they were up doing the same thing.

"Would you like some coffee, Dad?"

He nodded yes. He held the phone up to his ear, and he dialed a number with one hand and went through some papers with the other. The most important part was about to happen. Your father was calling the radio station. There was a special code that only he and Mr. Walt knew, and your father would say it very slowly, word for word, so that no impostor could call up and cancel the schools anytime he felt like it.

The water boiled in the kettle on the stove, and you poured it in a cup over the instant coffee. You handed it over and then poured another cup for yourself with a lot of cream and too much sugar that wouldn't dissolve. You put a slice of bread in the toaster, and the toast popped up. You sat at the other end of the table and chewed the warm bread and drank the hot coffee with your legs dangling from the chair.

Outside it was dark because the clouds were thick and dark, and the only light that filtered through was a dull, yellow light that made everything look deeper and somehow rounder than before. You felt something different when you looked outside because of the way the weather was, with the wind and the dark colors and the damp air that was warm and cold at the same time, and it was something like loneliness, though you weren't lonely. You were right there, sitting with your father, who was important because he could call off schools and because he and Mr. Walt had a special code. And it was good to be with him so early, just after dawn, because he was kinder than usual as he sat there with his folders and papers and pencils.

Your father finally got Mr. Walt on the phone. He had to wait because Mr. Walt was getting calls from all over. And then Mr. Walt picked up the phone and your father began.

"I am calling from my home at Forty-seven Prospect Street . . ." and he continued on. In a moment the schools would close, and except for the storm, it'd be over. You'd go upstairs and wash up and get dressed. Then you'd watch some TV, and later on, after the storm had died down, you'd do some errands. Your mother would send you to the store. Your father would make plans for the cleanup. Everything would go back to the way it was before the storm. It'd feel like a Christmas afternoon, and your father would be tired and cross. He'd yell about the mess in the yard, about the leaves and the sticks that were everywhere, and he'd blame you for what the hurricane had done. He'd complain how you never cleaned the yard right, and your mother would tell you what a disappointment you were because your father needed a son who could do lawn work.

You drank the sweet coffee and finished the toast. Your father hung up the phone and made some notations on a white piece of paper. Upstairs you could hear your mother's footsteps as she walked down the hall, and it was only after your father spoke your name a third time that you stopped daydreaming and turned away from the window and the yellow wind blowing under the trees and started up the stairs to start the day, waiting for a hurricane that'd blow over your house and leave everything a mess and pretty much the same.

ONE WALLENDA WALKING

The first sound is some nameless K number thing with the strings going *che che che* in rapid sixty-four strokes. It's music, and I wonder how Mozart got into my room.

The phone rings. I speak to somebody in the dream language of monosyllables, breathing yes and breathing no.

Fatigue settles in the bone, invades tissue and fat, pins my body to the mattress which continues to undulate like the sea. If the music stops the sea will grow calm. Maybe then I will walk on water.

I drank until closing, and when I walked home the sky was mottled with blue and, at the horizon, a line of rose clouds.

I'm late, and the best I can do is string together a few unconnected thoughts, like one of those skinny "the-plums-were-delicious" poems where each word has its own line, and the whole thing fails to resolve itself, leaving me to tease meanings from not-so-subtle sounds.

I'm very late, and it was Mary who called to make sure I was up. She said she'd call me at work, but I won't be there. If she were my boss, she'd fire me.

———

I turn and groan, and the sound I make is the sound made by a head of stone with acid in its stone breath—a morning sound—a veritable lark.

Finally, I am no longer asleep. Whatever moves I make mimic, then mock the whole notion of waking up. Everything hurts.

I step into the shower, and the hollow feeling in the center of my stomach makes the water feel colder than it really is. From reservoirs in Sullivan County it strikes the back of my head and sprays like a circular fan over my hair. My hair continues to fall and gathers like cobwebs on the surface of the milky water.

The woman in the apartment one wall away continues to play Mozart: violins, piano, bassoons, and trumpets. I want to kill her.

I dry myself and scrape away the beard. Soap falls in watery globs to the sink. The mirror clears, and I see myself. Then the phone rings and I rush to answer it. My feet are damp on the parquet floor. I leave tracks of water and reach out my hand to pick up the receiver. Then I stop. I don't want anyone to know I'm here. If I pick up the phone, my excuses will be gone. I won't be able to blame buses or cabs or traffic. I won't be able to act like it wasn't my fault, like it was some act of God or tragedy or something, anything, some unknown circumstance in which I played the innocent victim, just a bit player caught in something larger, a mistake, just one of those things: a door on the Number 2 line that wouldn't close, a crazy Pakistani cab driver who hit a traffic cop, a bus that struck another bus, an accident, any kind of accident, something I didn't cause. But if I pick up the phone and say "hello," then it's me. Then I'm the reason

why I'm late, then I'm the one who chose to drink until closing, long after Ray had left with Diane, and I had acted all
tough and hard, drinking doubles as long as the bartender
would pour them, spending my money. And the phone rings
seven, eight, nine times before it stops, before the silence
settles in the apartment with the mattress on the floor in the
alcove, the TV on the secretary's chair, and the afterglow of
one oboe walking like a dead Wallenda on a wire of unwanted sound.

I look at my clothes. The shirts are at the cleaners. I forgot to
pick them up, so I've got nothing pressed except an old shirt
wrapped in plastic. I had it pressed a year ago, but because
it's a cheap shirt made from cheap material I've not worn it. I
take it from the wrapper. There's a musty odor as I put it on.
It's a size too small around the neck, and it pinches as I try to
button it. I take the poplin suit from the hanger. It's not supposed to be worn after Labor Day (or is it Columbus Day?),
but I wear it because it's clean, and it's still hot outside as the
weather on some news update talked about summer temper-
atures in September and a trough of low pressure sitting off
the coast of Bermuda. I find the right tie, a muted red tie that
won't draw attention. I take a paper towel and rub my loafers.
I look in the mirror behind the closet door. I'm still young.
I'm still handsome. That's what I tell myself. I lean forward.
I put my face right up to the mirror. I check my eyes, but
with the dim morning light I can't tell if they're red or not.
My face is flushed, and the skin looks dry, and I remember
Ray walking out the door with Diane, and I remember how
good-looking she was and the way she put herself right up
under his arm.

The phone rings again. Whoever's been calling doesn't believe me when I tell them that I'm not here. How do they

know I'm lying? How do they know I'm here? Excuses won't work for them. I put a comb through my hair. I check to see if I have my keys and my wallet, and I open the door.

When I was a kid and nervous about something, I'd stop whatever I was doing, and without letting on in any way that I was doing it, I'd ask God for help, and I'd mean it, even during those times when I didn't think I believed in God, and I knew it would work. So as I turn the doorknob and look back across the room to see if I've forgotten anything, I pause, and get ready to say it—a prayer, a thought, anything. But then I don't say it because something in me won't admit that anything's wrong. So with the phone ringing and the apartment empty, I close the door behind me and wait for the elevator like it's nothing, like I'm ready to walk through anything.

DOGS WITHOUT HEADS

The receptionist doesn't know me. She calls ahead and sends me through a green door that separates the waiting room from the corridor where the partners have their offices lined up in order of importance. The decor is modern, sleek, New York, all money with clean, sharp angles and track lighting. There's the sound of keyboards clicking and the hum of printers and the bustle of attorneys and secretaries and paralegals charging the halls. It has the look of a campaign with purpose, and the lights seem bright after the waiting room, which was dark and green and comfortable.

A tall woman named Lois introduces herself. She tells me to follow her for processing. She says I missed the orientation session they held for the first-year associates. I walk behind her. She's older than she looks. She doesn't carry her height well. There's a lot of extraneous movement here, a persistent drift, and she makes up for all of it with her tight and forbidding face.

I start to explain about some trouble with the subway, and she asks which line. I stumble. I tell her the Number 4 line. She says she didn't hear anything about it on the radio, and I say it just happened, and I'm in deeper than I want to be with this subway excuse. She brings me to an office on another floor, which is empty except for a desk and a bookshelf. She hands me some papers for insurance and payroll information. I thank her profusely, too much, and she tells me to relax as if she knows that's what I need to do. I stand.

I say it's great to be here, but she's gone without a word and I'm sitting in a cubicle with papers and a ballpoint pen.

At first there's no sound, and then as time passes I hear the traffic and the voice of a girl who stands on Park Avenue and screams at people. I open my door and look down the corridor. I ask a secretary who's sitting there where I can get some coffee. She tells me about the coffee wagon that comes around mid-morning. She says I've missed it and that I'd have to go to the cafeteria in the basement, which isn't an easy thing to do because you have to know which elevator in the elevator bank goes to the floor below the ground floor. It's a long explanation, and she loses interest about halfway through. Then she asks if I'm one of the new associates. I say I am, and she returns to her typing. Lois is standing behind me. She looks at both of us. She asks if I've finished the forms. She says Larry Ackerman was supposed to show me around, but that he was called away to an emergency meeting with a Japanese client downtown. She says I'll just have to fend for myself for a day or two, and she tells me to follow her downstairs to the floor where many of the partners are. She brings me to the office that is directly under the first office I sat in. She says, "This will be your office." She says after I get settled Carol Schneider will see me about a research project. Again I thank her for her kindness and again she ignores me.

I open and close some drawers, getting a feel for the place. I play with the calendar sitting there, tearing off all the pages between June and September. I wonder who used the thing before June and where they are now.

The office is in the middle of all the action. There are people walking by. One partner who looks familiar starts calling for someone named Allen. I listen to them as they begin the incomprehensible language of credit agreements and letters of intent. Something should have been done that wasn't done, and with the soft sound of the secretaries clicking away on Chiclet-shaped keys, a quiet tension circulates through the corridor and seeps into my office.

I wonder what I should be doing. There's a legal pad and some pens on the desk. I date the day in the top right-hand corner. I stare at it. I rub my eyes. My head doesn't hurt as badly as when I first walked into the place, but there's something else going on as my system seeks to right itself. I have this feeling that if I move too quickly in any one direction, I'm going to trigger an enormous upheaval of pain, and I'm not sure whether it's that suspicion or my empty stomach that causes the false sense of fullness accompanying the mild nausea.

Outside my door another conversation begins quietly in hushed and conspiratorial tones. The partner who was looking for Allen was a man named Lester. He's gone now, but Allen's standing there with a woman. The woman asks, "What did Lester want with the letter?"

"He's crazy," Allen says. "He's pissed because ComTran said they were going to go for the fifty and Lester says they reneged and now he's trying to take my head off for having the letter prepared for fifty when he's—"

"I thought he said the letter agreement was bullshit and he didn't want them to have it."

"He did. But you know what it is. He hates Marty, and Marty and Mark just finished the Brooks-Bollo thing, and Marty's been critical of Lester and this looks bad. Now I got to run the whole agreement with the inserts, and Phil has tickets for the U.S. Open."

"Why don't you get one of the new people to proof it?"

"Is that who they are?"

"Who?"

"The new associates?"

A third person joins them. He's overweight and impeccably dressed. He has a high-pitched voice made strong by his weight.

"Did you see them?" he says. He's incredulous and superior. "Where does Warwick get these people?"

"I saw one," Allen says. "Maybe he's one of Abe's friends?"

"Didn't they hire back anybody from last summer?" the woman asks.

"I thought they hired Hanley, but I didn't see him this morning."

"Hanley," she says, trying to remember somebody.

"Well, the first thing they should do is advance them a week's salary and get somebody to take them over to Brooks and get them some decent clothes."

"C'mon," Allen says.

"Allen." A voice calls from down the corridor. It's Lester again. There's more trouble. I hear Allen say "Shit." The three disperse. None of them look in to see me, and I remove the stupid smile I'd prepared for them in case they had.

Outside my window the young woman on the corner of Park and Fifty-fourth continues to scream for charity. A secretary enters my office and asks my name and hands me a note. It's a telephone message from Eddy. He phoned to wish me well on my first day. I hold the note and try to dial out. It takes two times and one too many stupid mistakes. Finally it goes through and the receptionist for Herring & Green answers. I ask for Mary Bain, and when Mary answers she asks if I made it to work on time. I say no, and she coughs. It's the sound she makes to put an end to the conversation. She's busy. I tell her I think I'm ready to begin, but it doesn't mean a thing to her, and she hangs up the phone while talking to somebody in her office.

The September sun is unusually bright. The corridor is quiet. Most of the secretaries have left for lunch. I'm hungry, too, but I don't know if I should leave. I worry that if I leave they'll never know who I am or that I'm here. The phone rings again, and before I answer it I wonder how this is going to turn out, and the fact that I can't get comfortable at my desk isn't a particularly good sign.

They find me about three o'clock. There's a flurry of introductions, and some of them get my name right. They all say they'll be by to give me work. At least three of them say "Welcome aboard." The fat guy takes a long look at my tie, but when he sees my shoes he settles down. Allen's pretty distracted throughout the whole thing. The others come and go so quickly I don't get their names. Lester stands at the door. He's talking to Allen. Then the fat guy, whose name is Joe, introduces him. Lester's mood changes immediately. I think: This is a guy who's used to introductions. He takes my hand, and his body lets loose with about a million alpha waves smoothing the area with this enforced calm as he speaks in a low, FM-DJ molasses voice. I look at his eyes, and they examine me to see if I'm nervous or intimidated. He sizes me up, and, after he takes whatever he wants from the introduction, he returns to Allen. Then his mood changes back to the hyper, almost angry mood the others had talked about all day. I tell everybody how good it is to be here, and I wait for one of them to give me something to do, and I believe one of them would have, if they all hadn't been so busy.

It's late afternoon. I've been sitting here for hours fooling with pencils and paper. There's an electric pencil sharpener on the file cabinet. It's broken. I spent some time trying to fix it. It's still broken. I'm not very good with mechanical things.

Something's going on again, but I don't know what it is. Joe Monti, the fat, impeccably dressed guy with the thick hair and the high voice, is the messenger boy for Sherwin.

Joe tells Allen that Lester and Sherwin can't afford a fight with Marty right now. I don't know who Marty is. His office is somewhere on sixteen. It seems a lot of people have their offices on sixteen and that a lot goes on on sixteen. Marty sounds like a wild man, and I can tell by the way everyone talks about him that they're all a little scared of him.

Allen does all the talking for Lester. At least, every time he opens his mouth to Joe Monti it sounds like he's telling Joe where Lester stands on things. There's so much of this stuff going on I wonder when anybody has time to do lawyer's work, and as the day goes on, I realize I'm not even sure what "lawyer's work" is.

I wait for the research assignment from Carol Schneider, but it doesn't come. The phone doesn't ring. It hasn't rung since five, when it was somebody looking for somebody else. Then, around five-thirty, something else happens: A woman stands in my doorway and stares at me. She smiles as if she knows me. I say "Hello," and she says "Hello," and then she's gone. It's strange, but it's nice, too.

I sit with the yellow pad, and I doodle little drawings. I draw a dog first. It doesn't start out to be a dog. At first it's just a pattern of lines going round and round like a sand dollar. Then I add two dots, and for a while it becomes a shark. Then I add some more stuff, mistakes really, that I overwork with a lot of short strokes. And just when I think I've got nothing but a big splotch of graphite, I see that I have the outline of a dog with a tail but no head. So I add the head, getting the nose wrong, and end up with this fairly good-looking cocker spaniel. I put on the final touches and then look at the time. It's five forty-five. I figure it's late enough to leave. Departure times are a tricky thing in law firms. Billable hours are the measure, and you can't bill a thousand hours a day if you leave with the staff.

But I've got nothing to do, and nobody to bill if I stay. So this departure's tricky for appearances only. I think about first impressions. Somebody in my past once said: "We end as we begin." But it seems ridiculous to sit here for another hour drawing dogs without heads. So I walk to the door of my office. I look down the corridor. There's no one there. The secretaries have gone. There are some lights on in the offices along the way, but I can't hear anybody. Nonetheless, I employ the "distracted departure," which I make up on the spot. It's the "eyes-locked-to-someplace-faraway-fumbling-through-my-jacket-looking-for-my-keys-or-something-I've-lost" departure, a direct, though modified, descendant of the "crazy-white-man-walking-through-Harlem-at-two-in-the-morning" walk, designed as a deterrent to unwanted interference from bystanders and the environs.

I turn the corner by Mr. Westphall's office. In ten or twelve steps I'll be past the green door and out of here. I'm fumbling through my pockets like I've lost just about everything I've ever owned. I'm jangling keys and slipping my glasses off and on again. I'm caught up in this major distraction. It's working. I've already passed two associates and neither one looked at me. I'm only five steps away. The keys are out now, and I'm running them through my fingers. I say "Goddammit" like something real bad has just happened. I move on. I'm just a step or two away. I put the keys in my pocket. I reach for the door and I hear:

"Where are you going?"

I turn.

"What? Oh, I'm . . ." My hand jangles the keys again. I try to think of a question. I say something to myself, and I wish I had a legal pad. If I had a legal pad it would look like I was still working, still busy, too busy to be interrupted. I say something about a problem. I keep it real vague. Whatever the problem is, it's far off and hard to pin down. I think maybe he'll go away. Maybe I'll get out of here. Two steps, an elevator, three blocks, and I'm in a bar on Third Avenue. I give it one more sound-over-my-shoulder-fumble for my keys.

"I'm Mark Stillman," he says. He's a short guy with thin lips and reptilian eyes. His suit is padded about the shoulders and tapered at the waist; it looks a little like Joan Crawford's suits from the forties. His hair is puffy and translucent about his ears and pulled tightly over his narrow head. On top it's dull, wiry, flat hair, and it remains in place with a defiant resolve, sprayed and brittle, as if warding off all movement of wind, breath, exhaust, or nature. He tries to smile in deference to some auto-response of office etiquette, but it would have been better if he hadn't tried because the attempt only reveals the dissociation between his curiously dark eyes and whatever it is he does with his mouth when his lips pull away from the bottom edge of his upper teeth.

"Come with me," he says, and there's no avoiding it, no getting away. I try to introduce myself. But he's not interested in that. I'm one of the "new guys." That's all he needs to know. It seems that he's been looking for one of the "new guys."

"Marty needs bodies tonight," he says, turning again. "We're on sixteen," and I follow him and descend the stairs.

We head down an empty corridor. There's some commotion coming from the corner office. A tiny woman in a yellow sundress says something about some "son of a bitch" who can't be trusted. She's exasperated by what's going on, and as we approach she raises her hands as if we're late for an appointment.

"Who's this?" she asks.

"I got one," Mark says. "Lester's not going to get all of them. Not tonight."

"The only reason this is happening," she says, "is because

he knows Westphall's made up his mind, and nothing's going to save it for him, not even the ComTran thing."

"Mark! Get in here!" a voice calls from inside the office.

"Wait here," Mark says.

"OK," I say.

He stops and turns.

"Don't get smart," he says. "Just wait here."

"OK," I say again, and he enters Marty's office and closes the door behind him.

The tiny woman looks at me, and then walks away, bouncing on the small balls of her small feet, slapping a laminated menu from a neighborhood deli against her thigh.

I sit at a secretary's cubicle and spin this way and that in the secretary's chair. The secretary's placed small photos of her husband and little girl on the wall above her computer screen. Her husband looks like a guy in the trades. He has thick hair and a mustache. In one photo the three of them are posed before a Christmas tree with lights and icicles. The little girl wears snowman pajamas with reindeer feet.

Time passes, and from behind the closed door I hear somebody screaming into a speakerphone. He's swearing and then laughing and then swearing again. After a few minutes the door opens and Mark Stillman stands there and looks at me. He says nothing and closes the door again. I continue to wait there. I figure I can wait as well as anybody else—as well as any of the new associates. I don't see how waiting here, when I've been told to wait here, can hurt my career.

"All kinds of good stuff going on today," a voice says from behind me.

I turn. It's another lawyer.

"I'm Larry Ackerman," he says. "You're the new guy on seventeen. We've been looking for you."

"Well, here I am."

"Come with me," he says. "Lester's got some minutes and stock pledges that need to be drafted. We're all in the large conference room."

"I don't know if I should."

"What?"

"I mean—if I can."

"Why can't you?"

"Mark Stillman told me to wait here."

"So what are you doing for him?"

"I'm waiting for him."

"Waiting."

"That's what I'm doing. I mean, that's what he told me to do."

Larry looks around the empty corridor.

"Is he in there with Marty?"

"Yes."

"Well, don't worry about him. Around here you go where they need you the most, and tonight Lester needs people to do things."

"You sure?"

"Let's go," he says.

"Maybe I should poke my head in—you know."

"I said: Let's go."

I get up and feel the interior catch of indecision, the first crack in an otherwise smooth tablet.

"We all work for the same firm," Larry Ackerman says, walking with a brisk military gait. So I leave the secretary's cubicle with the Christmas photo of a happy family and follow him to the large conference room with Mark Stillman's admonition sounding like the after-shadow of something I'm bound to hear again.

MOZART RITORNELLO

The conference room is huge and well lit and the conference table is littered with papers and books and Styrofoam cups and soda cans. The room is so large it swallows up sound, and although it's crowded, nobody can disturb the general quiet because when people speak it's as if their voices are gathered in small, cellular pockets that brush against the walls and rise and disappear in the shallow glow of the lights overhead.

Joe Monti's on the phone in the corner. He's stretched out in one of those fancy office chairs, and he's slung real low in it with his legs crossed at the ankles. His high-pitched voice goes into paroxysms of very good phony laughter. He says, "Don't get me involved in it," and he cups his hand over his mouth so that nobody will hear him. Then he says, "I'm only here for Sherwin; I know the guy's crazy," and then it's a "what," another "what," and a final "what." He laughs and says "You bastard," like he's real familiar with the person. He can swear and get away with it. It's not even swearing. It's just the way the "big boys" talk.

The room is swathed in the odor of old pickles, onions, and the remainders of cold plates ordered from a deli. I start down one side of the table where Larry Ackerman has directed me to go. Then Larry stops by Allen Ballantine's chair where a number of associates lean against the wall. They're taking notes as he hands out assignments for the night. I'm only halfway to the end of the table and I wait for

Allen to say something to me. I look eager. I look ready. I look to the end of the room where Lester stands before a white board with a blonde who's wearing English schoolboy glasses.

"Larry," Allen says, "I've got Helen and Steven doing the resolutions for ComTran's subsidiaries. Balkoni talked to Preston at Citibank and they want new UCC 1s on Commercial's condos in Florida and upstate. They also want copies of ComTran's liens on the properties in Miami. They're being real pricks about it. Lester talked to them and said he'd get them what they wanted if they gave in on a few other things. But we need time for everything else."

I can see Allen's mind begin to wander, as if certain unexpected problems, emerging with the predictability of chaos, are enough to set him off center. Then he sees me, recognizes me, and looks away. "Larry," he says again, repeating the name as if to make a clean start, "what I want you to do is to get Vierps and a couple of associates and take care of the new stuff that came up today. There are about twelve pledges and a few sets of minutes for each of the subsidiaries." The phone behind him rings and interrupts him. He picks it up. Larry points to an open chair and tells me to have a seat. I listen as Allen goes crazy on the phone. Whoever it is wants something, and Allen thinks it's an unreasonable request, and he doesn't say "unreasonable," he says "fucking unreasonable." Everybody in the place can hear him as he screams at the idiot on the other end of the line. I watch him carefully. He's this little bit of a guy with Bob Dylan hair. He knows that everybody's looking at him, and he's enjoying this. It's a trip for him. For once in his life he's beating the shit out of somebody else.

Lester hears what's going on, and he looks over the rims of his glasses and points to Allen. He draws a line with his index finger across his throat, and Allen brings the conversation to a close. There's a buzz in the place over the latest outburst. Lester takes an ashtray and bangs the table three times to get everybody's attention. The buzz falls off, and there's quiet except for the intermittent rush of Joe Monti's laughter. Everybody looks at him, and he hangs up the phone. He puts his hands up as if to say he's sorry. Then everybody turns to pay attention to Lester.

"It's at this time in the deal," he begins, "when all the loose ends seem to be snapping in the wind. This is the time when it's good, even necessary, to slow down, to step back, and take a look at where we are and where we're going. The most important question each of you can ask yourself right now is 'What am I doing here?' If you can answer that then you've still got a handle on what this deal is all about."

He takes off his glasses and turns to the board behind him. Another phone rings someplace in the room. He tells his assistant with the schoolboy glasses to tell the night operator to hold all calls for twenty minutes. Then he begins to outline the fundamentals of what the ComTran deal is all about. He talks about the recession, the abuses of the past, the need for creative but sound business practices. He talks about the corporate structure of ComTran, about the proxy fight the management barely survived. He talks about assets, the properties in Florida and four other states. He talks about financing. He talks about the several banks that are involved. He uses different colored markers on the white board to designate different lines of responsibilities. He's like a professor lecturing to a large classroom of eager graduate students. No one speaks. Everyone watches him and waits for the scratch of the blue marker that will signify each person's particular responsibility.

"And down here," he says, "as collateral for the line of credit to the subsidiaries in Pennsylvania, we'll need stock pledges drafted up as soon as possible."

I want to write this down. This might be what I'm supposed to do. I look over the table for an extra pad, but I can't find one, so I memorize where he drew that line with the marker. I'm eager. I'm ready. Christ, I'm on board.

"It's like Mozart," he says, and when he says this everyone looks at each other with knowing looks because Lester, the polymath, is famous for cross-discipline leaps of reference.

"Just the right number of notes," he says, "not too many, not too few. If the deal is done correctly there'll be just enough documents for each of the transactions—not too many, not too few. And in the documents there'll be just enough words—not too many, not too few. This isn't an exercise in cutting and pasting somebody else's boilerplate. These documents all say something; they all mean something, and you can't hope to draft them unless you have some idea what they actually say, what they actually mean, and how they fit into the deal as a whole. So when the time comes to close and the papers are signed and everybody goes home happy, each and every one of you will be able to do the closing binder, not because closing binders are easy assignments— they're not—but because each of you will know what this deal is all about."

The room is silent. Lester made sense. He took the time to include everybody in the project, and now everybody has a place, a duty, a job.

The phone rings again. The twenty minutes are up. Everyone goes back to work with a sense of willingness and purpose. Even I feel it, and after I leave for the library with Bill Vierps and two associates, I feel good about working late. I figure maybe there is a place for me here. I figure maybe I don't have to worry about losing my job on the first day just because I got drunk last night, just because an imaginary subway broke down, just because I'm supposed to know things I just don't know.

TALES FROM THE COUNTER-REFORMATION

When Eddy calls and says it's a big thing, I don't understand what's so big about his getting permission to come to New York for a party for some old Jesuit who's supposed to be famous because he ran the school newspaper for ten thousand years and taught some writer who made it big when he wrote a book about cops and robbers in Boston. But that's because I don't appreciate the kind of life Eddy's living in a seminary with the Jesuits and their rules about where they can go and what they can do when they get there. Eddy's serious about it, though, and he says he'll be in New York late Saturday afternoon. He says it'll be a good party, and that I'll have a good time, and I don't have the heart to tell him I couldn't care less about some old Jesuit.

On Saturday afternoon Eddy meets me on the East Side with a guy named Rick. Rick's a nondescript skinny guy with a big head. He's from New Paltz and after the introductions he drinks his beer and doesn't say much. Eddy looks pretty much the same, although I take my time looking him over to see if he's changed at all. I don't know what those priests do in there, but I have my ideas, and if my ideas are right then the things they do in there are the kind of things that could change a person.

I order more drinks, but Eddy switches to soda and I think how this is different from the old days. Then I slap him on the back and ask him again what life is like in there, expecting he'll laugh and give in and order another Manhattan. But he sticks with the soda and pulls back from the forced camaraderie, saying little, being circumspect as ever, damning no one unless he does it with faint praise. And then he tells me about this guy named George, who's what they call their "Novice Master," which is just another word for boss. As soon as Eddy mentions George's name, Rick looks up from his mug of draft beer and says, "The less said about George the better."

Eddy keeps it up, though, telling me what an "unhappy" man George is and that it's the kind of unhappiness that can make a man mean and hard and brittle. He wants to say more, but after this small and uncharacteristic outburst, he doesn't feel comfortable going on about it with Rick there. So he says something calm and sensitive instead, as if saying something calm and sensitive will make everything all right, as if he's got a license now to say calm and sensitive things since he's studying to be a priest.

"I thought he made you a perfect," I say.

"Prefect," Eddy says.

"Well, things can't be so bad if he made you one of those."

"I'm not the prefect anymore," Eddy says. "That was just a temporary thing. Now this guy Pedro's the prefect," and he stares into his soda and doesn't say another thing.

We drink through dinner, and Rick's had enough beer to loosen up. I say we should take a cab to Fordham because I have the money. Eddy says no, that in the "spirit of poverty" he and Rick should take a subway. I'm thinking this is all fine and good; I'm thinking this is a regular piece of work; I'm thinking this is one hell of a script for the new millennium; and I'm thinking this is bullshit. Because this is New York, and it's Saturday night, and who gives a shit about the "spirit of poverty" when I've got a pocket full of money. So I'm a little pissed because the night isn't working out, and it's the first time Eddy's seen me pissed with him, and he realizes he's being a jerk, and that there are considerations in this world other than the spirit of poverty. So he says "OK," and Rick says "Fine," and I settle up with the bartender, and we start up Third Avenue to hail a cab with a driver who gives us his own little piss-and-moan about Fordham being in a bad neighborhood and then about the "fuckin' Mets" and then about everything else that happens to be on his mind.

The Jesuit residence is a Victorian mansion, an Anglophile's 3-D dream with all kinds of gingerbread this and gingerbread that and stand-up brass lamps throwing their caramel-colored vapors over oak-paneled walls and bookcases, stitched together with the skeletal frames of iron lace.

The well-heeled alumni are packed into two sitting rooms with fireplaces and oil portraits of saints from the Counter-Reformation. The crowd spills out of the first room into lesser clusters of polite social drinkers, standing in the hallway and across the hallway into the library. Most of the Jesuits have gathered in the kitchen, and the room is full of noise. We enter the kitchen and Rick passes me, because he sees somebody he knows, and it's obvious he's happy to get away. In a moment he's gone, swallowed by the crowd, as it reduces him to a part of some greater whole. This activity of unbridled inclusion threatens to consume me, too, as I momentarily disappear into the anonymous cluster of men wearing plaid shirts and khaki pants. I stand by the keg near the sink. I pour my first beer, and the struggle eases a bit, because with their attenuated defense stretched over the room like expanding spheres of clerical radar, they somehow determine that I'm not one of them, and like the rejection of foreign material from a host organism, I imagine myself being politely expelled as they move aside to let me pass.

Eddy leads me to the room with the alumni guests. He talks to a gentleman in a blue suit and to his wife in a plaid skirt, black turtleneck sweater, and one tasteful string of small white pearls. Eddy tells them about his life as a Jesuit, but it's a different story from what he told me, because what he's telling them is the party line, what the well-heeled alumni want to hear, with just the right touch of self-deprecating humor so as to ease any anxieties they might have about some of the more severe aspects of life in a celibate order. The guy's name is Todd, and he says how impressed he is with "them," meaning the Jesuits, and with their "fine history" of teaching even the most difficult students.

Lisa, his wife, looks tired. She's had enough of the self-congratulatory small talk. She asks me if I'm a Jesuit, too, and before I can answer Eddy's introduced me as his best friend from law school. I shake hands with Todd, and he's ready to bust, because he's a lawyer, and he's got about a million questions.

"Westphall, Sellars," he says. "Citibank. Real estate. Lester Bartok. ComTran," and I'm about ready to call the verb police, because Todd is obviously an aficionado of advanced small talk. "We did some work with them a few years ago," he says, "when the REITs made a small comeback."

"Great," I say, and it seems to be the right thing to say, even though it's the same as if I'd said "Oh, yeah," or "So what," or "What's a REIT?" because the beer has just kicked in, and I've hit that Moog-point of the eternal om where life is as easy and as distant as a far-off English countryside, and guys like Todd can stand there and talk business and REITs and networks and contacts all night long.

Lisa can't take it anymore. She's bored. And despite Todd's best efforts, the conversation stutters and fails. Todd tries to hide his disappointment with his wife, but even Eddy's hard-pressed to move it along while the ever-encroaching emptiness of what-really-happens-at-parties-like-these sits at the edge of the room waiting to remind everyone the only reason we're here in the first place is because a couple of hundred years ago Ignatius of Loyola decided to give up a life of parties like this.

I excuse myself and make my way through the dark library, which opens onto another room with bay windows. A small man sits in an oversize altar chair and reads from a book with page ribbons and holy cards to a group of Jesuits and civilians and a number of young people sitting in those light, fancy, sleek model wheelchairs I've seen in hamburger commercials. Rick is there at the edge of the room. He tells me that Father Sullivan was the chaplain for the disabled students and that's why the room is crowded with all the people in wheelchairs. He whispers all of this so as not to disturb Father Sullivan's recitation of the poems he wrote in his youth, when he'd stayed behind with a skin condition and a vocation while the other boys went "over there" to fight the Hun. Then this girl sitting in a wheelchair next to us looks up and stares at Rick. I figure she's one of the students he talked about. At least she looks young enough, all dressed in black. Rick sees her, and he shuts up. Then she looks at me until I smile and turn my attention to the priest.

The poems are short, and they march along with a certain predictability. The rhythms don't change, and after I hear him recite two or three I can feel the rhyme from a long way off, and I can predict the word before he says it, and the predictability gives this false impression of high art. He speaks and he acts with self-effacing modesty, especially during the applause that follows each recitation. But he holds center stage like a conquering Caesar, and when a young guy in one of those electric power chairs says something in a loud and unintelligible voice and threatens the priest's hold on the crowd, Father Sullivan counters with a long statement that brings everyone's attention back to himself. He starts another poem about armies in the night along the Seine and the footfalls of cavalry and a man named Stuart. I've had enough, and I start to leave and almost bump into the young woman dressed in black. She moves in front of me and catches one wheel of her chair on a narrow runner for the sliding doors to the library. "Damn," she says loud enough for everyone to hear, as she struggles for a second, her small but strong arms all but lifting her chair and placing it down a few feet away in the center of the library. She's got a bleached-out crew cut and a perfectly shaped head. She's wearing huge earrings. She stops in the library and whispers, "His poetry sucks," and I agree with her. I ask if she's a student, and she says she just looks young. "I didn't even go to Fordham," she says. "The only reason we came to this thing is because of my boyfriend," and in the light made warm by the cinnamon-colored wood of the library her boyish face is perfect with large, dark eyes.

Her name is Cindy and she tells me she's a graphic artist. I ask her about her artwork, and she asks me if I've seen the ads for this imported vodka with the bear and the good-looking model. I say yes, even though I don't remember them. She says that's the account she almost landed, but didn't because she thought ads with big brown bears and blonde models were bullshit. I say, "Yeah. Bullshit," and she laughs because she knows I'm too busy staring at her to know what I'm saying.

Eddy joins us as the poetry reading breaks up, and the guests begin to scatter. The library fills up with the same kind of relief and chatter heard in the back rooms of wakes. The students in wheelchairs move silently across the floor and gather in clusters by the hallway. Some of the guests stare at them. One lady walks up to where they're sitting. "You people," she says. They turn and look at her. Her smile is stretched across her face like a mistake. "You people," she says again, and she shakes her head with that "I'm-just-so-proud" look. Then she steps away. She says, "Charles, I want you to come here and meet some very brave people," and with that Cindy rolls her eyes and says, "I'm outta here," as if the word *brave* is some evil invocation of telethon etiquette. She leaves the room and I follow her, and the others disperse behind us, but not before the woman begins to ask long and inappropriate questions.

"That stuff happens," Cindy says. "Most people think we're Martians or something, and of course they stare. Sometimes that's OK, really. Especially the kids. But you'd be amazed what some adults ask. Real personal stuff. I mean real personal."

We're sitting in a small room off the patio near the back of the house. From where we're sitting we can watch the party in the large room with the fireplace and the oil paintings. The air outside is cool, and the wind turns the leaves so that the pale underside of each leaf shines in the cold glow of the garden lights. It's peaceful, and we don't say much. We just sit there, glad to be out of it. But then there's a crash in the kitchen. We hear a shout and the sound of a scuffle. Eddy walks quickly to the kitchen and then back to where we're sitting.

"That jerk," he says, and he tells us that it's some crazy German Jesuit named Dieter who drinks too much and gets drunk at every party and ends up picking fights. The commotion dies down, and two guys with plaid shirts walk a third guy with a plaid shirt across the lawn where he bends over and retches once and throws up in the bushes.

Father Sullivan enters the room overlooking the patio and

the back grounds. He says, "I see old Dieter has graced us with his Germanic wit." He thinks he's Noël Coward, acting urbane, debonair, and almost-British, dismissing the whole thing as if it were a trifle, a common rage among artists, normal, all to be expected from that *Deutsche* rapscallion.

He takes the chair next to where Cindy's sitting. She's a little unsettled being so close to him, but Father Sullivan wants to be the avuncular charmer. He sees Eddy, and Eddy offers some guarded but certain praise. Father Sullivan just takes it in like it's his due. His cheeks puff a bit as he tries to restrain the smile that wants to break his face, and it gives Cindy a chance to push herself away. She comes around next to me, and I offer to get her some punch. "Only if there's a lot of vodka in it," she says.

When I return, her boyfriend is sitting there. He's trying to impress Father Sullivan with a poem he's written. "It's a good poem," he says. "I just want to recite it."

"Maybe another time," Father Sullivan says, and he's not even trying to be polite about it.

"Really, Father, I wrote it special for tonight."

Cindy watches this and she's embarrassed. The priest wants no part of her boyfriend or his poetry. For Cindy's sake, I wish he'd just stop. But the kid keeps it up. Father Sullivan tries to fix him with this withering look. It doesn't work. The kid's had too much to drink, and he's oblivious to all the signals. He continues to interrupt the procession of well-wishers who've come to praise the old man, and then, when the tension is about to break with something more than a priestly admonition, the kid begins to recite the poem. Cindy listens to the first few lines and then turns away. It's all too embarrassing. She gives me the high sign to follow her, and I help her up one step as we head out onto the patio. The last thing I hear before we leave the room is the priest's voice. He talks about the importance of language and how "this" poetry, meaning Cindy's boyfriend's poetry, doesn't do a thing. He says that "Poetry," meaning capital-*P* poetry, meaning his poetry, doesn't need this kind of "tripe," and I can feel the sting in the word past the French doors and across the plain, flat stones.

We make our way down the long patio running the length of the house. There's some lawn furniture there and a planter with a gargoyle's head. I point to it, but Cindy's too upset over what's happened. She's more sensitive than I thought. She says that she warned him about the drinking and about trying to impress people with his poetry.

In the distance from across the grounds we see three figures. Two walk on either side of a third. They're helping him walk off some speech-slurring anger. Half the words are English, and half the words are German. It's Dieter and the two other guys with plaid shirts. Dieter says, *"Scheisskopf"* and something else, and he's just another drunk with a vocation. A fourth guy joins them and relays some message and then walks toward us from across the field. It's Rick, and he's wiping his hand across his forehead. He's upset over what happened in the kitchen.

"That guy's a maniac," he says, and he tells us how he was just standing there, drinking a beer, minding his own business, when crazy Dieter started to push him across the room. "At first I thought he was joking," he says, "but it wasn't a joke."

"Don't worry about it," I say, "and whatever you do, just ignore Father Sullivan."

"What do you mean?" he asks.

"I mean don't bother talking to him about poetry."

"Why not?"

"Trust me."

Eddy joins us. He's been looking for Rick.

"He does something like this every party," Eddy says. He

says that he and Rick should head off. He says that some superior thought it might be best all around.

"I guess so," Rick says, and though I don't like him, I feel sorry for him and a little shook up over the way these guys treat one another.

"I'll call you next week," I say to Eddy, and I shake Rick's hand. One of them says something about a "disaster." They look at Cindy and they say good-bye. She just raises her eyebrows and says good-bye, and they're gone.

"And they call us Martians," Cindy says, and we wait for the party to end as the wind scrapes the tops of the fir trees with a rustling sound, and the last crickets of the season make one hell of a racket scratching the sound out of their legs.

SMALL TALK

S olomon Isaacson, one of the new associates that everyone made fun of because of the way he dresses, is a
star now because, at a closing on Friday when the whole
thing was about to blow up and the bank officers were about
to walk away from it, he, meaning Solomon Isaacson—who,
like the rest of us, was just supposed to stand there and
place documents into files and make sure the big boys had
enough ink in their Mont Blanc big-dick pens—struck a
blow for the liberty of each and every overeducated, over-
paid, overeager associate and remembered some obscure
point of procedure, which in a world of one million to one
actually applied, and took the forbidden step of pulling Mark
Stillman aside and, in a brave display of tact and candor, told
him the deal could be saved. At first Mark Stillman went
nuts, and not in a good way, his face all blanched out with
this "Who is this guy?" expression, wondering where Solomon
Isaacson got the stones to presume anything, let alone something that the big boys didn't know. But then something registered and Mark's features relaxed as the import of what
Solomon had said clicked somewhere behind his blue-black
almond eyes, and with the look of a man who had just
caught his breath, he stepped forward and informed the big
boys and the bankers and the lackeys that the deal could go
forward because of some subparagraph of a subparagraph,
which he identified by rattling off a series of numbers and

letters in that monolith of boilerplate and conditional clauses codified as the New York Lien Law. So with the ABCs reworked and restated, the bankers returned to their seats, and the discussion continued, and by five that afternoon the deal closed with signed documents and a few of us conspicuously left behind to clean the room of excess paper, soda cans, broken pencils, and the garbage of a catered lunch from the Star Deli.

Solomon Isaacson now walks with short steps through the library. He sees me and asks what I'm working on. I tell him a hangover and the Perry Ellis ads in the second section of the *Times*. It doesn't register, and he launches into something about a Second Circuit opinion that just came down reversing *Monoghan* v. *Bank of Japan*. I listen like I couldn't care less, and it's not even rude because he's oblivious. It doesn't matter what I say, or don't say, and I wonder how long he'll go on like this, talking to me as if I'm listening when he knows I'm not listening, presuming, nonetheless, that I'm interested in what he has to say about an opinion that's unknown to me. Then I realize that this is his way of socializing, of making small talk. I figure he must think his newly acquired celebrity affords him the opportunity, even the mandate, to make this kind of small talk. But I want to disabuse him of this notion, because I suspect the real reason he's going on like this is to determine whether I'm a threat or not, to determine whether I'm smart like he is, whether I'm capable of remembering the impossible numbers and parentheticals by which deals are saved and reputations are made. So I just stare at him. I put on my best dumb Vermont cowface, all heavy and still with dumb comprehension, the eyelids at half-mast, the mouth as noncommittal as the flat line of a deceased heart patient, and with my blood pressure reduced to the phonic blip of an Indian Sufi, I go blank as Buddha and I say "Yeah," one inappropriate and nonresponsive "yeah," and return to my paper as he watches me with all six of his little refracted eyes suspended like pebbles of peppercorn in the lenses of his glasses. He can't pretend that I haven't blown him off, that I haven't poured water over the sugar of his hail-fellow-well-met charade, so he just turns and walks out of the library with a short wave to Pat, the librarian, who doesn't even know who he is.

Pat sits in a cubicle of glass at the end of the library. She's a large woman and she's got very red nails. She's married to Antonio who's a librarian at Herring & Green, the fancy firm downtown where Mary works, and Pat talks about Antonio as if he were as fancy as the lawyers from Harvard who work there and run the world. Antonio's from Queens. He was a tough kid, but now he's responsible and mature and still street-smart. My friend Mary says he's a "dude," and that you can see it in the way he talks to the guys in the mailroom, where there's a lot of back and forth, and Antonio says things like "Forget about it" in the drawn-out way toughs from the boroughs speak.

Pat says that she and Antonio like to play country music, but she's careful to distinguish between bullshit country music and real country music, and what she means by "real country music" seems to have something to do with the size of their black hats and the number of sequins the singers allow themselves when they're singing those heartbreak songs from the hills of Tennessee.

"We go there every October," she says, and she's talking about this music fair in Upstate New York. She says, "Antonio played with The Flat Box Boys, and they said he was good enough to do it full-time." Then she tells me about the weekend they've got planned, and about the country inn where they stay. She tells me about the fiddle player for The Flat Box Boys. She says that he's more than "real," he's "authentic," and that he learned from some "good ole boy" in some Indian-sounding chick-a-whatever county buried in the panhandle hills of West Virginia. Then she asks me if I want to go to the music fair with her and Antonio. She takes me by surprise, and she tells me how we can do it with accommodations at this inn. I cough and look for a way to ease out of it, to say no without hurting her feelings, and I'm relieved when her friend Susan, who's been standing behind me, excuses herself and walks into the small office.

"What's this stuff about fiddlesticks?" Susan asks, and Pat starts in about how she invited Susan last year and how Susan didn't go and how she and Antonio never invite a person twice. Susan goes, "Spare me, Pat," and I can see that she and Pat are close enough that Susan can poke fun at the country music thing, and Pat won't get mad about it.

"C'mon, Pat," Susan says, "let's get those papers filed," and she's mimicking Mark Stillman, who's her boss and who's known for bossing people around and for Susan ignoring him when he does. Then she looks at me, and there's this laughter in her that starts somewhere down deep and burrows up and reaches near full force just before she speaks, as if there's some terribly funny secret she knows concerning just about everything.

Susan's the woman who stood outside the door of my office on the first morning and said hello to me, and seeing her now, up close, I know that I don't know her, even though she does look familiar from sometime long ago.

The library phone rings, and Pat picks it up and places her hand over the mouthpiece. She points to me and then to the door. She says, "No. He just left. He was doing some research. Some of his papers are still spread out on one of the tables. Yes. If he comes back I'll be sure to tell him. All right, then." And she hangs up the phone.

"Carol Schneider's looking for you," she says, and I wave good-bye and leave the library and press for the elevator.

I'm in a hurry, so the elevator doesn't come. I hear the bells going off one or two floors below me and then one or two floors above me; and still the elevator doesn't come. I picture Carol Schneider in her office calling all over the firm, looking for me, wondering where I am, getting angry.

The library door opens and Susan joins me. I introduce myself, and she says she knows who I am and that I went to school with her husband.

"I did?"

"Yes," she says. "He was a quarterback on the football team," and she tells me his name again, and I don't remember it, though I act as if I do.

"I remember his name," I say, "but wasn't he a year or two ahead of me?" and we talk about nothing, she naming names, I pretending to know them, saying they all sound familiar, though none of them sound any more familiar than names from a Dublin phone book.

The bells pop and there's the intermittent rush of air as the elevator plummets away again behind the closed doors. Then I say something that strikes her as funny, and the laughter I'd heard in the library starts again, and it's as if she's trying to hold it in, but can't hold it in, because it's just too funny, and in the way that genuine laughter sometimes portends a bond of long-standing familiarity, I feel close to her, as if we do know one another, and it unsettles me in a pleasant way.

Finally, the elevator doors open, and Solomon Isaacson stands there, loaded down with file folders. He gives us a look, and we get on the elevator. The doors close, and she makes a face, and I make a face, and the elevator drops one floor. The doors open and I turn to say good-bye, and she winks at me, that kind of "I know more than you think I know" wink, and I'm about to wink back, because I figure I know a few things, too, but my eyebrows are all the way up there, and I can't get it all in sync before the doors close and I'm left standing there in the hallway with the receptionist staring at me.

SMALLER TALK

C arol Schneider has short legs, so when she sits in the huge chair behind her huge desk in the huge office from which she has emerged only three times since she made partner four months ago, her feet don't touch the floor, and she gives the impression of a frisky child enjoying her time in a high chair. When she speaks, her entire body bounces in sequential increments from her feet to her legs to her thighs, through her waist and up to her chest and finally, the movement having doubled itself with each passage, explodes its jittery self down her arms and her hands, which gesticulate madly while her talking head bounces on her shoulders in a display of cheerful and self-satisfied competence.

"So. We meet at last," she says, and the sunlight strikes the mirrored windows of the Citibank Building one block away. The room is too warm with the bright, reflected midday light. I squint and begin to feel the heat. I'm wearing my new suit. It's a wool blend, and it's too hot for this time of year.

"You were here last summer," she says.

"No," I say, "I clerked at Fine and Akers."

"Fine and Akers." She can almost taste the words. "In real estate?" she asks.

"No," I say, "litigation."

"Litigation," she says, picking up her head. "Good lawyers, Fine and Akers. Real estate. Commercial work. But litigation? They're not known for their litigation."

"Well, I . . ."

"Good firm. Bad department," she says, almost to herself. It's the first test, and I almost miss it before I know it's a test. She wants me to get with the program. She wants to say that "Welcome aboard" stuff. But she wants me to agree with her, with everything she says or thinks and especially with her thoughts about Fine & Akers, because her thoughts are critical, and she knows I haven't given it up until I agree with her when she's being critical. She wants me to say: "Right. Good firm, bad department." But I don't say it, because I don't agree with her, because I kind of liked it at Fine & Akers, because I thought it was a pretty good department with pretty good lawyers. They treated me all right there, and I think maybe I should have gone there full time, even if they didn't offer top dollar, even if they don't have the big reputation. So I say nothing. I let it pass. And she lets it pass. It's awkward, and then it's time for business.

She begins to talk and the words come quickly, words about business and corporations and financials and real estate—all kinds of words. It's a whole new vocabulary, and I wish I could get back to the small talk, because then I'd know what the words mean.

She looks at the ceiling. She talks about some deal that made everyone crazy, and then she stops talking. Her body settles, she grows still, and I try not to stare at the round ball of women-of-Iowa hair sitting atop her puffy face.

"So, why'd you choose corporate?" she asks, and we're back to the small talk, and my answer's right there. It's the perfect setup, and I'm tempted to say: "Good firm; good department," and score with wit and style and that subservient cool bosses lap up like warm milk from saucers of gold. But I don't say it. Instead I get a little carried away with myself. I try for something more subtle, not so facile, something more substantive, even meaningful. So I shrug my shoulders, and, without any appreciation for how stupid I actually sound, I say, "I don't know, just thought I'd see what it's like."

She doesn't say a thing. Her eyes go from blank to dark to blank again. Her lips begin to pucker in this pout like something preceding a storm, and the speech she's about to give wells up in her, shaking her, moving, volcanic, her body holding forth, then exploding in a torrent of arm-waving, finger-snatching, head-bobbing words, and the last thing I remember before the weight of language buries me with legalese, wraparounds, buybacks, and parentheticals is: "You'll need more focus than that," until, struck blind from the sun off the windows of the building one block away, I scribble something in the midst of the ominous *whirrrrrr* of Chinook helicopters putt-putt-putting over my head, because Carol Schneider's voice has become the Doppler effect of trouble. I almost duck with the circular rush of imaginary blades, while scratching pre-Colombian symbols on the pad resting on my lap: half-words, really, a vowel here, a vowel there, one issue in that "if-you-can-read-this-you-can-get-a-good-paying-job" consonant-laden speed writing, last seen on the inner walls of metro buses and subways, the mention of a precedent, some background, some foreground, a reason for the assignment, another reason why I shouldn't live, and I might as well be attempting the translation of some preliterate Asian dialect.

She pauses and sips from a cup of tea, and I look up from time to time, instinctually raising my eyebrows, nodding my head, movements that say: "Yes. I know what you're saying, exactly, no problem, that's it, correct, of course," my head-nodding, ass-kissing, suck-up face frozen in that creamy obsequiousness the confused employ to fool their enemies.

Then Bill Vierps knocks at the door. She motions for him to enter. He walks behind me and sets some papers in front of her. Her eyes go over the documents. Her hand runs over the second page as if she's scanning it. She looks at Bill and back to the papers. Bill Vierps towers over her. He's not nervous or intimidated at all. It's as if he knows she's reading exactly what she wants to read, and a smile creases her lips. She turns to him again and says nothing as her hand slowly scrapes the third page and then the fourth. Finally she says: "Has Mark seen this?"

"No," he says.

"Good," she says. "Make these changes here and then bring it to Marty. Tell him I told you so."

"Sure," he says, and he leaves the office.

"Just a paralegal," she says, "but he's worth three associates."

"Right," I say.

"Have you met him?" she asks.

"Briefly," I say. "The first night I was here."

"ComTran?" she asks.

"ComTran," I say.

"Oh," she says, pausing, regarding me again. "So you're the new guy on seventeen?"

"Yeah. I guess so. I'm the new guy on seventeen."

She sits there. She stares at me. And then she moves again.

"So," she says, "you'll have that for me on Monday?"

"You bet," I say, and I act real confident, and I leave her office trying to remember the first thing she said to me, thinking that if I could just remember that, I might be able to clone the whole assignment from the detritus of what's been left behind in a shorthand for aliens.

THE BUSY AND THE DEAD

When I return to my office, the secretary I share with about twenty other people tells me there's a message for me, and before I sit down the phone rings. It's my cousin from Syracuse, and she asks me some more questions about my family and things that happened when I was a kid. My cousin's a psychologist, or at least she's going to be a psychologist, depending on just how many initials she needs to string after her name before she can call herself "Doctor." She's pretty close to getting her Ph.D., though, and I know she can hang out her shingle as soon as she writes this dissertation on her favorite head-case, which happens to be me.

I tell her it's Friday afternoon and that I've got work to do, which is true as far as it goes, though nobody really works on Friday afternoon, and everybody's got the act down where they look busy without being busy. But I want to impress my cousin with that "I'm-just-too-busy-to-talk" talk, knowing full well that in New York City either you're busy or you're dead; and I want my cousin, who's sitting with her cop-husband and her cats in a brick house in Syracuse, to think I really am busy. I want her to have these images of skyscrapers and Park Avenue and people crossing intersections, hailing cabs, walking hurriedly, briskly, with purpose and drive, getting busy or getting to places where they'll get busy, so that all of it will somehow be important, even glamorous. So, as I remove the paper clips from the inside curve of a rubber band and dismantle the miniature catapult I'd designed that morning, I tell her that before Syracuse is buried in snow, I'll travel to her place for a weekend and tell her a thousand stories about life in my hometown.

She says OK, because it's just a "footnote."

I say, "Just a footnote."

She says, "The point I'm trying to make needs a footnote, and you're always good for a quote."

I say, "For a footnote."

She says: "I remembered something that happened in high school. Freshman year, or just before. You told me about it."

"I can't remember," I say.

"You will," she says.

"High school," I say.

"Yeah."

"A lot happened in high school."

"I know."

"But nothing really happened in high school."

"Sure," she says.

I say, "Look. I've only got an hour to turn some documents over" (and I think about the phrase "turn some documents over"), and I tell her to expect me sometime soon and that I'll tell her what I can, though I don't see what good it will do, acting all humble and self-effacing, knowing full well that being the head-case I am I can probably do her a lot of good.

I hang up the phone and watch the shadows start up the second half of the buildings on Fifty-fourth Street. From below I hear the girl who screams at the top of her lungs for people to put money in her tin can. She screams: "Please give to Cerebral Palsy," and she stretches the words all the way out until they don't even sound like themselves. It makes me angry and sad, and it goes on as the shadows rise over my head, and in the dark valley between the buildings the lights start to come on down the avenue.

Outside my office there's not even the pretense of work anymore. Everyone's standing in office doorways watching Phil Wessen pretend he's a world-class tennis star as he swings his racket from his ankles up to his knees, talking about some European tennis brat like he knows him. I stand in the doorway to my office, and I watch them watch him.

Phil's talking to Allen, the skinny guy with the Bob Dylan hair. Joe Monti's there, too, and Joe can't stand it, being this close to the "in-crowd," so he just keeps talking in the background, hoping that Phil Wessen will include him in the conversation. But Phil Wessen doesn't include him. He's only talking to Allen, ignoring everybody else, though not really ignoring us, because he knows the only reason we're all standing there in the first place is because he's invited us to do exactly that—to stand there, to watch him, to admire him, to think that maybe someday if we work hard enough, look good enough, pull the strings long enough, we, too, will be able to stand there on a Friday afternoon and talk about Forest Hills and somebody's backhand.

I catch myself smiling one of those involuntary forklift smiles when Allen tells Phil about some Czech who can hit tennis balls harder than anybody else in the world.

"Better than Connors at his best," Phil says, waving the racket, inspecting it with his fingers, pulling the strings down as if doing that actually does something.

A few secretaries continue their typing, though it's slower and less manic as everyone approaches the last half hour of the day. Solomon Isaacson turns off the light in his office and puts on his fedora and starts to leave, and nobody says a word because Solomon Issacson's important enough to leave early on Fridays. Mark Stillman almost bumps into him as they turn the corner near Mr. Westphall's office. Mark says something to him, and then starts down the corridor where he almost takes it in the face from Phil Wessen, who's swinging his tennis racket like he's serving to some imaginary person in Allen's office. Mark Stillman ducks and passes with a sour expression. He's definitely one of the young Turks, and he takes himself so seriously that he's got nothing in common with Phil and the tennis set. Some lawyers dismiss him because he's a drone who works around the clock. But that's a crock, and even Mark would say so because if he worked those hours, he wouldn't have time for his "babes." Mark Stillman calls girls "babes." He says things like "Hey, babe," and "Ciao, babe," and I wonder what's a person to do with a guy who says things like "Ciao, babe," and isn't kidding when he says it.

Mark Stillman continues down the corridor. He sees me and I smile my pecking-order smile, which is not unlike the forklift smile, except it's a shade more restrained, signifying a sense of place and diplomacy. But when I see Mark Stillman's eyes I realize such fine distinctions are wasted on him and that there was no need to smile at all. He stops at my doorway. I can smell his breath.

"I don't forget," he says in a whisper.

"Don't forget what?" I say, unable to remember what he can't forget, but I'm saying it to nobody, because he's left for Carol Schneider's office, where they'll plot on how to handle Marty.

By the time he reaches her office, dismissing the lot of us (even Phil Wessen, who'll have to vote someday on whether Mark Stillman should become a partner or not), the import of "I don't forget" begins to radiate an uneasy heat. I start to sweat and struggle to maintain my false front.

"Marty's going crazy," Mark Stillman says as he enters Carol's office, and I'm stuck there, in my door, mugged and rocky, unable to move until Phil or Allen break it up, wondering who has the courage to move and ruin their career, because nobody really wants to stand there and listen to somebody talk about himself in the language of white balls and rackets and lines drawn with chalk.

This happened when you were a kid:

You went to the Catholic school, and there were about a million nun stories. Some of them were true. Most of them weren't. But something happened after you went to the Catholic school. It happened during the summer before you went to the high school, which was a public school and didn't have any nuns or nun stories.

It was late August and Sheila Donovan was the prettiest girl in town. She'd been dating older guys for years, and she knew everybody, and everybody wanted to know her, and one day near the end of the summer she called you up and invited you to her party, and the invitation surprised you and flattered you.

Your hometown was a tough little mill town, and although the locals weren't all inbred with sliver-eyes and banjos, you all knew one another, and the reason you all knew one another was because there was only one high school in the whole town. So whether you went to the Catholic grammar school or the public junior high, sooner or later you all ended up in the same place, which was kind of like this feudal society of landowners and peasants, broken down and held together by its cliques and circles. The first time you heard the word *clique*, you thought of the sound. Then you thought it meant a group of friends. Only later did you learn what it really meant, because there was a clique and Sheila had invited them to her party, too.

Sheila Donovan wasn't in the clique. She didn't have to be in the clique; she was so good-looking she was better than the clique. And she didn't need them in the same way that they needed her, because she had everything they wanted. So Sheila was above all of that, and whatever crush you had on her was more like an altar boy's devotion from far away and not very real. It was more than enough that she knew your name and had thought to invite you to her party. It was more than enough, until that one time, when this thing happened and then it wasn't enough.

Your father drove you across town, and you showed up at Sheila's house, and the crowd was there, and it was as if you'd entered a different world. You didn't know anybody because they'd all gone to the public schools, and they didn't give a shit about nuns or nun stories. They were civilians, city kids who'd never had to wear uniforms. They looked older and experienced. The boys all had that Continental, mature look. They looked older than their years. The girls were all good-looking, even when they weren't good-looking, because they all looked like they belonged, and that was enough to make them look good.

Sheila introduced you around, and you said hello and talked about things you didn't know about because you wanted to fit in. The guys stood in a group near the garbage can that held the ice and the soda. They drank soda and told private jokes, and the girls stood on the other side of the lawn and talked among themselves. Some of them sat in lawn chairs, and it was easy and innocent as music played from two speakers sitting on the deck in the back of the house.

You sat in a lawn chair under a tree because you figured it was best to remain still and a little aloof, off to the side, quiet, passive, watching the show, waiting. But then a girl sat next to you, and you started to talk, and the conversation went from light to funny to close, and she flirted with you and it felt good.

Then Sheila called for everyone to line up for a party game. The boys stood in one line, and they were supposed to toss eggs over a net to the girls who stood in another line. The girls were supposed to catch the eggs and toss them back, and everybody was supposed to take a step back after each toss until the distance between the boys and the girls was too far, and the eggs would break, and there'd be screaming and laughter. You were Karen's partner. That was her name. And you played the game, and after a while you dropped the egg, and it broke, and the guys who were too cool to play the game just stood off to the side and watched. Some of them watched Karen, and some of them watched you.

After the cookout a breeze came up from behind the trees, and Sheila said that everybody should go downstairs to the recreation room under her house.

It was a dark room, and everybody gathered around the bowls of chips and the buckets of soda. You noticed that it was harder to talk to people than it had been when you first arrived. You didn't mind, though, because you were a newcomer and you'd met Karen, and she seemed to like you, and you knew the others would like you, too, as soon as they got to know you.

The darkness outside pressed against the windows, which were set high up in the walls below the lawn outside. You walked to the back where there was an alcove. You saw Karen there. She was talking to a girl named Linda. You interrupted them, and it was obvious that they'd been talking about you. Linda left, and you asked Karen what was wrong. She took a step toward you and put her arms around you, and everything that was warm and tender and pure and soft and caring welled up in you, and you were only thirteen, and you were happier than you had ever been. Then she told you the problem. She told you that she had a boyfriend and that he'd been watching you and that he was angry. You told her not to worry. You told her to let things take their course and that in a day or two you'd call her and talk about it. She pulled away from you and said OK. She walked away, and you just stood there thinking about it. You were only thirteen, and you knew that life could be perfect.

You walked back to the main room and then, as if a sudden breeze had blown through the place, you watched everyone run past you up the stairs to the lawn outside. Before half of them had run away you started to move along with the crowd. You didn't know what was happening. You thought it might be another game. Halfway up the cellar stairs you turned to somebody running next to you.

"Where's everybody going?" you asked.

"Outside," he said.

"What for?"

"There's going to be a fight."

"Who's gonna fight?"

"You are," he said, and it felt like someone had kicked you.

They formed a circle, and they pushed you into the center. You stood there and looked for the face of the person who wanted to fight you. Somebody called for Joey, and you looked at him. You had met him an hour or two before. You had said something that had made him laugh. You wanted to say something else, but you didn't know what to say. So you just stood there with a hot and hard feeling in your stomach. You looked at Joey's handsome Italian face, with the high forehead and the long straight nose. You looked at his eyes, and you saw how mad he was, and you saw that it was half genuine and half manufactured for the benefit of the crowd. Some of them called for him to take you on. Some of them called you names. Some of them just watched, and you turned around and felt foolish, and the heat that rested across your chest rose up, and your throat scratched, and your upper lip began to quiver as all the nerves in the tip of your nose grew so sensitive that it felt like the night breeze was going to tear it away. You tried to talk, but your voice was high and uneven, and then someone said: "He's not worth it," and the crisis passed as the circumference of the circle broke apart. They made their way back down the stairs to the recreation room. You heard them as they left. Some of the girls looked over their shoulders. One of them asked, "Who is he?"

After the last one descended the cellar stairs and pulled the door shut, you stood in the backyard, and the heat broke like a fever, and you felt it pour across your eyes. After several minutes Sheila Donovan, the most beautiful girl in your hometown, opened the back door to her house and called your name.

You didn't answer her. So she walked across the lawn in the dark and called your name again. Then she saw you. You were sitting on the lawn by a fence that ran along the side of her house.

"Come back downstairs," she said. "Everybody's calmed down now."

But you didn't know what to do, and you didn't answer

her, and you didn't go downstairs again. You just waited for your parents to pick you up, and you had to fight everything all over again when they asked you if you'd had a good time. And you said, "Yes." You said that you'd had a very good time.

WHAT WE MISTAKE FOR FREEDOM

S usan, the woman with the can't-keep-the-laughter-down voice, the woman who's married to the quarterback-law-partner-god, the woman who works for the dark-eyed-ciao-babe-lean-and-hungry Mark Stillman, is crazy about me. I don't know how I know this, but sitting here with Susan and Pat at this table at this fancy bar in the building where we work and listening to her tell Pat how much she's in love with her husband, I know she's in love with me, and I don't know whether to be happy about it or not. Pat just goes along with it, though, and she says how lucky Susan is to have a husband like David, and then she says how lucky she is to be married to Antonio, and when she says it about Antonio I know she means it, but the more Susan nods her head, the more I know she doesn't mean a thing she's said about David.

I order more drinks from a waitress who's dressed like a man, who looks like a man trying to look like a woman in men's clothes, and after the third round Pat's uneasy because she's not used to drinking this way. Susan's up for it, though, and I figure there's got to be a math to this whole physical attraction thing, a way of measuring it that has less to do with intuition and subjectivity, and more to do with math and probability, based, as it is, on one habit of the species, which is to seek out those who remind us of ourselves. So, given this belief in the Darwinian equalizer of like-to-like, I look at Susan, and she's either the exception that proves the rule or my theory fails, because as much as I'd like to think otherwise, I'm not good-looking and she is, and I can only wonder about her husband, or why she feels the need to sit here and convince herself that she's in love with him.

Susan continues to talk about life on the East Side. She talks about some restaurant where the waitresses sing. She says how she and David went there and how he spent the entire night on the phone with a client. She tells us how angry she was, and the underside of the story is how she's hanging by her fingernails to a way of life that's not working for her, a way of life that happens to include a superstar husband who's a brilliant god with money. I'm a little troubled by it because I realize that if she is attracted to me it's probably because she sees in me everything she doesn't see in her husband, which is just another way of saying I'm not a superstar-brilliant-god-with-money. So I look at her again. Her eyes are lowered and her voice is soft. I think I know what she's saying. But I can't be sure. There's a message here, but it's a hidden message, and it's a mixed message.

A couple of months ago, before Eddy left for Upstate New York, he wanted to take me out for a fancy dinner somewhere in midtown, in that area of the city that is even richer than the Upper East Side. I got all shook up and upset about it, because I found the whole thing kind of morbid; although I didn't tell him this, I saw his going into the seminary as a kind of death, and I wasn't into memorializing his passage from civilian life to the forbidden dark life of seminarians on a country estate in Upstate New York with a fancy last supper. So I balked at it, and this upset him. But I was stubborn, and I refused to do it. We compromised on an almost-fancy place on the Upper East Side, and it was a place I knew pretty well. They served us drinks, and I turned it into just another night on the town, which was what I'd wanted in the first place. And it would have been just another night on the town except for the conversation we had around ten o'clock, which was the last hour before the drinks took their toll, and I stopped making sense. Eddy started talking about the reasons why we do the things we do, and he told me the story about when he was a kid and his parents left him alone in the house for the first time. It occurred to him that no one was there to place any limits on his behavior—that he could do anything he wanted to do and that nobody would scold him or reprimand him. He said that he felt completely free and overwhelmed and exhilarated with the sense of open space and the possession of time that was his. And then the feeling faded, and instead of feeling free and easy and open, he felt an enormous weight and pressure because there was nobody there to tell him what to do. He felt a responsibility to be very careful, even more careful than when his parents were there, and he ended up sitting in a room with the television turned off, wondering who was watching him and thinking it was God.

"It was then I knew that right and wrong has nothing to do with laws or rules or punishment or authority," he said. "It has to do with freedom and what we mistake for freedom," and although I listened carefully, I didn't understand what he was saying, and I didn't understand why he wanted to be a priest for a God who was always watching him. But as I sit here with Susan, feeling the things I'm feeling, I've got this conscience thing banging away like a migraine, because Susan's married, and there are rules about married women, and I might be free, but I'm not that free, and I remember what Eddy said about freedom, and I wonder if there's some special reason for remembering it now.

The drinks keep coming. Pat says she has to leave, and we say good-bye to her, and after she leaves I ask Susan about her husband. She tells me they met in high school, that it started as a friendship because he was going with this girl who went to Miss Porter's and summered on Nantucket. "Then she was in this accident," she says, "and after that she moved away to another city where there were better facilities for her. It was a tragedy, and it tore David up, because he was in the same car when the accident happened, and he came away with nothing."

"But you two were friends."

"I went to Mount Holyoke, and he was a football star and I always felt comfortable with him."

"Maybe that's where I've seen you."

"Where?"

"Mount Holyoke. My roommate had a sister there; we used to go there for parties."

"Maybe," she says.

"You look familiar."

"That's what Pat says. That's what everyone says."

"So you've been married since college?"

"Law school. We got married his second year. I saw him through the whole thing. Worked as a secretary to help support us."

"Why do you work now?"

"Just for something to do. And it's easy."

"Working for Mark Stillman is easy?"

"Mark's easy. Have you done anything for him yet?"

"Not yet."

"Well, if you're working for Carol Schneider, sooner or later you'll work for Mark Stillman. He was very jealous when she was named partner. They were in the same class, and he acts like he's her best friend but he's always plotting something. He and Marty, they're working on this deal. I don't know what it's about. Nobody does, and nobody wants to get near it. They make money, so Westphall and the others let them go their way, but nobody wants to know what they're doing."

At the bar, Allen Ballantine and Joe Monti and Charlie Anton, another associate from the firm, are drinking from martini glasses. They know Susan, and Joe Monti waves to her. Allen Ballantine ignores us, because he's too cool to wave to a first-year associate or a secretary. Susan waves back to Joe Monti, and a second later, as Charlie Anton tells his story, Joe Monti's head explodes backward with high-pitched laughter. Susan tells me that Joe Monti's the horniest guy in the firm and that he's asked out everybody at least once.

"Including you?" I ask.

"Once," she says, "though it really wasn't like he was asking me out, because he knows I'm married, and Sherwin's his boss and he does some work with my husband, so Joe didn't want to get into that. It was one of those harmless after-work dates. He figured he'd try it. He's a pig, really. But then they all are."

At the bar Charlie Anton tells another joke. Allen's sipping from his glass, listening, but not really. Joe Monti's the intermediary, and Charlie's really working. He's known for his stories and he's pumping this one. Joe's laughter is about to take his head off, and there's this rapid-fire repetitive cackling going on that I can hear four tables away. Charlie moves the whole thing to a climax with some broad-shouldered physical humor, and Allen has to step away from the bar to get a better view of it. But physical humor is tough to sustain, and I can hear the quality of the laughter change as it becomes less genuine and more a show of force, a kind of one-upmanship bonding, which is what happens when jokes lose their humor, and guys try to outdo each other in showing how funny they think the joke is. I watch Charlie make a final, though anticlimactic, thrust with his fingers over his glass, and the three of them shake their heads with that final breath exploding, huh-huh-huh-huh, as Joe's wicked high laughter dies away. Then they all just stand there bonding the shit out of one another.

Susan asks me where I live, and I tell her, and she says I'd do better if I'd stayed on the West Side. She says how she doesn't like New York anymore and that she doesn't think I'm like the others, which I take to mean the group that's gathered at the bar or her boss or all the others at the firm or at her husband's firm as they scramble their respective ways upward to the point where they'll spend less and less energy to affect more and more, until they do just about nothing to affect just about everything. Then she asks me what I want to do with my life, and I cringe because her question takes the conversation perilously close to one of those "important things in life" conversations where losers solve their problems by recasting the perspective. I remember that for better or worse this is the profession I've chosen, and I can't understand why she needs to be reminded of it.

Ray arrives with a subdued flourish. He cuts a good figure, and he puts forth one of those unobtrusive handsome faces, as if he'd picked each feature from the column headed "least likely to offend." Everything about him suggests the care he's taken to blend in, to raise no questions, to attract only a certain kind of attention. His suits are taken from the middle of the rack. He wears those horn-rim I'm-a-lawyer glasses, and he creates the impression that he'd give some solid, middle-class Irish girl from the boroughs a peck of kids with even features and moderate athletic abilities. Although it's the image he clings to, he's told me that it's also the image he hates because he feels trapped by it for all those cliché reasons people love to indulge when they're secretly and inwardly very secure with something they know will never change.

Ray looks across the table and sees Susan. He doesn't know who she is, but it only completes a false impression he's held from time to time that I have a way of attracting girls. We both know it isn't true, though sometimes, when he's not feeling too sure of himself, it's as if he wants it to be true, because if it were true it would give him a better anchor in the changeable currents of the Upper East Side.

Susan takes one look at him and sizes him up in a second. She says that we look like we could be brothers. I figure I should take it as a compliment, but somehow it doesn't feel like a compliment. He takes a seat and orders drinks for the table. Susan declines. She says she has to go home. She says good-bye, and Ray stands as she gets up to leave. I figure it's the polite thing to do, so I start to get up, too. Then she places her hand on my shoulder. I sit down again, and she leans over and kisses me on the cheek. She leaves the table, and I sit there as if I've been struck.

"What the hell was that?" Ray says after she's gone.

"What do you mean?"

"That."

"What?"

"The kiss on the cheek thing what."

"Nothing."

"Nothing."

"Nothing."

"When they pat you on the back it's nothing," he says. "That wasn't nothing."

"It was nothing," I say, and I turn, and Allen Ballantine is staring at me with this strange look on his face. Charlie's playing to Joe Monti now, but Joe Monti's staring at me, too. And I figure maybe Ray's right. I figure maybe it wasn't nothing.

THE TEMPLE OF DENDUR

The best thing I can say about last night is that I didn't get arrested. I don't remember much, and what I do remember is like a scene that's been broken down into a series of first and sometimes-painful impressions. In a place on Third Avenue I stood behind some bald guy and pulled the hair over his ears all the way out so he looked like one of the Stooges. In another place I wrapped myself in a roll of tissue paper and walked around the back room like the Mummy, making Mummy sounds, which are these low grunts with a little Egyptian thrown in. Then on Seventy-seventh Street I made Ray lean against a discarded bureau, telling him to assume the position, saying "Spread 'em," and things like that, fooling people who walked by that it was a real bust, saying I worked for the Federal Bureau of Investigation. Then there was the party we crashed on Second Avenue where we met this Melanie Griffith look-alike who'd gone to St. Mary's in South Bend and who couldn't wait to meet Ray because he reminded her of some guy she'd met at Notre Dame. I kept saying, "Notre Dame? He thinks he went to Dartmouth," and the whole thing was pretty pathetic and, except for the Mummy thing, not very funny.

On Saturday mornings I always wake up with a hangover, and hangovers make me feel religious. So every Saturday morning, after I wake up and do what I have to do to get myself up and out the door, I head to this church on Lexington Avenue where the priests kneel on these kneelers around the clock in front of the altar. Everything in the church goes on around the clock, even the confessions. So I go there with my hangover, and I make a confession, and I say the same things I said the week before, hanging my sins on this scaffold of scrupulosity, all of it heightened by the chemically induced anxiety of electrolytes seeking balance in a body with a tortured liver.

I usually get a different priest each time, and the priests are French Canadian, and they give me absolution with accents. But today I get the priest I had last week, and my confession is the same as it was last week, and I think he remembers me as he gives me a lecture on alcohol abuse, saying that the kind of sugar that's in alcohol can affect the way a person behaves, not only when they're drunk, but especially when they're sober. So I'm kneeling in this dark cubbyhole with the light striking the profile of his pale face, and I'm expecting to hear the usual ten Hail Marys and ten Our Fathers, when he gives me a biochemistry lesson instead.

The little window closes, and I'm left in the darkness. I leave the confessional and sit in the back of the church. I say whatever penance is necessary to clean up the mess I'd left in my memory from last night. Then I drop a few coins in the poor box and hand ten dollars to one of the homeless sitting with her bags on the steps outside. I do it because I still feel guilty. There are things I can remember and things I can't remember, and the things I can't remember bother me the most.

I head up Lexington Avenue to a Greek diner. It's always empty except for the young Greek and his sister who make the food. The food's not good, but I prefer the emptiness and the silence of the place to a crowded place with good food. I drink tea and eat toast with jam that sits in small glass cruets. I order a muffin, and the crumbs fall and roll over my plate. The air is colder outside, and in the darkness I think of those Edward Hopper paintings, and I wonder why diners are such lonely places.

After breakfast I go to the museum. I pay what I want, which is what the sign says I'm supposed to do, and I stand for a moment in the Great Hall. The ceiling is four stories high, and the sounds rise like the heat and are taken far away where they probably bounce around and make a racket someplace overhead. Down here, though, despite the crowds and the movement, it's relatively quiet.

I turn to the right and pass under another arch, where the security guard asks me to stop. He can't see my admission button so I pull the lapel of my jacket. He just looks and then looks away. He's an Indian and he's wearing a blue turban, and when I pass him I'm in the Egyptian wing with the mummies under glass and the statuettes and the jewelry they put in the pyramids for the pharaohs to play with in the land of the dead. I head through the gallery and enter the huge open room where there's an ancient temple standing on a plaza of black marble, all of it surrounded by a moat where kids and lovers and others have thrown their coins for good luck. There's a mother there, and she takes her child's hand and they point to the top of the temple. She tells him something about Egypt, and I pass by and leave the whole ancient thing behind me.

I retrace my steps and head up the staircase to the galleries on the second floor. I cross through this passageway with harpsichords from the seventeenth century. I walk up a sloped ramp and down a short corridor to a huge room filled with the Impressionists. The room is packed. Everybody loves the Impressionists. People look at the Impressionists and they figure they're getting their money's worth; they figure they're looking at real "Art." They figure, sure, they might have clouded a few things over with all those primary colors, but a person can still recognize what they're looking at. They didn't go too far; they didn't break things down to the point where they're not things anymore. They don't scare a person off with that abstract stuff, which might or might not be a cruel joke.

I once stood next to a class of high school kids staring at a Jackson Pollock drip painting. One kid said how he "could do that," and then another kid said the same thing. That was how they dealt with it. What people figure they can or can't do has a lot to do with what they consider to be "Art." A lot of people might think they can do what an abstract artist does, but none of them want to talk about what an abstract artist does—because it's out there, resistant to words and logic, articulated only in those unctuous epigrams and metaphors made fashionable in the sixties when shorthand was mistaken for wisdom. And it's scary, too, that abstract stuff. It's the tennis-without-the-net thing, a visual free verse, a kind of aesthetic agoraphobia. So people disparage it or patronize it or say nothing at all, saving (perhaps inescapably) all their praise for the safe harbors of Impressionism, where trees are still trees, and churches might change their color but not their shape, and apples have more character than statesmen.

In the far part of the room where the Postimpressionists hang, I look at a Van Gogh. It's one of his more tortured pieces. Two beautiful ladies with frosted hair, flat, narrow feet, and bags from Bergdorf stand in front of it. They point to things. They nod their heads, staking claims to common ground and the security of easy agreement. One says "how wonderful" it is. The other talks about Van Gogh like he's a movie star, and I think how Van Gogh couldn't give his ear away to a prostitute, and I think what a difference a hundred years, some genius, and an untimely death make in the desirability game.

I leave the Impressionists and Van Gogh, and I sit on a couch by the cafeteria. There's a stone column from Greece there, and when the people come off the elevator and walk around it, some of the children try to touch it. The guard is a kind black man with a Jamaican accent. He says, "Don't touch, little children." There's the noise of plates and glasses from the cafeteria and the sound of shrill voices as people find one another and leave to eat something or go to the second floor to look at the paintings. But I just sit there. I'm not looking for anybody. That's what I tell myself. I tell myself that I've come to the museum to see the Rembrandts. I love the Rembrandts. They're deep and dark and warm, with gold and yellow and white paint dripping off them like spackle. The faces of the old Dutch peasants have the biblical look of wisdom, and looking at them makes me proud to be a human being again, because they connect me to a species more substantial than the faces of the people screaming about parking places and tickets and reservations and all the other things that take up so much time and energy in this city.

So I tell myself that I'm here for the Rembrandts and to walk off a hangover in the midst of things that are beautiful. I watch the people as they come off the elevator and make their way about the great stone column that once held up the Parthenon. Then a light overhead strikes something like chrome. There's a muted flash from across the circular space, and I ignore it and then look again, and I see her. It's the girl from the nasty Jesuit party. It's impossible not to recognize her as she moves along in her wheelchair, stopping, then moving again with her boyfriend, the wild and impetuous poet.

I wait for them to recognize me, but it doesn't happen. They pass by me, and although my eyes meet hers, nothing seems to register as they hurry off down the hallway to the Great Hall. I debate whether I should follow them and introduce myself again, but I don't know what to say. I figure she doesn't remember me. I made no impression once, and I wonder why I should make no impression twice.

My hangover begins to loosen a bit. I don't go completely white when I stand up. I want to move away from the quarter-moon couch where two women from Long Island talk about beauty as if Titian himself had tinted the copper color of their spooled hair. I try not to think about her, but she's not easy to forget. I remember her name, and the way we talked at the party when she felt as alienated as I did.

I start down the corridor, and when I reach the Great Hall, I see them again as they head off to the Galleries of Egyptian Art. I watch the back of her head as it disappears under the archway to the shadows there.

I pass through the Great Hall and enter again the gallery with the mummies under glass. I raise my lapel for the Indian guard. I enter the dark exhibit of ancient artifacts and monuments signifying promises that have been kept for centuries, and I realize that being accepted has everything to do with power and with everybody wanting to be somebody in a city that's so crowded it's harder and harder to be anybody at all. I pass by a case of gems and a gold collar for a queen. I think how most of life is spent solving the problem of why we feel the need to build monuments to ourselves, and there's this notion of freedom which has nothing to do with pyramids or the embalmed remains of our past, but has everything to do with the flight of birds over pyramids in a desert.

I stand in front of the Tomb of Purneb. I imagine the dusty remains of a man of power, and I think how crazy it all is, this obsession with appearances and status that makes us carve from inert stones tombs for our bodies that lie as inert as the stones that house them, and temples for our spirits that reside elsewhere. I think about Ray and how it might be time to put him on notice that we are beginning to have less and less in common with one another. And down another corridor, by the painted wood exterior of the coffin of Khnumnakht and a model of a boat that once sailed the Nile, I walk out onto the wide dark plaza, brilliant under the windows and the afternoon sun shining over the Temple of Dendur, and I see her again, by herself, oblivious to this co-incidence, which was born centuries ago, as she points to something very high up and very far away.

ZERO-DEFECT APARTMENT

B runo, the doorman, is on duty, which means he's working a double shift, which means he needs some extra money, which means he lost his shirt in a card game with Francis and the Colombians. Bruno really shouldn't be out there, meaning out there in the world, because he just can't see when he's being done or taken or talked about or laughed at. So he just goes along with his huge body and his oversize Mount Rushmore head set like a determined block of first impressions on his very broad shoulders.

He sees me coming down Seventy-fourth, and he turns with his great blue topcoat and the military officer's hat. He's trying to remember something. I can see it in the frown on his face. He knows my name, and I wave to him, and when I'm close enough to hear him he says:

"There was a girl here."

I ask him to repeat himself, to tell me more.

"I don't know," he says, the small brown eyes clouding over in the huge face.

"A girl," he says. "A pretty girl. She came by about an hour ago. Asked if you were here, and I rung up for you."

"Did she leave her name?"

"Yeah."

"She did?"

"I forgot it."

"What did she look like?"

"You know—a girl."

"Yeah. I know. A girl."

"Yeah. Pretty. Blonde hair. Not too tall. Smiled a lot."

"Smiled a lot?"

"Yeah."

"Was her name Susan?"

"Susan?" and his eyes go for a trip around the universe, and I can only guess what's going on in there.

"Was it the girl who was here the other day?" Now I'm talking about Jeanne. "You know, the girl with the long dress and the glasses," and it's like I'm giving him cataracts because everything's gone cloudy again, and he's trying hard to remember, and I'm afraid he's going to hurt himself.

"Remember," I say, "she asked you your sign?" and with each detail I bury him with another layer of confusion, and somebody will have to do an archaeological dig to bring him back to Bruno-speed.

"Never mind," I say, and I ask him about the poker game with Francis and the Colombians. His eyes open and grow dark.

"I shouldn't play with them," he says. "It never goes right."

I take the elevator to my apartment. There's music from the apartment next door. I think it's Ravel, but it's not, at least it's not the one piece of Ravel I know. Then the music stops and starts again. This is opera. Somebody's voice goes way out there. I wonder if aliens pick up on opera singers. Dogs do. One good aria can drive a dog nuts. I listen until the voice descends and a duet begins in the lower registers. I've never seen this neighbor of mine, but I know it's a girl, and she loves her music.

I live in a zero-defect apartment. It has no furniture, and nothing on the wall except a sign that says there hasn't been an accident here in twenty-three days. It's just a studio apartment with two alcoves. There's a small TV on a chair and a mattress on the floor, and except for the TV there just isn't any way I'm going to bump into anything, no matter what condition I come home in.

I open the door, and the apartment is dark, and against the muffled backdrop of opera I hear the distinct and sharp beep of the phone machine. I strike the machine and wait for the tape to rewind. It clicks again, and then a scratchy sound precedes the recorded message. I listen to the voice. It's my cousin. She's got another question. She says I might be more important than a footnote. She asks about something that happened before my mother got sick. She says the weather in Syracuse is cold and that they've predicted snow flurries. I make a note to call her. The tape beeps again and the second message begins. After two words I know it's Susan. She says she dropped by to see me. She says she's home. She wants me to call her if I get in before five.

I sit there with my head in my hands. I play the message again. This is the time when anticipation gives way to dread. There's something wrong about this. I mean, I just went to confession, and I don't know what the rules are about a message on my answering machine from a married woman. But then again, this is New York, and I don't want to stay in, so I call her and she answers. She's happy to hear from me. She'd like to go out for an early dinner. She lives ten blocks away. We decide to meet halfway at this Chinese place.

When I see her, most of my anxiety goes away because she's so pretty, and because I can tell by the way she waves at me that she's genuinely pleased to see me.

We walk to the restaurant, and the host seats us, and the waiters come around with their three-steps-away Chinese civility. We order drinks, and she says we'll be ordering a few more before we have dinner, and I don't know if she says this for herself or for me. Either way I don't complain. The thing about being with her is that I don't feel in any hurry to be someplace else.

I ask her about her husband. She says he's away again on business, and she tells me just how demanding life is for a junior partner.

"They work like slaves for seven or eight years," she says, "and then when they make partner it doesn't get any better. Sure, there's a little more money, and the prestige, but they work harder than when they were associates." Her voice trails off. I can see that life on the home front has suffered.

I do some calculations in my head. I try to figure out how old she is. I nod and look at her and act like I'm listening to every word she says, but in the back room upstairs I've got the solar calculator out, and I'm plugging in numbers and looking at her eyes to do age checks on the lines there.

"So, tell me about your family," she says, and it's like walking off a cliff for me, because I've got about five ways of talking about my family, and I choose the one I want depending on how well I know the person I'm talking to. With Susan I take the middle route, which is the one where I talk more about my hometown than my family. It's the story of the boy from the modest background who wants to make something of himself, and after a bit I've blown right by the family stuff, except for the essentials. Then she tells me about her family, and how she's the oldest, and how it was always important to do everything right, and how being right all the time has made it a very safe life. But now she wonders about all the things she's missed out on because of the decisions she's made.

"Whenever it was the choice between the proper thing and the spontaneous thing," she says, "I always went for the proper thing, except once on a trip to Spain after college. I got away from everybody, even David, and I only did what I wanted to do."

"Sounds like fun," I say.

"It was wonderful," she says, "and then I came back, and David was off to Columbia, and I started work, and we planned things."

"Did you live together?"

"Technically, no. I mean I had my own place, though I spent most of my time at his place."

"And you helped him through law school?"

"Nobody knows that. You see, David comes from this 'wealthy' family, which really isn't wealthy. Back then his father ran into some problems, and I helped out a bit."

We order more drinks, and the hangover that's been with me all day finally disappears. There's a deep-down relaxation in the muscles as I sink into the cushions and listen to her tell me about married life. She says that marrying David was the right thing to do, because no girl in her right mind would have turned down the opportunity.

"And the thing about it," she says, "is that with everything he's got, he's really a nice guy. I mean he's a genuinely good person," and as she says this, I know that this marriage is dead, because this "genuinely good person" stuff is the married equivalent of what a girl means when she says, "Can we still be friends?"

The waiter brings more drinks. There's no pressure to order our meal, but Susan picks up her menu each time he stops by and looks over the columns and says we need more time.

She moves on to other topics, and most of them have something to do with me. So I give her the kind of "tell-all" that disguises itself as self-examination, though it's got very little to do with that since it's more concerned with creating something new than with analyzing what's already there. I can't help myself when I embellish things, when I tell her that I ran a little faster, spoke a little more clearly, made the room laugh a little harder than I did, and it's as if I'm trying to make myself better than I really am in order to justify why she finds me attractive. At one point, after I go on about something particularly good that happened at the *Law Review* Christmas party, I realize that I'm over my head. I realize that I'm sitting here entertaining a married woman, and that I'm attracted to her, and that she's attracted to me, and that we're going to be out for another couple of hours, and that after we eat our dinner, we're going to take ourselves home, and then what . . .

The thought of the "then what" part has always caused me a little anxiety. I don't have a big reputation for this sort of thing, and I always have to drink more in order to ease the whole thing along, hoping that nature—that big-brother and spirit-guide nature—will miraculously take over, and like the blind groping in the perpetual darkness of inexperience I'll be able to find what I'm looking for in a flurry of gyrations I would have choreographed differently.

The waiter comes again, and we order our meal and drink our drinks, and after dinner when he asks us if we want more tea, I say no. I say I'll have a Scotch and soda for the road, and I look at my watch as if I might have another appointment. She picks up on all of this; she knows that I'm a little nervous. It doesn't upset her, but it does amuse her, and after another fifteen minutes of sitting there and looking at one another, we leave the place and stand on Third Avenue. She says, "Why don't you let me see this apartment of yours," and I'm a little flustered, but I don't want it to show, so I say something like, "You don't really want to do that," though I say it in this tone of voice which sounds like I'll do whatever she wants to do. I know I've got these scruples about things, but when it comes to a married woman I've got scruples I didn't even know about. She's persistent, and she's walking with me, and we're kind of heading in no direction as we drift across Third Avenue. Then there's nothing left to do, and we have to go either north or south. I say, "Why don't I walk you to your place," and she says no. She says she wants to see my place, and I can't think of what to say, so we start heading north. We pass three bars, and I suggest we stop off for a drink in each one. She says no, and we get to Seventy-fourth Street, and we turn east, and I tell her there's nothing to do at my place. "I don't even own a stereo," I say, and she tells me to relax, and she puts her arm through mine and now she's leading me. When we reach my place, Bruno's standing there. He approves of this. He thinks this is a step up for me, and he makes a little extra effort with the door. We're inside, and then we're standing at the elevator, and I start to say something. She says, "Relax," and my mind is going very fast, as if it's trying to think about anything but this; and finally, after we enter my apartment, and she sits on the mattress on the floor, I get up the nerve to tell her what I really think. She just looks at me and says nothing. Then she tells me to sit next to her. She's older than I am, and I feel like I'm this young kid who's being told what to do.

I say: "Susan."

"Come here," she says, and she draws her hand across the place next to her.

"Susan, you're married."

"Come here," she says. "I've got something to tell you, and I want to tell it to you when you're close to me."

So I get up from the secretary's chair, and it's like this phony struggle with myself, and I feel this weight on my shoulders, and I sit down next to her, and she lowers her shoulder to come up under my arm, and I put my arm around her, and I hold her, and she tells me how she thinks she's in love with me and that she's been in love with me since the first time she saw me in my office. I can't believe what I'm hearing, and I'm a little dizzy with the drink, and I wonder if I'm having an MSG reaction to the Chinese food. I tell her I'm flattered. I tell her that I like her, too, but that I've never been in a situation like this, and that I can't do a thing about it, meaning her feelings, as long as she's married.

She draws herself closer to me. I can feel the warmth of her body as she turns to me and tells me to stop worrying about all of that. She says something about me being a good Catholic boy, and this kind of pisses me off, and I tell her it's got nothing to do with that. I tell her it's because I can't imagine hurting somebody else, and that being with her can only hurt her husband, even if he doesn't know about it. This upsets her. She pulls away for a second, and I start to get up. But then she turns, and with her healthy and muscular body she takes my arms, and I'm off balance, and she forces me down on the bed. She starts to kiss me, and after a while the warmth goes out of it, and we're dealing with a different kind of heat. She wants her way in all of this. She's the aggressor, and I can't help but kiss her, thinking that if I kiss her hard, I'll be able to get on top of her. We struggle for a few minutes, until I hold her tightly and regain my balance. Then we stop kissing, and she looks at me. She's hurt and a little angry. She wants to know what's wrong with me. She wants to know what it is I find wrong with her. I tell her nothing. I tell her that it's because of the way things are, and that I feel guilty about doing this sort of thing under the circumstances. She looks at me, and she doesn't believe me. She starts to cry, and I hold her, and her shoulders move as she cries, and I feel terrible for hurting her, and I wonder if I should do something that I think is wrong just to make her feel good again. I don't like myself for these scruples over what's supposed to be right and wrong. And I wish I didn't think so much about things, and I wish I could just let things go.

After a while she stands up. I get her some water, and she regains her composure. She says she should leave. She says she's embarrassed. I tell her not to be embarrassed. I tell her I'm the one who should be embarrassed. I say all sorts of things to make it right again. But nothing really works. She grabs her jacket that she'd draped over the secretary's chair, and she leaves. I just sit there for a long time. I look at the sign on the wall. I check off another day. There hasn't been an accident in my place in over twenty-four days. I figure that's got to be some kind of record.

A DEAD MAN

eulah's from South Carolina, and she's my secretary, and she's got an accent, and some people think it's a special thing to have a secretary who has an accent, though they're the same people who say a Southern accent isn't as special as a British accent, which is why so many of the executive secretaries have this affected British accent, which isn't British at all, but is a cross between Masterpiece Theatre and overbite.

A lot of people in the firm have this thing about accents, especially the people from Connecticut who grew up talking with that flat everyman-Connecticut talk. It's like now that they've arrived and have entered the realm of what they consider to be a truly important class of people, with their royalist airs of wealth so great it abstracts itself out into the rituals and habits of apparently measured lives, they chat up this clipped and pristine talk where everything becomes stilted and trussed up in first-person plurals like a bad Dickens movie, a kind of cultural gigantism, an aesthetic of heroism and victory.

So the Big Boys talk like Fagin, and their secretaries sound like extras from the British Invasion, and I've got Beulah from *Gone With the Wind,* though I shouldn't say that I've "got" Beulah in the way that she's my secretary, because she's really not my secretary. She's just the person who answers my phone and does my typing if she's not typing something for somebody else. Beulah's always typing something for somebody else. She's the slowest typist in the whole firm. She even types more slowly than she talks. Charlie Anton told me she's still working on the memo he gave her when he arrived over a year ago.

It's not that Beulah isn't nice. She can be nice enough, with her Southern manners and the consideration she shows everybody. It's just that she's so honest, she's a little too informative about my whereabouts, and I've had to ask her more than once not to say, "I don't know where he is, he never tells me nothin'," on those occasions when she doesn't know where I am.

"But what am I supposed to say then when Ms. Schneider comes yellin' at me lookin' for you?" she asks me.

"Just say I'm in the library."

"But what if you're not in the library?"

"I'm always in the library."

"Last week you weren't in the library."

"That's true, but Pat will know where to reach me, so it's the same thing as being in the library."

"So you weren't in the library."

"Not technically, no."

"So you want me to say that you are when you aren't, then."

"No. Not really. What I want is—"

"'Cause I can't do that, 'cause if that's not lyin', that's too close to lyin' for this girl," and we go around with it, and Beulah continues to answer my phone with a "Mr. Who?" when she forgets my name, and I continue to hide out in this back room off the library where there's an old chair and a discarded air purifier.

———

Joe Monti says, "Good morning, Beulah," as he comes into my office. He sits in one of the chairs on the other side of the desk. He holds a cup of coffee, and he places the tips of his surprisingly small shoes on the edge of my desk. He smiles at me. It's not that he's taking liberties. He's a mid-level guy, and he can do what he wants, though in a way he is taking liberties, because I don't know him all that well, and I wonder what he's doing in my office. Then I remember that he knows Ray from someplace, and that after Susan left the bar Friday night, Joe parted company with the other Westphall, Sellars people and decided to tag along with us.

"I liked the Mummy thing," he says, and he laughs, and I watch him carefully because I'm trying to figure whether he's laughing with me or at me. I can't tell, so I just shrug and say something like, "Yeah, well."

"I mean it," he says. "You're a very funny guy," and he imitates what sounds like a Mummy grunt, and I wince with the memory of it.

He says, "Ray tell you about the party on Wednesday night?"

"The what?"

"Wednesday night. The party. With the girl Ray met," and I try to remember what invitations are out there, and I can't think of any, and I have to chalk this up as a first since Ray and I made this pact back in law school (when I was the one who knew about all the parties, and he was living with his folks in Brooklyn) that we'd tell each other about the parties we knew about, and that we'd go to them together, thinking it was a way to be certain of getting a lot of invitations as long as at least one of us was popular.

"I haven't talked to him since Friday," I say.

"Oh, well," Joe Monti says, "I'm sure he'll tell you about it," and it becomes clear that the horniest guy in the office is sitting there with his coffee and his brilliant tie and his tiny little shoes and double-breasted suit perfectly tailored to hide his gut, because he thinks that Ray and I can get him girls.

"That Susan's a great kid," he says, and the puzzle's almost complete. He's fishing for what was going on behind that kiss on the cheek in the Four Seasons, and I remember what happened with Susan on Saturday night, and I feel a little empty inside.

I say, "Yeah, a real brick," and he laughs, and I laugh, and over the sound of our laughter we're looking at one another with deadly serious eyes. My phone rings, and I pick it up, still laughing my phony laugh, still deadly serious. I say hello, and it gives him a chance to leave, which he does slowly, lowering his feet, holding his cup with both hands, rising slowly, mouthing the words "I'll talk to you," until he reaches the door, where his legs stiffen, and one arm goes out straight, and he takes a step in the frozen, halting gait of the Mummy, making the Mummy sound one more time before his body relaxes. Then he shakes his head and leaves with his knotted little ham of a fist stuck in the small of his back with a thumbs-up for whatever.

"What's so funny?" Susan asks.

"Oh, hi," I say with a kind of forced levity. "It was just a visit from the horniest man in America."

"Joe Monti?"

"Joe Monti."

"What did he want?"

"Who knows. He and Ray know each other, and we all went out Friday night."

"He wants you to introduce him around."

"I guess."

"Look—"

"Yeah?"

"I'm sorry about Saturday night."

"Don't be. It's all right."

"And . . ."

"And?"

"This is hard."

"What is it?"

"I want you to hear it from me."

"Hear what?"

"I left David yesterday."

"You what?"

"I left my husband yesterday. The marriage, it's over."

I listen to this, and I feel the evanescent yet unmistakably mild nausea of guilt. I think: This is my fault. I think: I did this. I think: I caused this.

"I'm telling you now," she says, "before it gets out. I don't want you to feel guilty or responsible."

"But I do."

"I knew you would, but don't. It was going to happen anyway. Saturday only showed me how close I'd come to leaving."

"Are you all right?"

"I'm a little numb, but I think I'm all right."

"I'll stop by later."

"Good," she says, and I hang up the phone and sit there, and I wonder how I get myself into these things. I think how ill-equipped I am for this kind of serious adult stuff, how it's for other people who like the emotional ups and downs of complicated things. I wonder what will happen. I wonder what she'll expect. I need a cigarette. Then I think I want some coffee. I leave for the library, where Pat's got a pot brewing. As I leave, Beulah asks me where I'm going.

"The library," I say.

"Right," she says, and I can't tell if she's being sarcastic or not, but I'm not in the mood to take it right now. I turn the corner, and I hear her voice again in the aftersound of what she said, and the "right" was definitely a "sure, you are," sarcastic kind of "right." I figure I'll have to speak with her about this. Then I reach the elevator and press the button, and I hear her voice again, and I get mad about it. I turn around and walk back through the lobby and down the corridor to my office. I stand by her desk while she answers the phone for somebody else. When she gets off the phone, I look at her. I say: "The library, Beulah. Just in case you didn't get that. I'm going to the library."

"Sure 'nough," she says, and she looks down, and she doesn't want to take it on, and I look a little foolish standing there.

Pat's busy arranging the newspapers in the rack. There's coffee in her office. I help myself. She says: "That's the last time I go drinking with you," and I forget that Pat had four drinks on Friday night.

I say: "You're a bad seed, Pat," and she likes this because she wants to be part of that Monday morning "aren't-we-a-bad-crowd" camaraderie.

I wait to see if she has anything to say about Susan. I figure there's some secret she's dying to tell me. Finally she asks: "Is something wrong?"

"What?"

"You look a little funny."

"No. Nothing, it's just that I heard some news this morning that kind of set me back."

"Good news or bad news?"

"Can't say, really."

"Well, what was it?"

I figure this is it. She knows, and she wants me to say something.

"I don't know, just something."

"Oh," she says, with her face raised up as if to say: "I know. It's confidential, but I can keep a secret, too," and she walks to her desk and drinks her coffee.

I stand there and thumb through the *Times*. The Perry Ellis girls are wearing sweaters this morning, big, fluffy 1950s-type sweaters. They look preppy and substantial, well-off, content, satisfied, maybe a little too thin for true preppies, but pretty, desirable.

Pat's phone rings. I watch her as she talks on the phone. I walk to the back of the library with the paper. I can see her through the glass wall. This is important. She looks at me. I hear her say "No." She rubs her forehead. She shakes her head slowly. She puts the phone down and waves to me. I point to myself. She waves again. I point to myself again. She hangs up the phone and says: "Yes, you. Who the hell do you think I'm waving to?"

I walk to her office and stand in the doorway.

"That was Susan," she says.

"Yes?"

"So what's the story here?"

"The story." I act dumb. I can keep a secret.

"You don't know?"

"I know," I say. I can keep a secret.

"It's crazy."

"I didn't do anything, Pat."

"Don't be so defensive. I'm not accusing anybody."

"I know, but I feel guilty about this," and I feel stupid trying to defend myself when there's no need. "I don't know whether I should feel guilty or not, but the fact is I do feel guilty, even though I know I didn't do anything."

"She's been unhappy for a long time. David's a nice guy, but he's a big shot now, and there just isn't much time left for their life together."

I lean against the window over a newly opened crate of CCH binders. The library door opens behind me. Solomon Isaacson and Bob Clark charge into the stacks. Clark's another one of the "comers." This place is overstocked with "comers," and they all charge at things like they're running down abstractions with one-syllable sticks.

Clark gives me a look. He knows he's a "comer" because there are "comers" and there are workers who aren't "comers," and there are ones who don't work at all, who are either "charmers" or complete "fuck-offs." Bob Clark thinks he's got me pegged. I figure he's probably got me pegged right.

"I better get going," I say to Pat, and she nods with her semiserious, guilt-peddling face, and I figure I better stop by Susan's desk on the way back to see if there's something I can say.

I turn the corridor after Bill Vierps almost knocks me over with his head buried in the book he holds over my head. I go, "Yo, Bill," and he grunts like he's busy. He passes by, and I look down the corridor, and I see Susan sitting at her station. She looks up. Mark Stillman stands behind her. He's got his hands behind her back. He's massaging her shoulders, a mini-high-backrub. He's got this pathetic little defiant look on his face as if what he's doing is OK. He sees me, and Susan makes a face that he can't see. The face she makes says, "Get this guy off me," and her eyebrows are lowered, and her eyes shoot straight to the ceiling, and because he can't see her, but can only sense her resistance in the hard way she holds herself, he continues to knead her shoulders, ignoring her feelings about all of this. He's wearing one of his grand-mal ugly suits, all dash and angle, aerodynamically dangerous with lapels so wide a stiff breeze could wind-sail him a couple of city blocks.

"Suzy's having a bad day today," he says, and he says it with an oiled and polished purr of language, the doctrinaire equivalent of a vanity plate, and I see her stiffen with each pass. I look at his watch and the other trinkets of jewelry and his almost-bald head. He knows that he can do this, because he's the boss, and the boss can do what he wants. He knows she's uncomfortable, but he's going to force it all the way, placing the burden on her to say something, to object, thinking that she won't say a thing, because, as bad as it is, it's easier to go along, to play his game. He looks at me. He knows I'm more than just a casual observer. I look at Susan, whose face has hardened into an almost-smile of resignation, because this guy who's wanted to jump in her pants for years has now taken the liberty to touch her. She stiffens her shoulders again, so that under his touch she doesn't so much pull away from him as she just grows smaller beneath his hands, contracting, freezing, folding herself into herself, as he, knowing that she has pulled away, removes his hands so as not to suffer the embarrassment of a more obvious rejection.

I ask if everything's all right. He says: "Suzy will be OK," and then he says something else, and I don't remember what it is, but I make an ill-timed comment, which isn't meant to be funny, and Susan, the woman who always talks with that keep-the-laughter-down voice, cannot keep the laughter down, and she lets loose with this explosive, hard laugh, and with that laugh Mark Stillman looks at me with his dead, dark almond eyes. He thinks that I've ridiculed him, and he thinks that Susan, his beautiful secretary, has laughed at him because of what I said, and in one instant all of the greedy, gaudy, rococo flourishes of gold chains, watches, bracelets, rings, the bluff and bluster, high-rise and puffery of his public self don't mean a thing, and Mark Stillman, the short kid who probably never got picked for the baseball team, and who's decided to fuck every poor son of a bitch who reminds him of that sad fact, knows that he isn't everything he wants to be, and in that same instant, as our eyes meet like duelists over Susan's almost-blonde head, he knows that I think he's a loser, and I know that I'm a dead man.

This happened when you were a kid:

Your brother was a star. He was a football hero. And every-body knew him because he could bend steel with his bare hands. He was a regular superman, and he was good-natured and smart enough—not so smart as to make any-body anxious, but smart enough to get by, and good-natured enough that everybody, especially the older people in town, talked about him and smiled or laughed and said, "That one," and passed him along, because he was a foot-ball hero, and he was OK.

One day in September he was home from New Haven, where he wore nice suits and embalmed dead bodies and drove in black limousines to and from cemeteries. He liked to tell jokes about what happened in mortuaries, and he was starting a new story when you told him that you wanted to go out for the football team. He just stopped and looked at you and raised an eyebrow. He said: "They're gonna kick your ass," and the way he said it was like a threat, and it told you how different you and he were.

It wasn't that you were too small. You were as tall as the other guys, but you were thin, and although you could be strong, in the way that skinny kids can be surprisingly re-silient, you never could rely on your strength, because how strong you were at any given time depended on where you were or who you were with, and you were never very strong in your hometown. There was always something that went on inside of you when you were in your hometown, and your brother knew this. He knew it wasn't "your" hometown in the way that it was "his" hometown. So he said: "They're gonna kick your ass," and he tried to scare you, and then to make sure that he had, he told you about a drill called Bull-in-the-Ring. "I made kids cry during that one," he said, and he laughed a little, and you knew it was just a matter of time, and the time passed.

It was a hot day, one of those days in late September that feel like August except for the difference in the way the light strikes things. The team had been practicing for about a week and you'd done all the running and the push-ups and the sit-ups, and you'd listened to Claude Bauer, a kid who'd stayed back a year in grammar school and who was bigger than everybody else, brag about the chance to wear uniforms and pads and the chance to hit somebody. Then the day came, and they gave out the uniforms, and you put on the shoulder pads, and you slipped the thigh pads in those short knee pants, and you tried on the spikes you'd broken in over the weekend, and you listened to the *clack-clack-clack* of the spikes on the walkway as everybody headed out to the field. Claude Bauer walked behind you, and as you hit the doorway he ran past you and almost knocked you over. Then Gerry Kolik bumped into you, and you were off balance, and with the helmet top-heavy on your head you remembered your brother laughing at you because he knew he'd scared you, and there you were, off balance and scared, knowing what was coming and not knowing what was coming.

Everybody ran around the field a few times. A few guys were banging each other on the shoulders—not because it was doing anything, but because they'd seen it on TV. You ran around and yelled with the rest of them, but you could hear your voice, and you knew it wasn't free and loose and crazy like the others. You could hear it, and it sounded weak.

Everybody lined up, and you ran at one another and the coach made you stop just before you hit. The whole thing was building up to the time when you'd all be tough enough to smack one another. You tried to get into it. You tried to make yourself loose and angry and hard, and as long as there wasn't any talk about the Bull-in-the-Ring drill, you felt OK.

The shadows got longer, and you were sweating, and the sweat got cool as the sun went down, and practice was almost over when Coach Marconi said: "Make a circle." Claude Bauer started to scream like a plugged animal, and the others took it up to show that they were as tough as he was. They made a circle, and you joined the circle, and everybody started to scream: "Bull bull bull bull . . ."

The first bull was a fireplug of a kid. Nothing could hurt him; he had no angles to break. He was built like a bullet, and he ran at one group on the circle, and they pushed him back. Then he ran where Claude Bauer stood, and Bauer picked him up and threw him on his back where he kicked like a beached turtle. Then he got up and ran again, and he was pissed, so he ran at Bauer and Bauer tried to hit him with a forearm, but the kid dodged once and caught Bauer off guard, and he had this head of steam, and in a second he was by him and out. That made Claude Bauer the next bull, and he stood in the center like a criminal picking his spot, and he eyed the edge of the ring where his buddies stood. He pointed to them and started to run at them until the last moment, when he turned and cut, moving fast for an oversize kid with no brain. He ran at Jimmy Burke, the poor bastard who stood on your right. Then he cut and ran toward Greg Sweeney, the poor bastard who stood on your left. Then he made his final cut and ran at you. He hit you with everything he had, and in less than a second he was over you and outside the ring. The cry went up: "Bull bull bull . . ." You picked yourself up and ran to the center of the ring. Your leg hurt, but that didn't matter. Nothing mattered—not even your brother and what he had said. You thought you were ready. You looked about the circle and somebody said, "Over here, pigeon," and then somebody said, "Stop picking the hair outta your teeth," and you heard them say "faggot," and you got mad, but when you got mad you got empty inside, not crazy and hot like you're supposed to get. You ran as hard as you could, but when you hit Billy McMahon, hoping he'd fall apart and let you out, he didn't even flinch. You were back in the center again, and the laughter went on, and something happened: The ring started to get smaller, because when you turned to run again you could only run two steps before Gerry Kolik smacked your head back. You tried to go at him, but there wasn't any room to get up the speed, and you could see their faces up close, and most of them were laughing and getting in their shots without risking a thing. This went on for a while, and you remembered what your brother had said, and the circle wasn't even a circle, and over your left ear you heard Claude Bauer laugh his stupid laugh and you felt the first thing you could call a real pain—a pain you couldn't ignore. It was in the small of your back, and you were off your feet, and the last face you saw was the quarterback's face. He was the hero of the team, and everybody looked up to him, and you admired him, and then there was the pain again, and then no pain, and then nothing at all.

That night when you got home, your mother was in one of her moods. You could tell things were bad, because when things were bad she'd wear her glasses so that the top of the frames covered her eyes in the way that she could see you without having to make eye contact. There was some slamming going on in the kitchen—just a plate or two, and then it was over. Whatever it was, it was like a storm that blew through the house and then went on to someplace else. Your father was home. He was reading the paper. The lights were on. It was dark outside. Your father noticed that you walked with a limp. "Are you all right?" he asked, and you said, "Yes." You said it had been a tough day at football practice, and he said you looked like a guy who'd played against your brother. "Now he was a bull," he said, meaning your brother, meaning "that one," and he read the paper, and you listened to nothing, because things had grown quiet again all over the house.

VANITY NIGHT

W hat we have here," Don says, "is the best goddamn studio in the city." He sits back in his chair. There's coffee in the black cup. The cup says: "Producer: Need I Say More." He picks it up and then sets it down again. I'm sitting in a chair to his left. Before us the soundboard extends out to either side with buttons and switches and dials. He pulls a microphone down from a flying boom. The mike is covered in foam and looks like one huge puff ball. He speaks to an assistant in the sound room beyond the Plexiglas window. He says, "Johnny, we got the gig at eight o'clock. An acoustic guitar, a voice. Straightforward. Tell Lesanne we'll leave plenty of room for the bass if they want to pay for it. Maybe an upright. Try for a 'Tupelo Honey' sort of thing."

Johnny waves from the sound room. The producer lifts the mike. It sails over his head and comes to a soft stop. He turns to me.

"We opened in the seventies," he says. "Produced a lot of disco for the clubs. Sixty-, ninety-minute tapes. Stamped it out. It was just a formula for the studio guys. But it made the money. By the eighties we could go for the good stuff."

He pulls a CD from the board behind him. He hands it to me.

"Do you know him?"

I look at the CD. I look at the name. I've never heard of this guy.

"Yeah, sure," I say, "I've heard of him. Everybody's heard of him." This makes the producer feel good. He sits up in his chair.

"You bet they have," he says. "He's big. And he's gonna be very big." Don takes the CD back and looks at it. "Fifteen hundred sales in the Rochester market alone. Christ, he's a national hero in Rochester. I got him airplay there, and in Cleveland, too. This stuff sells. Kid's a genius."

I say: "The kid's a genius."

"Forget about it," he says. Then he pulls the mike down again. "Hey, Johnny. I want to listen to the other kid's tape." He puts the CD back on the shelf, and he pulls a cassette from his leather jacket. Everything this guy wears is either leather or black, and he's about ten years too old for the leather and about five years too old for the black. He places the tape in the cassette player behind him. He fiddles with a few switches and a knob or two. The guitar comes up, and then the voice. It's William-call-me-B.J. I don't remember the song, but I know if I wait long enough I'll hear that dip he does with his voice, and sure enough, after about a minute he makes the change, and the voice breaks just so. Don, the producer, turns around and switches off the tape.

"You know this kid?" he asks.

"He's a friend of a friend."

"Who, the girl?"

"Yeah."

"You mean Jeanne's friend. This Mary person."

"Right."

He pulls an envelope from his pocket. He looks at something he's scratched there. "Mary Bain. That's right. She's the one paying for this."

"Right."

"Her and Jeanne are friends."

"Right."

"And you and Jeanne are friends."

"Right."

"So everybody's friends here."

"I guess."

"Then you can't tell me what you really think of this stuff."

"Well, I . . ."

"Forget about it," he says. "It's vanity night."

"Vanity night?"

"Yeah. Vanity night. We only open Monday nights if some-body wants to lay out a little cash to do a demo. Your friend, Mary, she paid for it; we're open."

"Vanity night," I say.

"Hey, don't get me wrong," he says. "The kid's OK. But this James Taylor stuff. I mean, it's for girls' schools. It's old. You know what I mean. Today it's a drum machine and a dancer. That's all it takes. Nobody sings their shit anymore."

"Nobody?" I say.

"Nobody," he says.

"Right," I say.

"This business sucks," he says. "But I love it."

"Yeah, well . . ."

"Music, man. It fucks people up. Ever since the Beatles. There ain't a kid alive who doesn't think he can't do that. Shit, man, the Beatles are older than me."

"And two are dead."

"Fucks 'em up, man. Everybody wants to be a fucking star."

"Yeah."

"You're a lawyer, right?"

"Yeah."

"What kind of lawyer?" He picks up his cup. It's empty. He takes one of those airplane nips out of his pocket. He pours it in the cup.

"Criminal," I say. I figure this will get his attention.

"Criminal law?"

"Right."

"No shit."

"No shit."

"What kind of criminal?"

"What do you mean?"

"You know: good guy, bad guy. What are you, a D.A. or something?"

"No. Defense. White-collar stuff. The big boys."

"No shit."

"Well . . ."

"You look a little young for that."

"Yeah, well . . ."

"So you, like, defend guys who steal from the stock market and banks and shit like that."

"Yeah. Shit like that."

"They're the fuckin' criminals all right. Fuckin' D.A.'s goin' after the Mob—that's nothin' compared to the criminals you're talkin' about."

"Nothing," I say.

"Lotta criminals in this business, too," he says. "And I'm not talkin' about that Dick Clark shit from the Pat Boone days."

"No?"

"No."

"Yeah."

"Like I say," he says, "it sucks, but I love it."

"You love it."

"I love it. Like catch this: I take my boy's CD up to Rochester. I know a few people there. I want to get some air-play. Break into a market. You think it's easy to break into a market?"

"No, I—"

"Hell, no, it ain't easy. It's a bitch."

"It sucks."

"Damn right, it sucks. But I take my boy, you know, to

three stations. You know what they say? You know what they want?"

"I know what they want."

"You know what they want?"

"Yeah, well . . ."

"Bet your ass you know what they want."

"It sucks."

"Sure, it sucks, but hey, like, I'm not gonna get the airplay."

"Hell, no."

"You do what you gotta do."

"Right."

"You do it."

"I understand."

"You understand, then?"

"Yeah, I understand."

"Hey, kid, you're all right."

"Yeah."

"But watch out for them criminals." He's laughing now, and Jeanne's standing in the doorway.

"What criminals?" she asks, and Don goes: "Forget about it," and I say: "Yeah, forget about it."

"Mary and B. J. are here," she says, and I get up and shake Don's hand and follow Jeanne down the hall to the waiting room. On the wall there are black-and-white publicity photos. I don't recognize anybody, even the ones that are supposed to be famous. One guy's got the cobalt-black hair and the lamb-chop sideburns and the Mafia aviator glasses and the silk scarf, and next to him there's a picture of four black guys with their blinding smiles and tight silk suits with short velvet collars.

"B.J.'s ready," Mary says, and she's changed her hair again, to one of those blunt-cut Dutch-boy looks where all the hair is the same length. She looks bigger than usual, and I figure it must be the trench coat with the belt.

"So you're ready, B.J.?" Jeanne asks, and William-call-me-B.J. just stands there holding his guitar case with decals from places he's never been.

"Let's do it," he says.

"Is Ray here yet?" Mary asks.

"Ray?" I say.

"I told him eight o'clock," she says, and I can't figure why she's looking for Ray, but I don't have the chance to follow up on it because Don, the producer, motions for us to follow him. He directs B.J. to the sound room, where he has Johnny set him up in front of a couple of mikes. The rest of us sit in the visitors' room off to the side. We can see what's going on through the glass, and we can see across the sound room into the control room. B.J.'s sitting on a stool under a red light. The lighting is pretty dramatic, like something off an album cover. In the control room, Johnny pulls the mike down and starts giving B.J. instructions about the sensitivity of the mikes and about not "pushing too hard." B.J. turns to us and makes a funny face that isn't funny. He's the center of attention, and he's loving it, but he's trying to act like it isn't a big deal, when he thinks it's a very big deal. He wants to do this forever. He wants to make it. Ambition surges through him like a drug. He wants to shed his bland fizz of a CPA's head. He wants the black leather, the cobalt-black hair, the aviator glasses, and a funeral in New York where cops stop traffic and groupies chant his name. "Fucks 'em up," Don said. "It really fucks them up."

"I hope I gave him the right address," Mary says as she turns from the window and doesn't look at me.

"Who's that?" I ask.

"Ray," she says, distracted, like I should know without asking.

"Ray," I say.

"Yes. Your good friend, Raymond."

"I thought you didn't like my good friend Raymond."

"Things change," she says, and there's an edge to it and this is new territory for Mary and me, and I tell myself I couldn't care less, that it doesn't mean a thing to me, but there seem to be a lot of things going on these days without me. I'm not in touch like I used to be.

B.J. starts the sound check for the levels for the first song. In the control room Don's on the phone, and Johnny's doing all the work. Johnny says: "Hit the lower strings again," and the speakers in the waiting room hum a second before they come on. Then the bass notes hum until Johnny draws back the volume. "Good," he says, and the mikes are so sensitive we can hear B.J. breathing.

Don's still on the phone. He screams at somebody, and Johnny holds up his hand, putting everything on hold until Don's through. Then Don slams the phone down. He says: "Do you believe the stones on that guy?" He shrugs his shoulders, draws up his jacket, and sits back. He says, "OK, what do we got here?" and it's almost time to begin.

Johnny points to B.J., and B.J. strums the guitar. It's one of the songs from the campfire at Mary's Labor Day cookout. Mary puts her head back and sways a bit with the music. Jeanne touches my arm and asks me to follow her.

"What is it?" I whisper.

"Out here," she says. "I have to talk to you."

From behind the door B.J.'s voice is lower now, but we can still hear him. The songs still sound the same. Jeanne leans against the wall with the photos. She puts her head back and sighs.

"This shouldn't take too long," she says.

"What shouldn't?"

"The session," she says. "Mary paid for three hours, but he'll be done in two." The top of her head touches the wall. "Folkies always start repeating themselves after a while."

"Yeah," I say.

She rubs her hand over her hair. Her glasses catch the dim light and hide her eyes. She looks Swedish.

"Have you talked to Eddy?" she asks.

"Eddy?" I say. "No. Well, yes. I saw him when he was in town."

"But not since then."

"There might have been a message on the machine one night. At least it sounded like him, though it only recorded part of it, and then I punched the wrong button."

"Well, I've talked to him almost every week now since he left."

"No kidding."

"No kidding."

"I didn't know."

"It just sort of started. I wrote him a good-luck note. He wrote a thank-you note and a little more. So I wrote again, and then he wrote again, and then there were a few calls, you know, one thing led to another."

"He's a good guy."

"He's having a tough time," she says.

"Is he?" and I remember the night at the party.

"He is."

"I thought so," I say. "When I saw him in September there seemed to be something."

"Did he tell you about his Novice Master?"

"His what?"

"A guy named George. The guy in charge."

"Yeah, he did." I remember our talk in the bar. There were things he wouldn't say.

"Well, this guy's made his life miserable."

"Jesus."

"Anyway, what I wanted to tell you was that Eddy's thinking of leaving."

"He is?"

"He's told me he's about had it, and things are getting worse and falling apart, and he's not sure what to do or where to go."

"Why didn't he just call me?"

"He's too embarrassed. He thinks, you know, like, here he did this radical thing, and now he's got to retreat, you know, change, do something else."

"Maybe I should call him."

"I don't know. Maybe it's best to let it go for now. I'm sure he'll be calling you," and she stands up straight. She has perfect posture. Her upper body rests casually on her strong legs. She takes her hand and touches my cheek. She says: "Sometimes I'm more worried about you than I am about Eddy," and she walks past me to the visitors' room.

Ray has arrived. He and Mary stand next to one another by the window and look out on the rose-colored sound room where B.J. sits on a stool and strums his guitar and sings his third song. Mary places her arm around Ray's waist. Then she takes it back and turns around.

"He's doing wonderfully," she says, and Ray turns and sees me. He doesn't give away a thing with the stupid salute he does.

"Who's that woman working the board now?" she asks, and she points to the control room where Don and Johnny are huddled in conversation, and this anorexic waif with a headband who appears to be running the show.

"That's Lesanne," Jeanne says. "Our resident flake." And I figure coming from Jeanne this means Lesanne has got to be a high-fiber breakfast cereal.

"B.J.," Lesanne breaks in, "three words: ecstasy, creation, equality," and it's time to worry when a hippie-retread starts stringing nouns together. But B.J.'s into this thing. He just goes, "Right. Right. I know what you're saying," and he speaks in this breathy Bob Dylan voice. Then Mary turns to Jeanne.

"She's not going to ruin this, is she?" Mary asks.

"Don't worry," Jeanne says. "Johnny knows what he's doing," and with that Johnny breaks in and talks to B.J. about sound levels again. Ray steps aside and asks me how I'm doing. I say I'm doing fine, and I say it with a look that asks: "What's going on here?" He just shrugs his shoulders.

Then Don breaks in on the mike to talk to B.J. He's not as easy as Johnny. He talks rough, and B.J.'s taken aback a bit.

"So, kid," Don says, "you ever think in one of your songs there, you take a break and do some talking."

"Talking," B.J. says.

"Yeah, talking, you know, Elvis did it there in one of his first songs."

"Talking," B.J. says.

"Talking?" Mary says. She doesn't go for this at all.

"Yeah, that's what I said," Don says. "I'm thinking about one of those parts where you, like, break off and talk against the music, and then you come back singing, like, with the chorus."

B.J. doesn't know what to say. He never thought of talking in his songs. But he doesn't want to offend Don or lose Don's interest. He thinks that if Don gets interested he might turn this thing into something more than just a vanity night. So he says: "Well, I . . . yeah, that's not such a bad idea," and Mary's out of her mind, shooting this look at B.J. like: "Don't you dare."

"Just an idea," Don says.

"Yeah, well, let's talk about it," B.J. says.

"Later, kid," Don says, and he picks up the phone again.

"It's a good idea," B.J. says to no one.

"You bet it's a good idea," Don says from the back of the control room, and he picks up the phone and starts talking again. This time he's screaming at some P.R. guy in L.A., calling him an idiot because all Californians are idiots for the usual reasons.

Jeanne opens the bottle of wine Ray brought to celebrate the session. She pours it into paper cups and passes them around. B.J. starts his fourth and last song. The same drop-in-the-voice phenomenon happens again, and hearing the fourth song I can't remember the first song. Even Jeanne picks up on it. She whispers that the hardest thing for any new songwriter is being able to write songs that are different from one another.

Ray and Mary stand at the window. They sip their wine. They move slowly to the music. Ray tells Mary just how great he thinks B.J. is. B.J.'s voice booms through the puff ball mike; his eyes are closed. In the control room Lesanne turns away and tries to talk to Johnny, who's trying to talk to Don, who's talking to somebody in L. A. In the corner Jeanne is stretched out on the couch. I just stand there sipping my wine. It's one of those moments in a crowd when everyone is taking care of themselves. I look at the back of Mary's head as she leans it on Ray's shoulder. I think how life is a constant surprise. I listen to the music easing itself through the small speakers suspended from the ceiling. I sit in a chair next to the couch where Jeanne lies with her eyes closed, and as the glare of the red light from the sound room billows out like the soft intimation of some out-of-the-way cocktail lounge, I wonder how much it costs, and whether the price is worth it, to purchase a few hours of vanity.

THE SUITS

It doesn't happen often, but it happens. There is the rare morning when I wake up rested with no hangover, and there's light in the room, and the place looks clean, and the shower refreshes me, and I don't have to put in an hour of reconstructive surgery. Like I say, it doesn't happen often, but because I didn't join Mary and Ray and Jeanne and B.J. for a late-night dinner with champagne at the Bow-House, I got home early enough to get to bed and to sleep, and then to wake without the crushing sense that I had succeeded once again in almost killing myself.

There's no one reason why I didn't join them. The Mary and Ray Show had gotten a little thick, not that I begrudge them whatever—which is what I say when I begrudge the hell out of it. It's just that I find it hard to take now that Mary's done the barrel-roll-180-degree change of mind and heart, and the whole thing makes me a little jealous. Mary's been my friend for years, and the fact that she never liked Ray always said something about her and something about me and something about Ray, and it gave me an edge, so that no matter how Ray treated me from time to time, there was always this dark, little incontrovertible chestnut of a fact sitting like a dense pellet of gravity in the back of his mind, reminding him that in certain circles I was accepted, and he was not.

I know Ray's a phony. I know I'm half-phony, but I've always enjoyed a certain sense of security in Mary's thinking that Ray's a bigger phony than me and not liking him because of it. But now I don't know how to feel with Mary liking Ray, which means she doesn't think he's such a phony, or that she's become a phony herself, or that I don't know how to spot a phony anymore, all of which says a lot about the kind of phony I've become.

"When did all this begin?" I asked her as we were leaving the music studio.

"I don't know," she said. "It just began," which is another way of saying: It began and that's all you need to know about it. "He's your friend," she said. "Why should it surprise you?"

"But you never liked him."

"Like I said," she said, "things change."

And of course Ray strutted around all night, throwing away his unobtrusive and insecure act for his I-think-I'm-in-serious-love act, because he knows he's landed a big one, knowing that whatever Mary lacks in beauty, she makes up for in status and money and pedigree and brains. Ray thinks he's become a serious contender. I could see it in the way he fawned all over William-call-me-B.J., telling him what a genius he is, saying he'd like to produce the next demo, though there wouldn't be any need for a second demo, since he didn't see how any record company could possibly turn down such a talent. And he said all of this while Lesanne stood there stringing her nouns together, as if normal conversation were a tone poem.

So I passed on the celebration, because I didn't think it'd be much fun with the price of admission being this earnest and studied homage to the best songwriter since Bob Dylan, and I arrived home in time to see Bruno, and I listened to him go on about some horse that didn't run very well, and I couldn't tell if he was surprised or not to see me sober.

Autumn does something to New York, especially in the morning before people have a chance to screw it up. The air from Canada clears it all out, and there's this brilliance to everything as the sun runs itself down the sides of buildings.

It's early, and I've got the time, so I decide to walk to work. There are so many people in this city; the streets are always crowded, and everybody's headed someplace, and most of them are headed to jobs like mine, jobs where they read things and write things and check off forms and hand things in for typing and wait for things to come back after a thousand other people do the same things with them.

Whatever happened last night in the city, on the streets, in bars and restaurants and cafés and bedrooms, it's over now, and new laws govern the way people behave. The kid at the bus stop with his name carved in the base of his skull who terrorized a bus terminal last night is just another office boy this morning, and he queues up, obedient, quiet, docile, allowing the old lady to go first.

This is the time of day when the people with educations and good jobs terrorize the people who've dropped out, or who haven't quite made it, or who live at the margins. This is the time of day that belongs to the suits; this is the time of day for white collars, the time of day when men who talk in the language of almost-math, a shorthand of numbers and mean analysis, exert themselves with metaphors of jungles and appetites, the time of day to wield power, or pieces of power, while the sun shines, while there's still time to get on it, to get ahead, until evening, when other values resume their hold on the city.

The buses pass by heading south and expel fumes of black exhaust that make the narrow avenue dark and foggy with a look of constant grime that not even the crisp crosstown breeze off the East River can remove. I cross at Sixty-third

Street, the upper edge of that part of midtown where the condos house really famous people who make it into the columns after they've given to some charity, with the obligatory splash of fashion and those freeze-dried satisfied smiles.

I hit Park Avenue, or rather the expanse of it hits me with the palpable presence of money and power. It is a great boulevard, as great as any in Europe. The wind comes up, and the sky is blue, and I pick up on the energy of the traffic, and the buzz of the power surging down the street, and I wonder: Is this all so bad? It's a beautiful day, and I'm a part of it. I've got money in the bank and a job that's better than most and a place to be and things to do. It's not so bad to be clean and clothed and rested and fed, walking in packs with others, going to our jobs, doing our work, advancing something, whatever it is, all of us a part of something and all of those somethings a part of something else, whatever it is. And I wonder again: Is it really so bad? I could have been born in some third-world country where everybody's homeless and hungry with their poverty, and I think how I could have missed some opportunities along the way. I could have stayed behind in my mean-spirited little hometown scrambling with the Jaycees just to get enough, just to get ahead for one more month, for one more week of net worth—all of it just to say "thanks" on Sunday because things are OK. But here, in the greatest city in the world, on a street with the little pine trees and the energy of beautifully driven people, I know there's real money and ways to spend real money. And I think of Mary and of Ray, and I wonder: What's so wrong with that? Two of my friends have decided to like one another. I wonder why it upset me the way it did. And I think how Jeanne is a good friend and how kind she is to be concerned about Eddy, who's having a rough go of it. And I think about Susan and how complicated that whole thing is, and how flattering it is, too.

I walk a little more quickly now as the sun strikes the building that used to be the PanAm Building, and the jeweled points of morning light shine in the windows like diamonds. The cabs crowd together until the lights change, and the horns start, and they move, and I plan my morning. I make an agenda. I'll work on Carol Schneider's assignment first. I'll finally get it right. Maybe even speak with her. Tell her that when I started I was too nervous, starting off on the wrong foot and all, but now I've found my bearings. I'm ready to start now in a good department, in a good firm. I'm going to get myself into this job. Tonight I'll work to midnight. And tomorrow night I'll work to midnight. I'll commit myself to it. I don't have to terrorize anybody in the bars at night because I'm scared of something in the daylight. I don't have to perform Broadway musicals in Third Avenue dives, because I want people to like me in my office. Things are going to work out, and if I start pulling it together, and the confidence begins to come back, I'll even call that girl from the party and ask her out and do something I want to do, just like Ray and Mary do things they want to do, just like Jeanne does the things she wants to do. I turn by the fountains in front of the Seagram Building. I watch others cross the plaza, and I look for people from the office. This morning I'm ready to wave to somebody. This morning I'm ready to say hello, to begin this thing all over again. The doors spin against the wind that wraps itself around the base of these skyscrapers. The elevator rings, and I go up with the smallest release of pressure on the drum of my inner ear. I breathe in the present sense of what it is to work high up in an office overlooking the canyons of the richest city in the world.

Just as I'm about to enter my office, Beulah tells me that Mark Stillman spent an hour in there with the door closed.

"What was he doing?"

"I don't know," she says. "The door was closed."

"Did he say anything?"

"Just to give you this," and she hands me a short handwritten memo on that "From the Desk of Mark Stillman" paper. It says: "Closing binder for the Brooks-Bollo deal by this afternoon." He signed it with his three initials scrawled like some knotted ganglia from Cell Biology.

On my desk two towers of paper stand precariously balanced against one another. I rifle the documents, lifting them at their corners, running my fingers down their sides. The stacks are composed of mostly one- and two-page documents. There are corporate documents, interspersed with corporate-contract documents, interspersed with letter agreements and their amendments, interspersed with bank documents, interspersed with collateral documents, interspersed with security documents, interspersed with things that look like geology studies, and then reams and reams of number documents with the numbers set in columns, interspersed with other pages of graphs and lines going every which way, and none of it, not one word of it, not one number of it makes the least bit of sense.

I look at the note again. It says: "Closing binder," and I know that a closing binder consists of an index and a series of documents sandwiched between two cardboard binders. Paralegals usually do them, and the paralegals who do them usually do them after having worked for months on the deal. Most of the time there's nothing to them, but with some deals, like the Brooks-Bollo Coal deal, the transactions are so numerous and involved, covering the interests of so many parties, putting the binder together requires some experience with the deal itself. And I know nothing about Brooks-Bollo except that it's one of Marty and Mark's deals, and that nobody wants to get near it. So with that feeling of weight and emptiness that precedes a task about which I have serious questions, I sit in my small office, which seems smaller than ever, and I stare at the papers in front of me, until a picture forms and I think that I'm being set up.

Outside on the corner of Fifty-fourth and Park the young woman screams at constant intervals: "Please give to Cerebral Palsy," and I can't help but hear it, and it won't stop, and I think how Mark Stillman made the assignment, and I remember how Susan laughed at the wrong time, and how in a second of laughter careers can be destroyed.

After staring at the papers for half an hour, I read the first document on the top on the left side. It's a three-page letter referencing a government form. I look for the form. It isn't there. I search through the first pile. About two-thirds of the way down the second pile, I find a form that looks like the form mentioned in the letter. The date is off by one day, but it could be the form. The real problem is that it was buried in the body of another document that doesn't have a thing to do with the letter or the form or anything else in the deal.

I start the process again, pulling documents off the top, attempting to make a list. Some documents have been broken up, torn apart, moved around, so that in one case I come upon twelve unidentified pages in the left pile that go with thirteen unidentified pages in the right pile. The sheer volume of the thing is bad enough, but these documents have been shuffled, and this is a task that's guaranteed to fail.

I go through the documents again, slowly. I try to make a list. By mid-afternoon, having skipped lunch, I've catalogued about one-third of it. There's always something missing, and I spend most of my time trying to track down missing pages and parts of things. Half the time I don't even know what I'm looking for.

By four o'clock it's clear that the Brooks-Bollo Coal deal is the name given to a series of deals—at least three, possibly four or five, possibly more. There are documents with parties named once, who then disappear, never to be seen again. There are loans made on top of other loans, and other loans made to secure those loans, creating an attendant pyramid of collateral, each with its own pyramid of documentation evidencing things that made sense to somebody a long time ago when the negotiations were as hot as the big bang. There are liens and mortgages and stock pledges and leases and things called wrap-arounds. There are government documents with their telltale boilerplate printed in type too small to read, with sentence structure too complicated to comprehend.

By five o'clock I feel that I've made some progress, that I can begin to draw an outline of the Brooks-Bollo Coal deal. But by six o'clock I discover another whole cache of documents in folders under my desk. At first they seem to negate everything I've reviewed, casting the deal in a whole different light. There's a history to this thing. Some of the documents are old and apply, if at all, as reference points for the operative documents, which are the scattered and hidden documents. I grow tired reading the endless reams of legalese. Everything begins to merge. Everything has too many words. The documents have been shuffled. Staples are missing. Pages of documents have been separated. I fear pages are missing. There might be no solution to this thing. I start again.

At seven o'clock I order in from the Star Deli. I order the Tom Hanks sandwich. I wish I was Tom Hanks. I haven't eaten all day. The sandwich is overstuffed and falls apart in the round aluminum tray. The french fries look miserable and are too cold to eat. A pain begins across my shoulders. I rub my neck. The odor from the sandwich tin and the salad dressing staining the napkins in the trash barrel fills the room. I feel greasy. I'd like to take a shower and change my clothes and start law school again. But there's no way back, so I just continue to list the documents in the folders. Then entropy sets in. I try to keep things ordered, but the office is too small. Papers start showing up where they don't belong—under my chair, across the air vents, behind the air vents, near the file cabinet on the other side of the office. The tendency toward disorder is too strong; I've entered another cloud of unknowing, more confused now than when I began this project.

At eight o'clock I take a walk around the firm. I'm looking for help, but I'm not sure how to ask for it. Joe Monti's in his office. His office is as neat as a nun's cell. He carefully makes small checks on the cover pages of mortgages stacked under the banker's green-shaded light. He looks up. Mozart is playing from the tiny, expensive speakers on the credenza behind him. I sit in the client's chair.

"You look beat," he says.

"I am."

"Late night last night?"

"Early night last night," I say, "but a long day today."

"It happens," he says, "but that's why they pay us."

He looks as crisp as he did this morning. I wonder how some guys thrive on this stuff.

He continues to lift mortgages from one pile; he makes a check and places them in a second pile. Every time he does this, he makes another check in his billable hour diary. It only takes him a few seconds to make the check, but at this rate, in one quiet night of paper shuffling, he'll bill enough hours for a whole week. I think: No wonder so many people have the leisure to stand around corridors talking tennis and all of that. This is how they do it. I figure there are tricks to this game. Then I think: Of course there are tricks to this game. There are tricks to every game, and this is just a game, a bullshit paper-shuffling game.

I ask him, "Do you know anything about the Brooks-Bollo Coal deal?"

"The what?" Check. Move. Check. Place . . .

"The Brooks-Bollo Coal deal."

"Is that one of Marty's deals?"

"Marty and Mark's."

"Then all I know is that I don't want to know a thing about it."

"Mark's got me doing the closing binder, and I can't make heads or tails out of it."

"Be careful with him," he says.

"Really?"

"Really," he says. "Have you talked to Bob Clark?"

"No."

"He did some work early on with it, then he got away from it, but you might want to talk with him."

"Clark?"

"Yeah."

"Isn't he a little rabid, I mean, you know."

"He's not a bad guy." He pauses. "Hang on a second." He pulls out his drawer. He has extensions listed there. He dials the phone and he waits.

"Hello, Bob? Yeah, well, I guess we all are . . . Three hundred last month . . . No shit . . . Yeah, well, the reason I'm calling is I was wondering: Did you work on the Brooks-Bollo Coal thing? . . . Yeah, Marty's deal . . . Right . . . the coal leases . . . A monster . . ." He looks up from the phone and winks at me. "You did . . . Right . . . uh-huh . . . uh-huh . . . No, I didn't know that . . . Well, that's not beyond him," and I wonder what's not beyond whom. "So that's the word on it . . . I'll tell him, because right now Mark's got him working on the closing binder . . . Right . . . That's what he's telling me . . . Can't make heads or tails out of it . . . He did . . . He did . . . No wonder, then . . . No, it doesn't make sense, but Mark does pretty much what he wants . . . Right . . . OK, Bob . . . Thanks, then."

He puts the phone down and looks at me. His eyes have that sickly, soft, patronizing look usually reserved for sick animals or condemned men. But then he thinks of Ray, and how Ray and I can get him girls. So he tries despite himself.

"Clark says it's a nightmare. It's actually seven deals in one, with a couple of side agreements that don't seem to fit in anyplace. The early stuff was poorly drafted, and they cut a lot of corners, so the documents won't be able to tell the whole story. Let's see. He says there were numerous parties and more than a few banks, though Citibank took the lead. And that's about all he knows, except for the bad news."

"The bad news?"

"Yeah, he says the word's out that Mark's got you on this one, and he doesn't want anybody else stepping in to help out."

"You're shitting me."

"That's what he said."

"Should I go talk with him?"

"Who?"

"Clark."

"Sure, if you want. But I don't think he'll be much help. He doesn't remember all that much about it, and he's not going to cross Mark on this one."

"Right."

"How about Bill Vierps?" he says. "He does these closing binders in his sleep."

"I don't know him that well."

"Well, it's a suggestion," and he returns to his papers, moving them, checking them, placing them, checking his book. I thank him for his help. I tell him we got to go out together again. In my own way I try to remind him that we can get him girls. In my own way I try to forget that I'm really screwed.

By nine o'clock, the list is almost two-thirds complete. Outside, the wind has picked up, moving the darkness around the skyscrapers throughout midtown. A light rain strikes the window with its pinging sound, and then as the rain gets heavier the sound sprays across the window, and the wind rises and falls in short bursts. The firm is very quiet. I've located another batch of documents in the second pile that has been torn apart and shuffled. I go from page 23 of one document to page 16 of a geologist's study to page 12 of a lease. On some of the copies the page numbers are missing, and I have to match up the holes left by the staple remover in order to place the pages in their proper order. The system works pretty well for a while, but then breaks down when the sentences stop flowing from page to page.

At ten o'clock Bill Vierps is standing in my doorway. Joe Monti must have called him. He has that sleepy-eyed expression, as if it takes all his energy just to be as tall as he is. He comes in and sits in the client's chair. There isn't much room for his legs.

He says, "I heard you got stuck with the Brooks-Bollo closing binder."

"Yeah."

"This it?" He points to the papers on the desk.

"This is it."

"Major problems with it?"

"Somebody shuffled all of this."

"They what?"

"I said somebody shuffled these documents," and I show him the pile I'm working on, and how I had to match up the staple holes with the staple holes, and how some pages from one document ended up in the right pile and some pages ended up in the left pile, and so on. He takes a look at them for a minute and the enormity of the problem begins to sink in. He sits back in the chair with his head toward the ceiling. He tries to stretch his legs.

"This is fucked," he says.

"I know."

"No. This is really fucked."

"So then I'm not crazy."

"I don't know about that," he says, "but I do know this is fucked." Then he tells me the nine to twelve things I have to do in order to pull this thing together. I'm tired, and I only grow more tired as he goes on about it, being a nice guy with his help, but burying me with it at the same time. I catch the first four or five things he says, and I'm a little embarrassed taking instruction from a paralegal. I feel inadequate doing this, even if it is quarter to eleven, even if I do need the help.

Bill goes on about the structure of the thing, emphasizing how he'd learned everything he had to learn about closing binders from this partner named Lester, who I met the first day and haven't seen since. Lester's supposed to be this great teacher. He's supposed to be a little crazy, too. Something about one too many trips in the sixties. But he understands that associates don't know shit, and that they have to be taught. Then Bill goes on about Article 9 for a while, and he's using shorthand, and I'm trying to keep up, and, as I'm writing this stuff down, I'm tempted to tell him to do it. I'm tempted to delegate the whole thing because I'm the attorney, and he's the paralegal, and someplace on the Great Chain of Being there's something that says I can tell him what to do, and he has to do it. I mean, I'm the one who sat through three years of lectures and read two million incomprehensible pages and took about a hundred ridiculous exams and sat one whole summer in a ballroom in midtown on the West Side with about ten thousand other ravenous graduates and sweated out studying for the bar exam and lost sleep and took the exam and didn't break down. I figure I'm not crazy; I figure I'll just tell him straight out as he goes on about something called a UCC 1. Then I realize there's no way. There's no chance of that happening. And although he's the paralegal, he has more experience than me, and he knows the place, and he knows this closing binder bullshit, and for once knowledge does mean power, and I need to know what he knows, because as far as he's concerned I'm just another poor bastard passing through a good department in a good firm with an associate's face and a new suit.

By eleven-thirty he's finished and gone, and I'm sitting here with the rain against the window. It'll be a long walk home. I'll never get a cab. I look over my notes. I've lost half of what Bill Vierps had to say, though I'm not sure how much of what he had to say was worthwhile, and how much of it was him just showing off. Like everybody else in this place, he talks too fast.

I throw some papers in my briefcase. I've seen movies where guys do this. Usually there's a sax playing when a guy does this in the movies. All I can hear is the rain. So I imagine the sax. My briefcase is a real beat-up thing. "Something for a real lawyer," my father said when he gave it to me. It was one of his old ones. It was a special present. It looks authentic. Something for a real lawyer. But tonight I don't feel like a real lawyer. I decide to leave it. It'd be dead weight in the rain. I'd just have to carry it back in the morning. It gives me the look, but that's all.

The rain lets up for a minute and then starts again, harder than before. I need a shower. I need some sleep. I figure I'll drop into a place along the way. Have a beer or two. Maybe a Scotch. Just one. Help me to sleep. The corridor is quiet. Even Joe Monti's gone. The mortgages sit in a neat pile on his desk. Overhead I hear a hum from the lighting fixtures. I turn the corner and from the end of the corridor I hear voices speaking Spanish. It's a Catholic language filled with oaths to the Blessed Virgin, words of hope. It's a language for poverty and drugs, too. A short man with a mustache pushes and pulls a vacuum over the carpet, and I think how everybody's got to do something. Yes, even at night, I think, everybody's got to do something.

POLITICS AND RELIGION

It took a week to complete the first draft of the index. Bill Vierps helped along the way. We used indexes from other deals as models. Beulah typed it, and I wasn't too concerned with her speed because there were so many changes. Mark Stillman complained twice, sending Solomon Isaacson in to say that when Mark said "ASAP" it didn't mean a week later. I tried to explain about some of the problems with the documents. Solomon Isaacson listened and stared at me. Then he said: "It's just a closing binder."

When it was finished, I brought it to Mark Stillman's office. Susan wasn't there. She'd taken some time off to "get things together." The temp was this young girl with flyaway red hair and a heavy chin. After she told Mark that I was waiting to see him, she said, "Go ahead on in."

Mark Stillman has a big office, longer than most, but narrow, too. He's placed large mirrors on one wall to give the illusion of space that isn't there. He sat behind his desk with papers strewn over everything. He looked up when I entered. He didn't say anything. He just took the index from my hand and started slashing it with his pen. "Who told you to arrange it this way?" he said, and before I could answer he'd drawn circles around whole groups of words and had directed them with arrows to other pages. He crossed things out. He deleted words and phrases. He moved things. Every now and then he'd look up as if to tell me that he should have known better than to pick the one idiot associate who couldn't do a closing binder. I started to tell him that we'd based it on other models he'd used, but all he heard was the word "*we*."

"What do you mean, 'we'?" he said. "I gave this assignment to you, not to a committee."

"Yeah, well, I was having some trouble with it, so I asked Bill Vierps to help me out. You know he's done a lot of these things, and—"

"Bill Vierps?"

"Yeah, Bill Vierps."

"Bill Vierps, the paralegal?"

"Right."

"Who said Bill Vierps could work on this thing?"

"Well, I—"

"I didn't assign Bill Vierps to this. I assigned you, and you're the attorney."

"Yeah, right, well, I—"

"Don't you think if I'd wanted Bill Vierps on this I would have assigned Bill Vierps to this?"

"I guess. Sure, but—"

"So where do you get off assigning other people to do your work for you?"

"Hey, look, I only—"

"No, you look . . ." and it went on like that, with him complaining and with me backpedaling, and then trying to stand up only to backpedal again, and all the time he's got this ballpoint pen slashing the hell out of the index, drawing lines like a road map. After he finished, he handed it to me. He said: "When you make these changes, bring it to Marty for his review."

Beulah spent a whole day trying to make sense out of what he'd written and out of what I'd written to explain what he'd written. Then it was ready except for typos and spelling. I corrected those, and it looked OK.

Marty's office was on sixteen, and it was my first chance to meet the guy that everybody talked about, but nobody wanted to get too close to. His face surprised me, because it was one of those soft, kindly, Doughboy faces with the hapless expression of a hurt dog. When he smiled he had this mild and charming manner, and he joked a bit as he looked at the index and then cut it to shreds, wondering out loud as to "who in their right mind ever decided upon this order for the documents," saying how it made no sense, reminding me that there were plenty of models I could have consulted. He took his own pen to it. He said, "This goes here and this goes here," and I tried to tell him that that was how I'd drafted it. But he didn't want to hear about it, and after he made a comment about the tardiness of the project, saying that he'd already heard from the client, I told him I'd make the changes right away. He said, "I know you will," and he wasn't friendly about it, and as I was about to leave his office, he told me to bring it to Mark for his review.

Maybe I was born yesterday, maybe I was born at night, maybe I was born last night, but it didn't mean a thing to me that I was going to have to go back to Mark Stillman with the same index, listing the documents in the same order as before. I just figured that since the changes came from Marty, Mark would have to accept it. So Beulah did the typing, and I proofread it, and Beulah typed it again, and when she finished I handed it to Mark, and he went crazy. He started screaming, and it was so loud that his temporary secretary got up and closed the door. He wanted to know how I could have the "audacity" not only to assign other people to do my work, but to ignore the changes he'd made. I tried to tell him what Marty had said and what Marty had done, but it didn't do any good as he took his pen to the pages in front of him. Then he sent me off with instructions to change the index again and to bring it to Marty for his review, which I did, having been born yesterday, having been born at night, having been born last night, thinking it was all just a glitch in communication.

Marty's round little Doughboy's face wasn't mild at all when he saw me in his doorway holding the third or fourth final revision. And when he saw that his changes hadn't been made (even though they'd been made and changed), he was pissed, and he stopped his meeting with Solomon Isaacson and a paralegal named Heidi to tell me just how pissed he was.

Most of that had happened by Thursday. But on Friday, after Beulah wants to kill me for making her type the same thing over and over, and after she tells the other secretaries how I can't be the brightest light in New York City, and after I trap Marty and Mark in the same room at the same time so they have no choice but to agree on the order for the index, I leave early and buy two bottles of Scotch and walk to my apartment, where I plan to hide out for the weekend. I'm worn out. Bruno holds the door for me and says I look tired and then motions to the lobby where Eddy's sitting, waiting for me with a couple of suitcases.

"What are you doing here?" I ask.

Eddy just shrugs his shoulders.

"This is a surprise," I say, and Eddy says: "Yeah, a surprise," and even though I'm in no mood for company, it is good to see him.

He's upset, and he tells me how things have changed and how he's left the Jesuits, not necessarily for good, but at least for a while, a "leave of absence," he calls it, to straighten out a few things. Then he says I look tired, and when we get to my apartment I crack open the first bottle of Scotch, twisting the aluminum cap with a snapping sound, and pour a shot into a coffee cup and drink it down, fighting the first impulse to gag on the heat of the liquor.

"It's been a bad week," I tell him, and before we get into what's happened to him, I tell him the story about being banged back and forth by the Nurk Twins with their stupid Brooks-Bollo Coal deal. He listens, and he gets to the bottom of it, saying that what's going on has nothing to do with coal deals or indexes or closing binders, but has everything to do with the stupid thing that happened when I said the wrong thing at the wrong time. I drink freely, and I offer to go out and get him what he needs for his Manhattans. He declines. He asks if there's anything besides Scotch. I tell him no, and he says he'll sip a glass of Scotch with ice and plenty of water. He puts the TV on the floor and sits on the secretary's chair. I sit on the edge of the mattress with the back of my head against the wall. I cough as something catches in my throat. I lean forward, then back again, and watch the light change and the apartment grow dark.

Eddy sips his drink and then places it on the floor. He puts his head in his hands. His hair is getting thin on top. We're both getting older, but it's a premature kind of aging. He picks up his head and looks about the room. He sighs once, and then he begins.

"When I was a freshman at Georgetown," he says, "there was this Father Mannion there, and he was working on his dissertation for his doctorate in theology. A lot of guys knew him because he was into relating with the students, and he'd have these wine-and-cheese parties in his room, and he was very careful about who he invited. He'd kind of like survey the freshman class and pick the guys who stood out in some way and who'd, you know, appreciate the fact that they'd been invited. I mean, he never risked asking anybody who wouldn't come. Anyway, the parties were boring and everybody drank and tried to be witty, and I got to know this guy, and he wasn't such a bad guy, though he could be a real asshole when he'd had a few. The story was that he'd been going to school forever, and that for whatever reason he just couldn't seem to complete his doctoral dissertation. I even heard one of my professors talk about it, you know, saying that Mannion should just go away, you know, go off somewhere for a year and just write it. But he didn't, and he was, like, this figure on campus, always showing up at the social scenes and the right political causes and all of that. Anyway, a few weeks ago we get this call from somebody at Fordham, and they invite us down for a day to tailgate and go to a football game. So a bunch of us sign out a car and head down to Fordham, and it's raining so hard we have to pull over about five times, and we finally get there, and it's still raining so we go to the residence, and these old guys are there, and they don't know what to do with us. So we're just hanging around, hoping the rain will stop, but it doesn't, and it's time for dinner, and we suffer through that with the old guys who don't know what we're doing there. And after that we get word that this Father Mannion, who's now a big shot at Fordham, has invited us to his room for one of his wine-and-cheese parties. We get there about eight, and a few of the other guys know him from someplace else, and of course I know him, and he remembers me, and we start sipping his wine and eating his cheese. But he's not drinking wine, he's drinking bourbon, and he's really drinking, and he's got half a bag on, and he starts in on us. At first we figure he's just trying to be funny, you know, doing that ribbing that means 'I'm a regular guy,' and then we realize that he's not trying to be funny at all, and that he's got this attitude. He says that we're intellectually inferior and that our training is bankrupt and that if we didn't start reading some 'Christology,' which is his favorite word, we'd be sued for malpractice, and he's going on and on, and everybody's kind of listening with their mouths open, looking around, trying to make out what's going on, you know, like, what is it that started this guy off on us? And by this time we're all drinking, and I'm drinking more than usual, and one of the guys there, Bill Abley, he tries to change the subject. He says that Rick has written this song, and that everybody likes it, and that Rick should sing it. I guess he thought it might ease things a bit, at least get Father Mannion off his horse. And Rick says thanks but no thanks, and Bill says, 'C'mon, Rick,' and it's kind of cruel, but everybody's drinking and Rick's a ham and finally he says he won't sing it, but he'll recite the lyrics, which he does. Well, you know how it is with lyrics, they never sound right without the music, and the whole thing falls flat and Father Mannion's sitting there, and he looks at Rick with this disgusted look, and he says: 'Aesthetically mediocre; theologically incorrect,' and he's, like, real pompous, and I can see that this hurts Rick, because he didn't want to do it in the first place, and he was just coming off that disaster with Dieter, and there's no question that Mannion's serious, that he meant to hurt him. So Rick is embarrassed, and he says, 'It's just a song, Father,' and Mannion says, 'I know it's just a song; and it's not a very good song,' and one of the guys goes 'Whooooaaaaaa,' you know, the sound like there's going to be a fight, and I pour myself another drink and drink it down, and pour myself another one, and I'm feeling a buzz and I'm a little pissed about it, and I break into the conversation and I say, 'You know, we should all listen'—and I say 'listen' like 'lishin,' which kind of gives me away—and I say we should all 'listen' very carefully to what Father Mannion has to say, because he's a world-famous theologian, and then I say that for most of his adult life he went to school and studied this stuff and when the time came for him to write his dissertation all of Georgetown waited for it to be published, and we waited and the faculty waited and the Vatican waited and the Cardinal waited and the boys at his wine-and-cheese parties waited and everyone just kept waiting and waiting and waiting, and then I looked at him, and he was white, I mean literally white, and I could see him all rolled up in his chair because he knew what was coming, and I just said it. I said: 'So when did you finally finish that dissertation of yours, Father Mannion?' and he just about had a fucking heart attack, and only one other guy in the room knew what the story was, but everyone knew something had happened, and it didn't take a genius to figure it out, and right after that we were all asked to leave."

The room is dark now. Eddy's just sitting there with the drink in his hand. He hasn't touched it, but now he takes one long drink and almost finishes it, saying he'd like another. I say something superfluous like I'm glad he told that asshole where to get off, and that part of being an adult is not letting other adults shit all over you. But he really doesn't want to hear that. It's not a time for victory clichés and jingoisms. He just wants to keep talking, to tell me what happened.

So he tells me how word of what had happened with Father Mannion got back to this guy, George, the "Novice Master," Eddy's boss, and how when things go wrong in there they tend to multiply, and that first impressions are lasting impressions and that it didn't help that he liked to drink, even though the drinking itself didn't really matter, because what really mattered was "going along" and not questioning anything. "If you don't go along," he says, "they pick up on whatever your vice is, and they make your life miserable. The fact is that you could do it with goats and they wouldn't care, as long as you go along with whoever's in charge."

So I ask him what this guy, George, had to say about it, and he tells me that George was pissed because Mannion was about to be named Provincial, which is like the boss of bosses. "And then, two weeks ago," he says, "they named him Provincial and this meant that George would have to answer to him, and George didn't want to waste any time showing him where he stood on things. So one night, I was sitting in my room with a half-pint of bourbon that Rick had left from his birthday party, and George walks in without knocking, and the rest of it was this 'You're an alcoholic' bullshit and a lot of talk about detox and AA and his duty to preserve the order from certain evils, and I was pissed because I hadn't even taken a drink from the fucking half-pint, and I told him so. But he didn't believe it, and I told him he was just playing politics with Mannion, and, well, that just about assured me my leave of absence."

"It's all politics," I say.

"I just didn't figure there'd be that kind of politics in a seminary."

"There's politics everywhere," I say. "I live alone and there's politics here."

Eddy finishes his drink and asks for another. In the kitchen I pour his drink with a little more Scotch. I turn on the radio and flip to an FM station that plays soft classical music. I put it on low. It's a conscious thing. I want there to be something soothing in the place. I want there to be something beautiful and comfortable and pleasant at a time like this. Eddy's real upset. I've only seen him like this once before, when his younger sister was in a bad accident, and it didn't look good for her.

"I fucked up," he says.

I hand him his drink.

"Forget it," I say. "I know you were serious about it, and I know you wanted to do it, but now forget about it. There's plenty of life out here, and we can make a go of it. It'll be good to have you back in town. I'm working. I've got plenty of money. We'll get some furniture, and you can stay here. And then when you find something I can help you get a place." And I keep going on like this, half meaning it, half knowing that none of it will get that far, because Eddy's too independent, and although he might not have them now, he'll soon have plans of his own.

He's quiet for a long time. The music from the radio is barely audible. In the apartment next door the recluse turns on her stereo. It's a Bach cantata. The voices waft up and recede like vapors. It plays against the music from the radio. I turn on the lamp at the foot of the mattress. I motion to the TV. I say, "You don't want to see the news, do you?" It's a leading question. He doesn't.

"It's like I'm the news today," he says.

"Me, too," I say.

"So what do you think about this alcoholism stuff?" he asks.

"What do you mean?" I ask. I'm not ready for this.

"You know, what do you think?"

"What do you mean, what do I think? I like to drink and so do you, but that's a long way, I mean, we're a long way from that."

"I know," he says. His voice is small, tentative, admitting something. "I went to one of those meetings."

"What meetings?"

"You know. AA." He stops and looks around. This is hard for him.

"Good," I say. "I think meetings are good."

"Hey, wait. I didn't mean to piss you off, but . . ."

"No. But you show up here after some bullshit I don't

know nothing about, and you lay your troubles here, and I listen and offer you drinks, and the next thing I know you want to talk about alcoholism."

"Forget it," he says, and he's hurt and he's pissed.

"What the fuck did they do to you in there?" I ask.

"I said forget it," he says. "I shouldn't have brought it up."

"Well, you did," I say. "It's out there now."

"It wasn't that bad," he says.

"What do you mean?" I say. "If it wasn't that bad, then why the hell did they put you out on the street?"

"I'm not talking about the Jesuits," he says. "I'm talking about the AA meeting."

"Well, that's none of my business," I say, and I back away from it because I just can't handle it.

We both sit there quietly for a while. The silence is awkward at first, and then it just becomes silence. The Scotch begins to work. I feel a little easier about everything. I figure I've got to say something.

"Look," I say, "I'm just a kid, and you're just a kid. Sometimes we think we should be more than that, but really that's all that we are. We're just kids. And that's half the problem here. They can't keep us in school forever, so they drop us out into the adult world with all these animals who've been around for years, and we're just kids, and they can pretty much do what they want with us. And that's the problem, and it's not because we drink too much or anything else, it's because the ones who've made it to the point where they're not kids anymore feel like they can walk all over us and put up about ten thousand hoops for us to jump through and not have to give a shit whether they fuck us up or not, because we're just kids, and kids aren't supposed to know shit. And all that talk about AA and being an alcoholic and all of that is just a lot of bullshit. It's just their way of getting you this time, because you told that rude shit to go fuck himself."

"Yeah," he says. "You might be right and all of that, but these guys are priests, and priests aren't supposed to do what everybody else does."

"Look," I say, "I got my own reasons for hating priests. And I know that people are pretty much the same all over the place, and that you're just as likely to meet a shit with a Roman collar as with a three-piece suit. People don't change no matter what they're wearing."

The phone rings in the dark alcove where it sits on the floor. I answer it. It's Jeanne, and she's looking for Eddy. I tell her that he's here. She asks how he is, and I tell her he's fine, and she asks to speak with him.

"Eddy," I say.

"Who is it?" he asks.

I tell him, and I continue on to the kitchen where I hear Eddy's half of the conversation.

"It's all right," he says. "No . . . This afternoon . . . No. I haven't called them yet. Maybe tomorrow . . . I didn't know that . . . So there's an extra bed there . . . You sure she's gone . . . Paris . . . Must be nice . . . No. I was never there . . . Well, maybe . . . I'll tell him, then . . . What time? . . . Sure, I can make it . . . I think so . . ." and he places one hand over the receiver as I leave the kitchen and holds his drink before his face.

"Do you want to go out to dinner tonight?" he asks. "Jeanne and Mary and your friend Ray want to throw me a coming-out party."

"I don't know," I say. "I'll think about it."

He goes back to the phone: "He says he'll think about it . . . No, I guess he had a bad week, too . . . I'll try . . . OK, then . . . nine o'clock . . . Right . . . Well, look, I was just thinking, if I'm going to stay, maybe I should hop a cab now and bring my things . . . Right . . . OK, then . . . Right . . . Right . . . Five A . . . See you, then."

He hangs up the phone and returns to the secretary's chair. He places his hand on it before he sits down. His Scotch is beginning to work, too.

"You don't want to go," he says.

"I don't think so," I say. "It's been a bad week."

"Yeah," he says.

"So you're going to stay with Jeanne."

"Oh, that," he says. "Yeah, well, she has an extra bed. Her roommate moved back to Paris."

"The model?"

"I don't know. I think so," he says, and we sit there. The conversation's over. This was the first stop, and now he's moved on to other things.

I say, "You didn't tell your folks yet?"

"No," he says. "They're not going to be happy about this."

"I guess not."

"What can I say?"

"Just kids."

"What?"

"Nothing," I say, and the light at the foot of the mattress has the too-warm yellow glow from the lampshade I bought in the Village when I was in law school. It's an old shade. It must have been made after the Second World War, when furniture and cars were round, and lamps were designed to spread light so as to give the illusion of warmth and security.

This happened when you were a kid:

You could swim fast, so you joined the swim team, and you liked it because all you had to worry about was going faster than the other guy and turning against the wall. The swim meets started in December and they ended in March. It was a winter sport like basketball, but you didn't get big crowds like the basketball team, and the girls who came to the swim meets were different from the girls who went to the basketball games. The girls who went to the swim meets were the girls who liked to watch you come out of the pool in those tight swimming suits.

Your father came to the meets, too, and although you didn't see him, others told you that he cheered for you when you swam.

One Friday night you were swimming against a team from Hartford. They were about as good as you were. You'd been following them in the Hartford papers. That's what you did. You'd follow the other team in the papers and the papers would print the times and you'd know what you had to do to win. You had to swim against a guy named DeLillo. He was a tall kid, and you were evenly matched though on your best night you could beat him. You felt confident, and you were wearing your lucky suit. It was a faded blue suit that you wore in the summer when you were a lifeguard. It wasn't maroon like the team suit. It was blue and different, and you believed it brought you luck. That's the way a kid thinks about things, so you wore it because it brought you luck and made you a little different, and the coach didn't mind, because it worked.

You swam against the kid named DeLillo twice that night. It was a good night. You beat him twice, and the team won the meet, and you'd worn the lucky suit, and you'd assumed that your father had cheered for you.

After the meet you walked to the parking lot to meet your father. It was the dead of winter. The sky was black with wispy winter clouds here and there. The snow was frozen in old piles of ice along the sides of the roads. The ice was everywhere and everything crunched underfoot when you walked. You felt the cold air in your damp hair, and before you reached the car some of it had frozen in the hair behind your ears.

You got in the car and waited for your father to say something. But he didn't say anything. He was upset. You figured maybe there was something wrong with the car. But the car started, and he said nothing.

Your cousin was having a party at her house that night, so he drove you there. When you arrived and were about to get out of the car, he said: "When you get home, I want to talk to you," and you knew that you were in trouble. You knew that you'd done something wrong. You just didn't know what it was.

Your cousin's parties were fun. She held them in the basement, which had been done over, and there was music and things to drink and things to eat. It was a good crowd because your cousin's crowd wasn't the "in" crowd and nobody had to make fun of anybody else. It was all pretty tame stuff, and you enjoyed yourself, though that night you were anxious and upset because you knew there'd be trouble when you got home.

Your cousin was a year older than you, and she had her driver's license, so she drove you home. Before you got out of the car you told her what had happened, and she was interested, because she wanted to be a psychiatrist, and she was always trying to figure out what made people tick. She offered a few theories, but none of them made any sense. She asked you what you'd said and what you'd done earlier in the day. She asked you if you'd smoked a cigarette or anything like that. She asked you about the teacher at school who'd given you detention and who was famous for having said things about your father. She asked a lot of questions and would have asked more but you said you had to go. She said good luck, and you walked up the sidewalk that went around to the back of the house.

The inside of the house was almost dark except for the yellow glow that came from the light in the kitchen and the light in the den. Everything happened in the room you called the den. The TV was there, and it was the room where your parents drank.

You opened the door and they heard you. Your mother said: There he is.

You walked into the den, and your father's face twisted with anger. Your mother's face was different: It was open and dazed with a look of surprise until her eyes struck yours, and you saw something different than anger. She was waiting for this. They'd been drinking for hours, and they were all worked up. So she started in, not at you, but at your father, reminding him how much you'd embarrassed him, how much you'd disappointed him. Your father had no choice but to explode, which he did with an anger that was half genuine and half manufactured. And he went crazy for a long time before you had an idea as to what you had done:

At the swim meet, when you had lined up for your second race, one of your teammates had said: "There he goes, showing off again. You'd think his old man couldn't afford to buy him a team suit." And because it was a small pool with the spectators crowded in on either side, your father had been sitting in back of this kid, and he'd heard what the kid had said.

"Who do you think you are?" he said, and he said it over and over. Then she said: "Who do you think you are?" And that went on for a while, and then there was some screaming about the money your father made, and about what he could afford, and when he got a little tired from all the shouting she'd remind him, repeating what you had done, repeating how you'd tried to be such a big man, when you weren't a big man, when you were just a kid. Every fifteen minutes or so she'd get up and go into the kitchen and pour more drinks, and while she was doing this he wouldn't say a word, not wanting to waste his energy while she was gone.

After a couple of hours he started to get tired, and with the liquor taking its toll, he leaned back, and his head dropped forward. When he did this she woke him up, and it started all over again. Then she looked at you with a look that said she could control the situation, that she could rile him up no matter how tired he was and make him scream whatever she wanted him to scream, and that this was her way of getting what she wanted, and that there wasn't a thing you could do about it.

It went on for hours, and by about three o'clock you started to get tired and you discovered that you could survive the whole thing if you just grew small inside yourself so that the person that was you became this dark little stone that resided somewhere deep behind your heart in the lower regions of your chest. The body that sat there was just a shell, and from deep down in the smallest, most precious place where you hid and protected your true self, you watched them dispassionately, viewing them from the distance of another reality, dissociated from the old lamplight and the sounds of anger, withdrawn, so that the person who took it was no longer you, but took it for you, and somehow the night ended with the darkness and the cold and a fatigue that never really went away.

MISSING

I t begins the second I arrive. Beulah tells me to go to Mark Stillman's office, which I do, telling the temp who I am. The temp motions me to the door, and I enter his office and stand a few feet in front of his desk. He doesn't look up. The index is in front of him.

"What's this?" he says.

"What's what?" I say.

"This." He points to the index.

"It's the index. You and Marty agreed to the changes. It's done."

"No," he says. "It's not done."

"As far as I know it is."

"Look at this," he says, and he tosses it across his desk. "Tell me what's wrong with it."

I pick it up. I do the cursory review. Then I put it back down.

"I don't know what's wrong with it," I say. "I listed what you gave me; it's in the order you and Marty agreed to."

"Don't tell me that," he says. "Don't tell me you listed what I gave you, because I gave you the Klein-Shorndorff Citibank Letter Agreement, and you didn't list that."

"I didn't?"

"No, you didn't."

"If I didn't list it it's because there was no Klein-Shoredoor Agreement."

"Klein-Shorndorff," he says. He says, "Are you saying you lost the Klein-Shorndorff Citibank Letter Agreement?"

"No. I'm not saying that."

"But I gave it to you," he says. "It was there with the other documents, and it's only one of the five most important documents in the whole fucking deal. It's the original. Do you know what I'm saying? It was the original. So what happened to it?"

"I don't know."

"It's simple," he says, although none of this is simple. "I had possession of it. I relinquished possession of it. I gave it to you. Then you had possession of it. And now it's gone. In my book that means you lost it, and I want to know what you're going to do about it."

"But I didn't lose it," I say. "I listed everything," and I'm going noplace with this. As far as he's concerned I've lost this letter agreement. Then I remember the mess in my office when the entropy set in and documents ended up everywhere. I think how it might be someplace, somewhere, behind a file cabinet, under the desk, in a drawer, down an air vent. I tell him I'll check my office again, and it's as if I've admitted responsibility for this thing. It's the wrong direction to go, because he's all over me, saying that it took two weeks too long to prepare the index in the first place, and that now it's probably going to take another two weeks to get the documents pulled together. Then he complains how the firm pays these prima-donna know-nothing first-year associates too much money and gets back nothing in return. I just stand there and take it, and then I ask him why he's busting my balls, and he goes nuts saying it's got nothing to do with "busting anybody's balls," but that it's got everything to do with incompetence and laziness and attitude. I look at him with his eyes all pressed up into these dark little lost-soul nuggets, and I'm about ready to tell him to go fuck himself, but I don't say it, because there are people standing outside his office. They can hear the shouting. They're drawn to it in the way spectators are drawn to street fights. And I want it to be over. I don't want this anymore, so I pick up the papers and leave the office. He's still screaming: "Tonight. I want this thing on my desk tonight," and I walk down the corridor, and I feel the eyes of others on me as I pass by.

I turn the corner and see Beulah down the hall. She sees me coming and lowers her eyes. News travels so fast in this place that she knows from three corridors away what's happened, and she's embarrassed for me.

Later that morning, Carol Schneider's secretary stands in my doorway. She watches me as I move another one of the eight boxes containing the documents from the Brooks-Bollo Coal deal. I look up and she tells me to follow her.

Carol Schneider's sitting at her desk. She's on the phone, and she's trying to lean back with that nonchalant talking-big-money talk, but she's just too short to carry it off, and she looks like a little girl trying to count the holes in the acoustic ceiling tiles. She's talking Eurodollars and a few other things that are very big, and she talks about who's going to take the lead since Wells Fargo backed out. This is varsity league business, but she's doing it all with this forced casual tone of voice, and she complains about Barclay's and calls them a "lacy" crowd. From time to time she lowers her eyes and looks at me, but she looks right through me, and I might as well not exist. Then she motions for me to close her door as she winds up the phone conversation with an implied threat that if some small bank in Georgia doesn't sign off on some agreement, there are plenty of ways for the big boys in New York to make life miserable for the banks in a particular

Southern state. Then she says: "They'll make Sherman look like Mr. Fucking Whipple," and she hangs up the phone with a "Back at you," which is what they all say now since it performs the necessary function without betraying any hint of the intimacy generally conveyed by a simple "good-bye." Then she looks at me as if she's trying to remember why she called me.

"Didn't I give you an assignment?" she asks.

"Yes."

"And when was that?"

"Two, maybe three weeks ago."

"Was it a three-week assignment?"

"No."

"Was it a two-week assignment?"

"No."

"What was the assignment?"

"It was a summary, like a training manual for bank employees about revolving credit loan agreements. I was supposed to do it after reviewing this agreement you gave me to read."

"And . . ."

"And I was supposed to have it back to you in a week."

"So where is it?"

"Well, I got tied up and real busy with this—"

"Wait a minute," she says. "Don't tell me about being busy. Everybody's busy here. That's what we do here. We get busy and we stay busy and we bill enormous sums of money to enormously wealthy clients who pay us enormous sums of money to stay busy for them. So don't tell me about busy, just tell me where the assignment is."

"I haven't done it yet."

"You haven't."

"No."

"Why not?"

"I've been working on this thing for Mark Stillman."

"And where'd you get the idea you could just start working for Mark Stillman?"

"It wasn't my idea."

"Oh."

"No. He just dropped this thing on me and it was a real mess and—"

"What was it?" she asks.

"The Brooks-Bollo Coal deal."

"That deal closed weeks ago."

"I know, but he wanted the closing binder, and . . ."

"And?"

"And it was a mess. The documents were all shuffled and out of order, and then he and Marty couldn't agree on the order they wanted, and they had me going back and forth like I was crazy . . ."

"You did say 'closing binder'?"

"Yes."

"Paralegals do closing binders."

"I know," I say, "but this was no ordinary closing binder. I mean, you had to see this thing."

"Wait a minute," she says. "I know Mark. He's one of the best attorneys in the firm. He's been here a long time, and he works on major deals, and he doesn't have a reputation for making a mess out of things. That's not him. I know him. I don't know you."

"I'm not saying anything about him," I say. "All I'm saying is that what he gave me to do took day and night for a week and a half and I haven't been able to get to anything else yet."

She leans back in her chair again. She starts counting those holes in the ceiling. I look up and connect a few dots myself. Then I look out the window. It's cloudy. I look across the street to the windows of the old Citibank Building. I see the people there walking around. The guys all wear white shirts. I figure the people in the old Citibank Building all have better lives than me. I want to be somebody else. I start to retreat inside myself, growing smaller, harder, almost invulnerable.

She turns to me. "How much do we pay you?" she asks.

"Well, you know, the going rate."

"The going rate."

"Right."

"That's a lot of money, isn't it."

"Yes, it is."

"And we expect certain things in return."

"Yes, you do."

"So. Just think about that," she says. "And I'll want that assignment on my desk tomorrow morning."

I leave her office. There's no courtesy in this. I must look beaten down. Outside I'm tired again. But inside I'm someplace else. Inside I'm safe; inside I'm just watching things.

It takes the whole day and all that night to complete the assignment. Around four A.M. I say: "Citibank wants a training manual; I'll give Citibank a training manual," and after the night temps leave I type the last five pages myself. I place it on her desk before dawn. The sky has that Claude Monet look, with all these colors running through it. The manual is a credible job, and I'm proud of myself, and I think how this "lawyer's work" isn't so bad if you remove the sabotage and the terror.

I arrive later the next morning less tired than I've been on other mornings. I feel like I've accomplished something. She said she wanted it on her desk, and it's on her desk. I plan how I'll send off the Brooks-Bollo documents for binding. I figure I'll let Mark worry about the Klein-Schulmann-whatever.

Outside my office, Beulah's standing there with the phone

on her shoulder. Something's not right. She's fumbling through papers. I say, "Good morning, Beulah," and she just turns and smiles that too-busy-to-say-hello smile. Then, when I enter my office, Solomon Isaacson is sitting at my desk going through the boxes containing the Brooks-Bollo documents.

"What are you doing?" I ask. I try not to be too belligerent about it.

"Mark sent me down here to go through your office to find the Klein-Shorndorff agreement."

He looks back into the box. He's got a copy of the check-list and he's marking it one document at a time.

"And what am I supposed to do while you're doing that?" I figure there's got to be some law about associates sitting at other associates' desks.

He looks up at me. He knows he can tell me what to do. If we were in a bar I could terrorize the hell out of him, but this guy doesn't go to bars. He goes to places where he's powerful. Maybe that's why he never leaves this place, and why I find it hard to stay here.

"I don't know," he says. He doesn't care what I do, and I sit in one of the client chairs and watch him as he goes through the files document by document.

"Do you have any idea what it took to put this thing together?" I ask, trying to make conversation and hating myself for making the effort.

"If I didn't know better," I say, "I'd say somebody was trying to make my life miserable."

He looks up at me. His eyes circle the area. He avoids direct eye contact. Then he goes back to work.

"These things were all shuffled and torn apart," I say.

He ignores me.

"Yes, sir, a real bitch of an assignment," I say, and the tone of my voice gives me away.

"It's just a closing binder," he says, and I want to kill him, with his stupid head bobbing over each document, his small fingers wrapped around that blue Bic pen as he makes his little checks on his paper.

The phone rings three times, but Beulah takes messages. One's from Eddy. Another's from my cousin. She's got antennae when it comes to trouble. And one call is from somebody I don't know.

I've got my feet up on the desk. I'm pissed. Solomon picks up his copy of the index and places two of the boxes back on the air vent and two more on the floor behind him. He looks about the office. "Do you mind?" he says, and before I can answer he's pulling open the drawers to my file cabinet.

"Wait," I say. This is going too far. He stops. He turns to me.

"Sorry," he says, "but I've got orders to do this," and he goes through each drawer in the file cabinet and tosses things about and moves them and pulls some out and places them on the desk and then goes through them carefully. I just sit there; I can feel the heat behind my eyes. I keep my feet up, propped against the desk in one of those high school poses of languor and disdain, and I'm thinking up ways to plot against this guy. There must be some way I can screw him, and then, as he steps from the file cabinet and opens the file drawers on either side of my desk, I stand up and tell him to stop. I tell him to close the drawers and to get out of my office. He just stands there, his hand on the long drawer under the desk.

"You heard me," I say. "Get out of my office."

"I can't do that," he says.

"Yes, you can," I say. "Just take two steps to your left and three steps straight ahead, and you're out of here."

"I'm sorry," he says. "Really. I've got nothing against you. But this is something I've been ordered to do, and Mark told me that if you make trouble over it I'm supposed to call him, and then all hell will break loose. It's easier this way. Really."

I stand there. Then I sit down again. I can't hate this guy. He's so far into this scene he can't see anything else. And, truth be told, he's doing what he can to be nice about it.

He says, "Here. We'll look through this drawer together, and then I'm done."

I look at him. They've beaten me, and he knows it. I walk around the side of the desk. My hand is shaking as I open the drawer. There are some pens, a ruler, half a roll of Tums, a few gold ink cartridges shaped like bullets, a dust ball, and a small photo of my father.

He looks through the drawer. He says nothing. He checks his legal pad. He looks at me. He's about to say something, but he turns and hurries out of the office.

Beulah stands in the doorway. She's heard the commotion. She holds the phone messages in her hand. She hands them to me.

"What's going on here?" Beulah asks.

"Nothing," I say.

"It doesn't sound like nothing."

"There's a document missing and one of the attorneys is trying to say I lost it."

"Well, I know about that," she says. "They called me this morning, and I'm supposed to go through this entire office with a fine-tooth comb and look for . . ." She looks down at her steno pad. She reads: "A three-page document that says 'Klein-Shorndorff' across the top. Now, where am I supposed to find that?" she asks me.

"Forget it, Beulah. It's not here. We already looked."

"Well, then, let me just come in and walk about a second or two so I can say that I did my job."

"Be my guest," I say, and she walks through the office,

taking three steps forward, turning, and turning again behind the desk.

"My goodness," she says. "How can you stand that all day?"

"What's that?" I ask.

"That," and she points down and out the window. "That
crazy screaming," and after she says it I can hear the girl
again: "Plllllllleeeeeeeeeeeeeeeezzzzz giiiiiive tooooooooooo
Surrrreeeeeeeebrallll Paaaaauuuuuuullllllllllllzzzeeeeeee."

"Oh. That," I say. "I'm used to it now. I can block it out."

"That girl could drive me crazy," Beulah says.

"Yeah," I say. "She could."

The procession begins before noon. The paralegals come
first. Heidi, the girl who works with Solomon Isaacson, starts
in with another paralegal named Jim. They're a little embarrassed and tentative at first, so I smile and act pleasant to
put them at ease. I figure it's not their fault. Then they lose
their timidity and tear through the place with their earnest
faces congealed into that hard, smug look of mid-level people from the home office. Heidi's just a Swiss collaborator,
but Jim's a good-looking Aryan with blond hair that he's
parted with a WASP daytime-TV part, just off center to the
top of his head. He's wearing round James Joyce glasses.
Someday he'll be a star, but he calls me "Mister," and I stand
in the doorway and wait for them to finish.

Larry Ackerman comes by about lunchtime. He says he
feels "terrible" about what he's been asked to do. He says it's
just one of those things. I tell him to go ahead. I tell him not
to worry about it.

"It's not here," I say after he goes through one box.

"It's not," he says.

"I've been through the place. Isaacson's been through the
place. Hansel and Gretel have been through the place. My
secretary's been through the place. It's just not here."

"Then what's going on?" he asks.

"I don't know," I say. "But whatever it is it's got nothing to do with a letter agreement or the Brooks-Bollo deal."

"I'm going to tell Lester about this," he says. "Maybe he'll be able to call off the dogs. He takes it personal when some of the assholes terrorize people around here."

I say: "Thanks." I say: "I could use some help."

The phone rings as Larry Ackerman leaves. It's Pat from the library. She says something "funny" is going on, because she's got strict orders to pick up all the papers and documents I might have left around the library.

"What's going on?" she asks, and I give her a sketch and she just goes "uh-huh" in these noncommittal little grunts, and the more I tell her the more she wants to get off the phone and get on the right side of this thing. She's not interested in risking her reputation by getting too close to somebody who's made the early casualty list, and by the time she's off the phone I figure she's got the second table from the back cordoned off with yellow police tape, and I know there's no way anybody's going to mess with the scene of that crime.

Bill Vierps knocks on the doorjamb about the time I'm ready to go for lunch. I say: "They got you, too," and he takes offense at the word "*got*." By the time I leave he's lifted the third box onto the desk and has removed the documents.

That afternoon, when I return, I have to sit in the client's chair again, because Bob Clark is doing what everybody else has already done. He says, "How the fuck could you lose a Letter Agreement?" and he's got these fanatical, blue-light, Stonewall Jackson eyes, and I don't want to get in his way, because he'd run me over if I did. So I don't say a thing, and I remember how the nuns taught us not to respond when falsely accused, because that's how Jesus impressed the hell out of Pontius Pilate. And I remember how I asked the nun:

"If He impressed him so much, why did he crucify Him?" And I remember how the nun said it wasn't right to ask questions like that.

Joe Monti stops by about mid-afternoon and he's got absolutely no balls about this, so he does this phony talking about girls and parties while he stretches his neck and looks all over the office, hoping to see something. When he feels he's done enough he leaves with that stupid thumbs-up fist stuck in the small of his back.

The procession continues all afternoon, with lawyers who look familiar and paralegals I've seen and don't know, and the word about what has happened has spread throughout the firm. People stop and stare at me when I go to the bathroom. Everybody knows who I am. But I walk with my head up, even though there's this tendency to avoid all eye contact, to look away, to look down. Finally, just before five-thirty, Susan comes to my office. She just stands there and looks at me for a while, the same way she stood there and looked at me on my first day at work.

"What's going on?" she asks.

"I didn't know you were back," I say.

"Are you all right?" she asks.

I don't say anything.

"Are you all right?" I ask.

"Better," she says, and I tell her the short version of what her boss has done, and how I've entertained the entire firm in my office. She asks if I'm certain that it began with the way she laughed.

"I don't know," I say.

"Maybe I could say something to him."

"Don't," I say. "It's too late now," and I get up to leave. She walks past me. I figure she might try to touch my arm or something, but she doesn't, and now we've exchanged places.

I stand in the doorway, and she stands in front of the window where the eight boxes are lined up in a row. I say good-bye, and she says good night. As I leave she does what everybody else has done. She bends over and picks up a box, places it on the desk, and begins to go through it. I shake my head. I can believe it. I can believe anything. She's a good secretary. She's obedient. She's left her wealthy husband. She needs this job. And she's got her orders. Everybody's got their orders. Anybody can understand that.

BLUE POLES

Lester Bartok tells me his real name is Bartkowski but that his grandfather changed it when he came to America.

"Either it was one of those changes that happened as a mistake," he says, "or he did it on purpose in honor of the composer. I never did know. He loved music, and my father played the piano. I only heard him play once, though. We had this upright, and my mother and sisters were teasing him, so he sat down, and he just started playing, something by Chopin, I think, and then it was over, and I never heard him play again. He taught accounting. Maybe he thought accounting teachers weren't supposed to play the piano."

Lester and I are sitting at a back table at Le Boeuf à la Mode. It's a fancy restaurant on the East Side. Lester knows the owner. She's from France, and Lester loves everything about France.

"I'm a Francophile," he says. "Every year I go to Paris for at least ten days, sometimes more, if I can take the time away from the office. The first time I went, I was in high school. My mother gave me this round-trip ticket, and I was nervous about going, not knowing the language and all. But she believed that after a certain point you're old enough to do certain things and that it's good for you, gives you confidence. She loved Europe, and I stayed with the daughter of a friend of hers who worked in the Australian Embassy, just a few blocks from the Eiffel Tower." And he tells me how he first walked through the city along the Seine and made his way by the Louvre and then to Notre Dame.

"I stood in front of it," he says, "and I was about a hundred yards away, and I thought: I can't get any closer, because there'll be lines or I'll need a ticket or something, or I won't know what to say. So I sat there and watched the tourists, and in the distance, up close to it, I could see that people were disappearing into it, and I thought: Maybe I can go inside, maybe I won't need a ticket, maybe I won't have to say some special French phrase. So I walked up to it, expecting somebody to stop me, but nobody stopped me, and I opened the door and I was inside, and it was dark and cool and there were these shafts of light that just poured through the windows, and the ceiling looked like it was about a mile away, and I didn't feel overwhelmed by it, because the scale was just right and there was a simplicity to it."

The waiter comes by and pours water in our glasses. He's very formal and very handsome. He asks if we'd like something to drink. Lester orders a vodka and grapefruit juice. I sit there wondering if I should order a drink or not, and Lester says: "Go ahead," and I order a Scotch and tell the waiter the brand I want. The waiter does this little bow and says: "Of course, monsieur."

"I guess the moral of that story," Lester says, returning to France and Paris and Notre Dame, "is that you shouldn't be afraid of going for something that you feel is beyond you," and he laughs to himself and then out loud, and takes a long look at me as if to tell me to relax.

He says: "You know, if you approach a city from a distance and pick out the tallest building on the horizon, whatever that building's dedicated to is what that society's all about. The tallest buildings used to be cathedrals, but today, in New York, well, we know what they are, and it could mean that lawyers are the new clergy."

He picks up his water and sets it down again. He looks at me: "So I guess you didn't know you had a vocation to be a lawyer."

The waiter brings our drinks. He sets them down on the clean linen. The glasses are wet and frosted. Lester picks up his. He says, "Cheers." I don't know what to expect with this guy. On the one hand he's as smooth as silk, a man who's very pleased with his own résumé, and yet there's something in the way he speaks about cathedrals and vocations and lawyers, as if it's a speech he's memorized and given before.

"I never thought of it as a vocation," I say. "I mean, when they asked me what I wanted to be when I grew up, I never said I wanted to be a lawyer."

"What did you say?"

"I said I wanted to be John Lennon."

"No."

"Yeah."

"So, why did you become a lawyer?"

"I never gave it much thought," I say. "I was a good student. I had the grades, and it seemed like everybody became a doctor or a lawyer or sold insurance. And I didn't want to sell insurance, and I saw a movie of an operation on a woman's ear and that did it for med school, so I took the law boards to please my folks."

"That's it?"

"There was one other reason." I pick up my drink, and it's the first real taste of the day. It goes down easy, which means it could be a long day of this sort of thing.

"And what was that?" he asks.

"What?"

"The other reason."

"There was this girl I fell for in college. She came from a wealthy family, and I figured if I was going to have a chance

with her I'd better become a professional, you know, successful and all of that."

"And what happened with the girl?"

"She ended up marrying her boyfriend. I don't know what
he does, but he had money, too."

"So, it sounds like you're one of those small-town boys
who comes to the city to make it big, marry the girl of his
dreams."

"Well, I don't know, I . . ."

"Don't get me wrong," he says. "I think it's terrific. I did
the same thing."

"Really?"

"Sure. I came from a small town outside of Buffalo. Now,
what's the best thing about Buffalo?"

"The falls."

"Besides the falls."

"The Bills."

"Besides the Bills."

"I don't know," I say. I drink again. He all but inhales his
vodka and grapefruit juice, and in a minute the waiter backs
us up with two more.

"The name," he says.

"The name," I say.

"That's right," he says. "Everybody thinks the name comes
from, you know, thundering herd buffalo."

"It doesn't?"

"No. It comes from the French: *beau fleuve,* beautiful river."

"I didn't know that."

"You can use it at a cocktail party."

"I will."

"Anyway, that's where I came from, and I went to a small
school there, and then the lottery nabbed me, and I was off
to Vietnam. Then I came back and finished up, and there
was this girl from New York, and she was in school there,

and I thought: Here I am a Vietnam vet with the fatigues and the Fu Manchu and everything else, and if I'm going to win her over, I'd better get my act together. So I aced the Boards and got into Columbia and here I am today."

"And what about the girl?"

"The girl?"

"Yeah, the girl from New York."

"I married her."

"That's great."

"Then she divorced me."

"Oh."

"Now she lives with a screenwriter in L.A."

"A screenwriter."

"Yeah, the guy does pretty well. Cops-and-robbers shows."

He finishes his first drink and half of his second. The waiter stands off to the side and watches. They know him here. This could be a long afternoon.

"So," he says, "let's take a look at where all this trouble started."

He figures we've circled around this thing long enough. This is his way to bring up the unpleasant stuff.

"It's Mark Stillman," I say. "He's got his reasons . . ."

"No," he says. "It's not Mark Stillman."

"It's not?"

"Just like the rebel," he says. "Straight to the ad hominem."

"The what?"

"Context," he says.

"Context," I say.

"What was your major in college?" he asks.

"English," I say.

"English," he says.

"Right."

"And what's your favorite sport?"

"I'm not much for sports."

"You're not much for sports."

"I swam a bit in high school."

"Swimming."

"Yeah."

"What about football?"

"That was my brother's sport."

"Tennis?"

"No."

"Basketball?"

"No."

"Golf?"

"No."

"So what do you do?" he asks.

"Oh, you know, I read a bit. Go to museums."

"Nightlife?" he asks.

"A little," I say.

"A little," he says.

"Well, maybe sometimes more than a little."

"Right," he says.

The waiter comes again. Lester's finished his second, and with the smallest move of his index finger he motions for another round.

"Now, a young guy like you comes along," he says, "and the first thing you do is make the mistake of acting the same way at the firm as you act outside the firm. You forget that once you walk into a bureaucracy, it requires a little change in attitude. I mean, most of them would starve their grandmothers if I asked them, but you don't have that junkyard-dog look. And the firm recognizes that. It sees someone who's a little different, and what happens? It begins the long, hard grind, and you either conform or you leave."

He stops. I listen with that lowered-eye, head-bobbing look of the teacher's prized pupil. I'm back in school again. I'm going to get an A. I don't want to interrupt.

"So, Mark Stillman," he says, "is nothing. He's just part of the process."

The waiter delivers the third round. Lester pauses. He takes a short sip and sets the drink down. The first two must have put out the fire he was feeling. I keep up with him, and the Scotch continues to go down easily. I start to feel the first click. This is something new. I'm not sure how to act. I look for guideposts while I can.

"And it's a question of process, a question of rituals," he says. "The firm has its own rituals. There's no way of stopping it. Luther tried to stop it, and you end up with committees."

He puts the drink down again. He fingers the glass. He's looking for the next tack. I sit there and wait. I don't dare say a thing.

"Last year I went to Arizona," he says, "to Sedona. It's like this mecca for all the New Age people, and it's all this hocus-pocus with their talk about vortices and power centers and pyramids, and everybody there has had about a hundred past lives, and all of them were Cleopatra or did time in her court, and one night this woman I was with convinced me to join them for this ritual where they walk on fire. So, the wind was blowing, and it was cold as hell, and one by one they lined up and walked across the thing with all these histrionics and high fives; and my friend, this woman who's out there dabbling in this stuff because she burnt herself out at Sullivan and Cromwell, she's got all these reasons why it's meaningful and important to walk on fire. Well, I told her she was nuts, I told her she was crazy, but then I thought about the rituals we perform every day at the firm: the off-color joke, the kissing up, the glad hand, having to laugh at jokes that aren't funny, Phil Wessen's tennis racket routine, and I wondered who's the one walking on fire."

He stops. He looks about the bar. He sees the maître d' and motions for him to stop by. The maître d' walks over and they talk about something in perfect French. The maître d' is named Paul. Lester introduces me. Lester says I'm a "true gentleman," and the maître d' does that same little heel-clicking bow the waiter did. Then he leaves, and a minute later the waiter delivers a bottle of wine, compliments of the house. Lester whispers that he's not that fond of wine, but it would be rude not to drink it. So he pours a glass for me and a glass for himself. It's dark and deep, and after the Scotch it tastes very sweet and cold.

"What's the great thing about tennis?" he asks.

"I don't know," I say. "I don't play."

"No. Really," he says. "Think."

The question is not a rhetorical one.

"The speed," I say.

"No," he says, shaking his head. "It's the language. Didn't you ever wonder where that word *love* comes from?"

"Well, I . . ."

"I mean, you miss a shot, and the other guy scores, and he gets points and you get *love*. I mean, where did that word come from?"

"I never thought about it," I say.

"It's French," he says. "When a player didn't score a point they'd give him a zero, but when they drew the zero they sort of flattened it out so it looked more like an egg, and the French word for 'egg' is *l'oeuf*, and the word came down to us as *love*."

"Oh," I say, and I do that nod like I'm really interested.

"Now, Phil Wessen, he'll strut around the firm because he's John Westphall's adopted son, and he'll carry that tennis racket of his and swing it around and act athletic and talk like a jock, but do you think he knows where the word *love* comes from?"

"No, I . . ."

"You know he doesn't. That's not his thing. That's not his

ritual. Being a prince, the heir to the throne, is part of his ritual, and heirs to thrones don't have to worry about the arcane origin of words. That's left to people like you, who worry too much."

"No, I . . ."

"No," he says, "it's true. You worry too much. I can see it. You're thinking: Here I am two months into my first job, and I got a senior associate all over my case, and then there's this partner who takes me out to lunch, and I can't make sense out of what he's all about."

"No, I mean . . ."

"I'll tell you what I'm about," he says. "When I started here, Phil Wessen was an associate, and for whatever reason he'd done something right, and John Westphall took a liking to him, and Phil could do no wrong, and he had this great reputation, and the first month I was here he just took one of those arbitrary dislikes to me, and for a while he made my life pretty miserable. So I had to fight back. I had to do things, I had to produce, because there was this thing out there, this reputation I had to overcome. But I did produce, and the years went by, and I stayed, and they made me a partner, and now Phil Wessen and I are partners. I'm not saying it's easy; I'm just saying it can be done."

"Yeah, well, I know it can be done, it's just that—"

"Look," he says, interrupting me again, "you know what the Poles and the Irish have in common?"

This is not a rhetorical question, and I know I don't have a chance of answering it correctly.

"The origin of words," I say.

"Not the origin of words," he says. "What the Poles and the Irish have in common is that we both come from occupied countries. We both know what it is to be under somebody's heel."

"Well, I never thought of it that way, but—"

"Of course it's right," he says. "And we've got this need to be somebody else. I mean, sometimes we don't even know who we are. So we attach ourselves to these little rituals, that aren't our own, just to enter the mainstream, like when my wife and I lived in Connecticut and I did the commute, and she did the ladies' clubs, and all the time we knew we were just outsiders looking in."

The waiter returns to take our order. Lester orders quickly, with an accent laced with the barest trace of the liquor he's consumed. I can't hear what he says, and what I do hear I can't make out. He looks at me and waits. There's this whole thing about what's right to order when you're out with a partner. The rule is never order onion soup because the cheese can be a big embarrassment and, unless you're particularly sure of yourself, never order anything with a sauce that can splash your tie. So I order the French onion soup and the filet with the béarnaise sauce, because I figure it's a good day to break all the rules.

Lester pours more wine. I lift my glass and drink some more, and then set it down again so he can fill it up.

"When I was young we didn't worry so much about fitting in," he says. "Back then the key was to be as different as you could be. There were so many of us we somehow got being an individual mixed up with being marginal. The reaction was too extreme, though. Everything was polarized out of bounds. That's why the fashions were so far out. The seventies was one ugly decade. And people forget how smug it was. When I got back from Vietnam I'd see the kids, same age as me, with the hair and everything, and they didn't know a thing about what had really happened, but they'd call me a baby killer, and until I let the hair grow and all of that, it was a time for crouching in corners."

He pauses. He remembers something. I take a bread stick from the basket with the French bread. I break it and the sesame seeds roll out onto the linen. I spread butter on the tip, and when I eat it the butter melts in the smoky bread taste.

He looks about the room. His eyes focus on things that are far away. "We only have four or five memories," he says. He looks down. "And we carry them with us always, and they order everything. They're like the scaffolding on which we drape all the chaos and the nonsense. They're like these blue poles that just stand there in a long row, and we touch one and then go off into the world until it's too much, until we come to another one, and we touch that one and stay with it until it's time to move on again, always returning, and always moving on again."

He looks up. The wine has touched him and the room seems darker than it really is. His eyes waver a bit. He looks away. He likes the drama in this. He wants to be a tragic figure. He wants to be thought of as brilliant and eccentric and honest. He works hard at all of this. It's all precious and a little forced. He doesn't even know me, but he's telling me I'm OK, and that the trouble with Mark Stillman is more because of my qualities than because of my shortcomings. It's a hard message to ignore. It's a flattering notion. I try it on, and then I reject it. After all, Lester might be a little nuts, and we might even share some common ground because of that fact; but Lester is also a lawyer, a partner, and an adult, and one should never rely too heavily on any one of those.

The waiter brings our food. We talk little as we eat. Lester stops drinking. He's a little withdrawn now. He feels he's said too much, allowed himself to be carried away with the shooters and the wine and the sound of his own voice. I feel the need to talk, not because I have anything to say, but because it's all become a little awkward.

The maître d' approaches the table and asks if everything is all right. Lester says everything is fine. The maître d' excuses himself and says that there's a telephone call for Lester. The waiter brings a cordless phone to the table. Lester says: "*Merci*," and he picks up the phone and speaks to Larry Ackerman. There's a major problem with one of the Japanese clients. Lester says, "The fucking government," and he's angry. He says, "Don't we have people in Albany taking care of that?" Then he tells Larry he'll be back in twenty minutes. He puts the phone down. The waiter comes and takes it away. He hands the waiter his card, and then tells the waiter to put everything on his account. The waiter says: "Of course, Monsieur Lester." Lester tells me he has to leave. He says: " 'I was a free man in Paris,' " and it's a lyric he's remembered and has said often. He stands up. He says: "You stay here. Finish your meal. Have a few more drinks on me. And when you get out from under Mark's heel, come and see me. We'll work on some projects. We'll give it a shot. If it works, we're both winners. If not, at least you will have had a fair shot."

I say, "Thanks, Lester."

"Fair enough," he says.

"Fair enough," I say, and I say "thanks" again, and for the first time in a long time, I actually mean it.

CRIP GIRLS ARE EASY

After Lester left the restaurant the French waiter had stories to tell about "Monsieur Lester," but I'd had enough of that, so I left a big tip, headed out the door, and returned to the firm by way of Third Avenue. I took my time and stopped at two bars along the way. I needed the time and the quiet to figure out what had happened at lunch. I realized that at the price of being human, Lester was a little crazy. He'd offered some help, even patronage, a shelter in the storm, but there was something strange about him, something uneven and unpredictable. All of that talk about France and cathedrals and vocations and the New Age stuff and Phil Wessen's tennis racket. It didn't make a lot of sense, and I wondered if his taking me out to lunch didn't have more to do with his need to be different than it had to do with any real concern for me. His speeches had seemed scripted and memorized. He'd played the role of the wise champion, the mature warrior, and even though he'd offered to help, I bridled at being taken in for reasons that had less to do with me and more to do with him.

By the time I return to the firm everyone has left for the day. I walk through the place looking for people, and except for a few faraway sounds, I don't hear or see anyone. I go to my office and it looks the same. There's a note on my desk from Susan. It says to meet her at Eaamon's on Second Avenue.

They're celebrating Bill Vierps's birthday. The eight boxes remain lined up against the wall. It doesn't look like anybody's gone through them, but I can't be certain. I pick up the third box and go to the section that contains the letter agreements. I hope there'll be a miracle like in the movies, and something will just appear with a flash of light and the sound of organs or thunder. I thumb through the papers. There are twelve agreements in the section. I check each one again. There is no Klein-Shorndorff Citibank Letter Agreement. And there is no flash of light or sound of organs or thunder. Then I remember the day Mark Stillman stood there behind Susan, touching her shoulders, and I remember her face, and I remember the way she laughed. I try to measure the damage and ask myself whether any of it can be saved. But the damage is great. I can tell by the way people act toward me, as if I had some terminal disease, as if I was one of those guys in combat who are deemed to be unlucky.

I place the box back down by the air vents. The girl who screams has left for the day. It's just another weekend, and even charities have to take a break.

My head feels heavy and wrapped in bunting. It's the wine that does that. The Scotch had started me off, but the wine dropped a blanket over it. I didn't feel the click, and it's questionable whether I will.

I stare at the telephone on the desk. There's a call I've wanted to make for some time. I debate the question again. I feel my head and the heaviness, and a heat begins like a wire in my stomach. I think about it. I pick up the receiver. I put it down. I pick it up again. I dial the weather. It might rain tomorrow. I dial my apartment. There's no answer, and then I hear my voice on the answering machine. I hang up. This is crazy. I haven't done this sort of thing since the first time I called the girl in college who drove me nuts, and then almost really drove me nuts. Finally I dial information. I know the number before I ask for it, but I ask for it again. It's the same number. She's still there in the Village. I write the number down on one of those yellow stick-'em pads. I stare at it for a while. Then there's some noise from down the hall. I hear a voice. It's Joe Monti. He walks by my office and looks in. I've surprised him. He was talking to himself.

"What are you doing here?" he asks.

"Nothing," I say.

"I heard you had lunch with Lester."

"Yeah."

"He's a trip."

"Yeah. Nice guy, though."

"Yeah, he's all right. So, are you going to meet up with Ray and me tonight?"

"Ray didn't tell me anything about tonight."

"It's a party," he says. "His friend Mary told him about it. We're meeting at the Lemon Lime around ten. You should stop by."

I say that I'll think about it. I stare at the open door after he leaves. I think about Ray and Mary. I think about how things change.

Finally I pick up the phone and dial three numbers and put the phone down. I curse myself for being a coward. I don't know why I'm so nervous about this. She's just another girl. But then something tells me to forget it, to move on to Eaamon's, to get drunk, to do what's expected and easy. But I dial the number again. It rings once, and I fight the temptation to hang up.

She answers the phone. She has a light and delicate voice, almost tentative, and it's different from what I remember.

I say, "Is this Cindy?"

"Who's this?" she asks.

"You might not remember me," I say, which is what people always say when they really don't think it's true, "but I'm the guy who talked to you at that party up at Fordham a month ago."

She pauses. She's either trying to remember or she's planning some way to get off the phone.

"Oh, yeah," she says. "The lawyer."

"Right," I say.

"Yeah, hi," she says, and she says it with that I-couldn't-care-less voice.

"Hi," I say, and the conversation starts slowly, a thin and slack line of words that grope uneasily but never stop completely. Finally, when the timing's right, or when I think it's not going to get any better, I ask her if she'd like to get together for drinks or coffee. She's not sure, because her boyfriend left earlier in the day all upset over something, and she doesn't know when he's coming back.

I say that we don't have to get together tonight, and she surprises me and changes her mind. Her voice changes, too. It's assertive again, the way I remember it. She says her boyfriend can be such a "baby," and that she can do what she wants.

"Why don't you come over here," she says. "I can make tea, and there's some wine."

"Tonight?"

"Why not?"

I tell her that I've got to meet some people for about an hour, but that I'll be over after that. I ask her what subway is best from midtown. She says, "I don't know; I don't take subways."

"Oh, yeah, I forgot," I say, and I feel like a jerk as I tell her I'll take a cab instead.

Eaamon's is a dark place, and it takes a while for my eyes to adjust, so I hear them before I can see them clearly, sitting at a large round table in the back. Charlie Anton is telling stories again, and Pat's there nursing her drink, swearing and determined that she's not going to have more than two, not after what happened the last time she was out with this crowd.

"Settle down with that stuff," I say to Pat as I approach the table, thinking she'll find it funny. But she doesn't find it funny. She just looks at me and gets very quiet. The whole table gets quiet until Susan pushes her chair over to make room for me. The dip in volume tells me just how bad things are. My problem with Mark has touched everybody here in one way or another, and their silence doesn't bode well for me. Then Charlie picks up the story he'd dropped in midsentence, and the others direct their attention to the punch line that gives them a reason to laugh.

"How was your lunch?" Bill Vierps asks.

"Who'd you have lunch with?" Susan asks.

"Lester Bartok," I say.

"He's another story altogether," Bill Vierps says.

"I heard he's crazy," Susan says.

"Who's that?" Pat asks.

"Lester Bartok," Susan says.

"Oh, him," Pat says, and she makes her eyes go in a big circle around the room.

"He did a little time," Charlie Anton says. "Took one of those long vacations."

"What kind of vacation?" I ask.

"Took a break, you know," Charlie says, tapping his temple.

"Went to Paris," Pat says, and laughs.

"Yeah, right—Paris," Charlie says.

"So how was it?" Susan asks.

"It was OK," I say. "He's a pretty smart guy," and I ask them if anybody knows where the word *love* in tennis comes from, and none of them does except for Bill Vierps, who had his own lunch with Lester Bartok about a year ago. I tell the story anyway, and Susan just sits there with this amused look on her face.

"So what time do we leave tomorrow?" Charlie asks, and Bill Vierps says that they have to be out of the city by seven, and Charlie does that cliché-cringe, like there's no way he'll be able to do it and still be civil.

"They're going white-water kayaking tomorrow," Susan says, and I ask what is white-water kayaking, and Bill Vierps describes it, and I can see somebody stuck in one of those canoes with their upper body plugged into some convex canvas on a narrow slip of hollowed-out wood with the paddles with the blades on either end. There's this talk of white water and blue death and of turning it over when the kayak tips, and it all sounds like a lot of work.

"What do you think?" Susan asks, and I say it sounds like fun, and she asks me if I'd like to go with them, and I say no, but I say it politely, not letting on what I really think about a hobby that dunks you in forty-degree water at a time of day when I'm still doing damage reports on any number of internal organs.

"I'm thinking of going," Susan says, and Bill Vierps leans over and tells her some more about the thrill of victory. After that she looks at me again. She says: "Why don't you come. It'll be fun."

I say, "You're really serious about this?"

"Yes," she says, "I am."

"I don't think so," I say, and Bill goes on again about how beautiful the river is and how "thrilling" it all is, and for the first time since I've met him he's lost that sleepy-eyed, world-weary, seen-too-much expression. He's excited, and Charlie's rubbing his forehead saying: "How did I ever get myself into this?" Then Bill Vierps pulls out the brochure he's carrying.

He hands it to Susan like he's closing a sale. Her eyes are all over it, bugged out and hungry, looking at it like the recently separated wife she is, just out there to do whatever's new and exciting, scarfing up experience like she's on spring break. She hands it to me. She says, "Look at this," and I take it from her and turn it over. Charlie says: "Careful there, now, don't lose it," and everybody groans with the joke, and I just hand the brochure back to her.

"So what do you think?" she says, and she's looking right at me. She's really asking; this is something she really wants. And I see myself stuck in a kayak from the waist up, freezing to death in white water and dark pools. I say: "No," and this time there's no question as to what I mean. She turns away. I've disappointed her again.

Charlie starts to tell jokes, and everybody laughs. After a while I excuse myself and leave with a happy-birthday hand-shake for Bill and a wave to the others. Susan gives me this look, but I don't explain myself. I just leave.

Outside it's almost dark, and the cabs have their headlights on. The traffic has eased a bit, but it takes some time before I finally hail one.

The cabdriver is this little Asian guy, and he's so short he drives standing up, raising his head over the dashboard, then lowering it as he aims for a spot somewhere down the avenue. When he reaches the place he'd aimed for, he picks up his head again, and, with the skittish movement of a desert gopher, aims for some other spot farther down the avenue. In this way he constantly pushes himself ahead of the flow, content with nothing but speed and the dangerous squeeze through seemingly impassable spaces. He's a maniac, and somewhere around Fourteenth Street I realize that we're going to die, but we don't die, and he gets us through it, and we reach the Village in about half the time it'd normally take.

I tell him to stop a few blocks this side of Christopher Street, and I stop off at a liquor store to buy a bottle of Scotch. I figure it's the least I can do.

I'm real nervous about this. I tell myself that the nerves have something to do with her boyfriend, and I think how I'll cast this whole thing as the arrival of "just a friend." I tell myself that's what it is: Cindy and I are "just friends." I don't want to date her or marry her or anything like that. That's what I tell myself, and I think how I'll visit with her the way friends visit, and that when I leave I'll be able to say: Now, that was a nice visit with a good friend.

I get a little lost, and I ask directions from a couple of guys who make gestures with overstated certainty. I figure they're putting me on. I wonder if I look as nervous as I feel. I think maybe I'm paranoid. People are strange. I'm strange. And this is the Village, and the energy is different from the energy uptown.

I reach her apartment building and tell the doorman her name. He eyes me with suspicion. He knows her right off, and he's a little protective of her. He makes a call and asks me my name. Then he speaks to someone on the other end of the line. He tells me to go ahead, but he doesn't look at me when he says it.

"Second elevator," he says. "First one's under repair."

I say "Thanks," and enter the elevator and push the button for the eleventh floor. The doors don't close, so I push it again and then again. Each time it gives off a little ring. I look at my shoes and wait, and then when I look up, the doorman's standing there. He looks at me. "Relax," he says, "it'll move," and with that the doors close in front of his hard face, half hidden under the visor of his doorman's cap.

Some trips take forever, and this one's like a transatlantic crossing. Time has slowed so much I actually start to worry about my breathing. I spend about an hour on eight and then an hour and a half on nine and ten never comes, and then it does, followed immediately by eleven and that soft, airy feeling under my feet. There's a sign dividing the apartments by alphabet letter, and her apartment is just down the hall. There's the odor of bacon. An old Creedence Clearwater album plays somewhere. Somebody's stuck in Lodi again.

I reach her door and stand in front of it, looking at it. The door has her name and only her name on it. I knock, and there's a long pause, and then I hear somebody. The door opens, and she's sitting there, dressed in black. Her hair has grown out a bit. Her face is still perfect, and her eyes still have that depth and softness. I put on that face that smiles too much. She catches it right away. She says: "You're not some kind of wacko, are you?" and I say no, as if there's some other response to that question. Then she takes a long look at me. I put out my arms, and then drop them. She looks at me again, and then she lets me in.

The apartment is large and clean, and the furniture is all spread out so as to make it easy for her to get around without having to worry about bumping into things. Her studio is in the first room with the windows, and there are three easels set up with watercolors in various stages of completion. The colors are mild, but the lines are strong. On a long table by the wall there is a series of cameras set in a row. Several photos are taped to the wall. The photos are mostly portraits, and some candid shots from the neighborhood. Some are powerful, especially three shots of an Indian family with their faces and huge, black eyes peering out and fixing the viewer.

She takes the bottle of Scotch and says "Thank you" and puts it in her lap and brings it to the kitchen. She tells me to have a seat and asks if I'd like a drink. I surprise myself and say no. She says she'll make some tea, and I sit in the dark room off the studio where there's a wide-screen TV turned on without the sound. There's no sign of her boyfriend, and later, when she joins me and asks me to help her with the tea, she tells me he came back earlier and that he was drunk, and that he started a fight and then left again.

"He won't be back tonight," she says, and she looks behind her and out the window as if to gesture that he's out there somewhere. "He does this every few months," she says. "Ties one on and starts a fight and then leaves with a big show about it. He'll be back on Sunday, begging me to take him back in."

"And you will?"

"I don't know about this time," she says, "but then I say that every time. His act is getting pretty old, though. But then he comes back, and I see how beat-up he is. I don't know. I tell myself no, but then I see him . . ."

"He drinks too much, too," I say, and I say it as a matter of fact.

"What is it with you boys?" she says, and she looks straight at me. "You hit the city and I don't know."

The phone rings, and she places her mug down and moves silently across the floor to the other side of the studio. I hear her say, "No, Dad," and she laughs, and then it's over. She returns, telling me how overprotective her father is, and that he's always calling her up from Chicago to see if she's all right.

"The hardest thing," she says, "I mean, the hardest thing was getting him to let me live on my own."

"He lives in Chicago?"

"Yes," she says. "I love Chicago," and she tells me how her dad is this executive for a big advertising agency, and she asks me about a certain beer commercial that's famous. She tells me that that one was his, and I'm impressed, and I tell her how much I like her photos and artwork. She turns and looks at all of it, surveying it with a slight smile because she's proud of it, too. Then her face turns real serious in the way that says she wants to cut the crap and the little dance we've choreographed as we sit here with our cups of tea and polite questions.

"So why'd you call me?" she asks.

"I saw you at the museum last month," I say, "and today this crazy partner said something about doing things that are 'beyond you'—or beyond me—and then I had a few drinks and got my courage up."

"So you think I'm beyond you?"

"I don't know if I'd put it like that," I say. "What I mean is," and I don't know what I mean.

"I usually get the wackos," she says "or the liberals who want to show how liberal they are, or the nervous guys who take me out once and then go off and become monks."

I don't say anything. I review the categories. I must be a wacko.

"Relax," she says. "I know you're all right," and she sips her tea and looks at me, and I lean back on the couch and hold the warm mug as it cools in my hands.

The network news is over, and the good-looking anchor with the thinning hair stops moving his mouth before the credits roll, and the commercial comes on with snow bunnies, and then the preview for the entertainment show from L.A. Cindy says she's been waiting for this because there's going to be a clip about some charity event at the Frick Collection.

"My father flew in for it," she says.

"So he's a celebrity?" I ask.

"No way," she says. "His agency had something to do with it. He told me he met some, though, and he thinks he got in front of the camera when they were trying to shoot the mayor. I want to see if they caught him on camera."

"Why didn't you go?" I ask.

"I wasn't invited," she says, and she fools with the remote control, turning on and then lowering the volume. "Anyway, it was formal, and I'm just not up for formal these days."

She hits the wrong button and we're looking at a local news show. She says "Dammit" and punches back to the entertainment show. Then as she hits the mute button the sound goes off, and a family car that looks like a race car climbs a hill somewhere in France.

"I saw you at the museum, too," she says.

"Oh?"

"I know that you followed me."

"I wasn't following you."

"Yes, you were."

"OK, maybe I accidentally ended up in the same place where you ended up, and maybe it wasn't like a total coincidence, but . . ."

"I said it was all right," she says. "I remembered you right away when I saw you by the elevator. I mean, that party was hard to forget."

"It was pretty bad."

"Richard went on one of his benders right after we got home. It was a friend of his who'd told us to go to it, all because of that priest who's supposed to be such a great poet."

"My friend Eddy, the guy who asked me to go to it, he left the Jesuits."

"Really?"

"Yeah. He couldn't believe they could be so rude. He's got a real sad story to tell."

"I bet," she says.

She flicks the sound on, and the blonde with the head-spinning smile talks about the latest in entertainment news: Another cocaine-addled kid with a good agent slugged some sleazeball photographer somewhere in Hollywood; another actress is pregnant, but promises to keep working; and there's this new singer from Brazil who does forbidden things onstage.

"It's all such crap," she says.

"What?" I ask.

"Celebrity," she says. "I mean, who cares?"

"I don't know," I say. "I figure it's because the world's too crowded."

"What do you mean?"

"The world's too crowded, so people feel they have to be celebrities, you know, stand out, just to be human beings."

"But who wants to stand out all the time?" she says.

"I don't know," I say. "I guess some people just like to be looked at."

"Not me," she says. "People have stared at me all of my life, and I've had enough of that kind of celebrity."

"I guess," I say.

"That's what I liked most about Richard," she says.

"What's that?" I ask.

"The first time he met me he looked at me, but he didn't stare at me. I mean, as screwed up as he is, he's never stared at me."

"What's the difference?" I ask.

"Between what?"

"Between looking and staring."

She says it's got something to do with the way she feels when it happens. "I know the difference right off," she says.

"I hope I didn't stare," I say.

"You did," she says, "but it was all right." She turns off the sound as a marching band in a hamburger commercial begins to play.

"You're really very shy," she says.

"I am?"

"You don't even know it, with the way you carry on every weekend."

"How do you know about my weekends?"

"I know," she says, and she shakes her head slowly. "After we met I checked out where you worked, and I know a person who knows a person who works there, and they don't know you, but they know about you."

"I had no idea," I say.

"There's a world that goes on outside of you," she says.

"I guess," I say, and I hold the dark mug to my lips and drink the tea. It's almost cool and very sweet. I put the mug down.

"So what else did you find out?" I ask.

"I know you're having a hard time in your job."

"I can't believe this," I say.

"This friend of a friend didn't elaborate, but they said somebody was making it hard for you."

"It's been pretty bad," I say, and I stare at my shoes. They're scuffed. The tassels look pretty worn. "Yeah, it's been something," I say, "but then I don't exactly have an El Cid tolerance for pain."

"A what?"

"El Cid," I say. "The Spanish epic? Arrow to the heart?"

"What?" She doesn't know what I'm talking about.

"It was before both of our times," I say, and she hits the sound button and the all-American host introduces the benefit at the Frick, saying how "all the stars turned out."

The camera cuts away to these famous people getting out of limousines. Then the camera settles on one actress. They interview her, and she talks with this exaggerated Brooklynese, because now it's chic to be from Brooklyn. I look at her, and then I look at the two people who are standing behind her. They're so familiar, I don't even recognize them. But the camera stays with the actress, and I see the two of them again as they emerge from the darkness of the background to the lights shining there. It's Mary and Ray, and they're smiling, talking with Mary's father and two others, holding champagne glasses, grinning like it's their birthright. I sit up like a shot. I look at the screen. I can't believe what I'm seeing. Cindy watches me from the corner of her eye as she waits to see her father. Then the camera cuts away to some grande dame who talks about how special rich people are for giving away what they don't need. Then it's over, and the face of the smiling hostess fills the screen with talk of some self-proclaimed supergroup's latest album.

I sit there frozen in front of the TV screen. Cindy asks me what's the matter.

"Didn't you see them?" I ask.

"Who?"

"Mary and Ray."

"Who are Mary and Ray?"

"Mary and Ray," I say. "They were my friends."

"They went to the Frick?"

"They were right there."

"So, that's good. You've got friends with connections."

"You don't understand."

"Understand what?"

"I used to be popular. People used to invite me to things, and they didn't even tell me about this."

"It was just a stupid benefit. There's only about three hundred of them a year."

"Yeah, but this means . . ."

"What?"

"You know."

"I don't know. I don't know what you're talking about," and now she's confused, because I can't explain why this bothers me so. She doesn't know me; she doesn't know that this kind of thing means too much to me; she doesn't know how much it hurts me to see people pass me by like I'm not important anymore. She's free of this sort of thing. She doesn't give a damn about being accepted in the cliques and circles that have haunted me for years. But I'm devastated, and I feel the emptiness that comes when things are about to end. Mary's taken Ray all the way up, and I feel like the drummer the Beatles left behind one month before they made it big.

"Tell me," she says. "Please, tell me what's the matter," and she's being kind about this, as if promising to make up for whatever I think I've lost. She comes up close to me. I look at her. I see that she is truly beautiful, with her perfect and delicate lines, like a model's face on one of those magazines the girls buy before they go back to school. And all I can do is look at her, because I can't explain how much it hurts to be a loser. I want to tell her, but I can't, and even if I could, I wouldn't, because explaining something like this, no matter how true and real it is, only shows how miserable I really am.

She asks if a drink would help. I say no. I try to settle down. But I can't settle down. I envy just about everybody in the whole world. I don't know what I'm doing here. I realize how impossible this whole "wacko" scene really is, with her poet-boyfriend out there in Dylan Thomas land, and how I blame it on that because I don't have it in me to take her just the way she is, knowing I would want it to be different, demanding changes and compromise, ever limiting our time together to small hidden places where I would whisper across the darkness.

I take her hand and tell her that she's the prettiest woman I've ever met. It comes out stilted and false, and she looks at me because she's got radar when it comes to wackos. And then I tell her I have to go.

"You don't really," she says.

"I know, but I do."

"Why?"

"I just do."

"Don't," she says. "I'll make some more tea; we'll talk."

"I'm sorry," I say, and I thank her for the tea, and when she asks me if I want to take the bottle of Scotch, I say no.

I take both of her hands in mine. They are fine and strong hands. We hold each other for a moment. Then I let her go, and I just leave.

WHERE THE LIGHT IS DIFFERENT
AND STRANGE

Because nothing happened on Monday or Tuesday, because the boxes sat there untouched and unmoved, because nobody came into my office to search the place, because nobody chirped or twittered after I passed by, because time had passed and other things had happened, because people had their own lives to live, I dared to believe that the problem with Mark Stillman and Marty and Brooks-Bollo was about to go away. But then on Wednesday, after I finish drafting two more minor documents for Larry Ackerman and send them off to typing, the six-foot-tall woman with the Amazon voice enters my office. She stands there and tells me to follow her. She says Mr. Westphall wants to see me.

"Mr. Westphall?" I say.

"Now," she says, and I follow her down the hallway to the huge corner office with windows on Park Avenue.

The sunlight pours over everything like something out of a space odyssey movie. At first the other people in the office are just silhouettes against the light. Then I see Mark Stillman standing in the back of the room, and I know I'm in trouble.

The office manager takes a seat to the left of Mr. Westphall's desk, and Phil Wessen hands him documents from the right. Mr. Westphall signs one document after another. He holds one up to Phil, who explains something, and Mr. Westphall nods his head and signs that one, too. Then he looks up; he looks at me; he asks Lois if she was able to reach Marty. Lois says that he's out of the office with a client, and Mark steps forward to say who the client is and where they are and just how close he and Marty are to finalizing one more megabuck deal. Mr. Westphall's eyes are blank and pitiless. He doesn't like Mark Stillman. I can only sense this, but it gives me some comfort.

Phil takes back the documents and pulls another one from the folder under his arm. He shows it to Mr. Westphall, and both of them laugh these small, dismissive laughs. This is something only they know about. This is a glimpse of the inside stuff. In some universe this is probably important. Then Mr. Westphall asks for the letter. Mark jumps up and says he gave it to Phil. Lois takes out her steno pad and begins to take notes. Phil pulls a folder from under his arm and hands it to Mr. Westphall. Mr. Westphall opens the folder. He looks at the letter and reads it silently. Everyone is very grim; this is not the green room for the Nobel Peace Prize.

He finishes the letter. He looks up. He asks me if I know about this. Mark Stillman answers for me. He says, "No, sir. I brought my copy straight to Phil." Mr. Westphall looks at Lois. He asks when he received his copy. She says, "Yesterday afternoon's delivery."

"So you don't know about this?" He's talking to me again. His face sags with weight and age. Large red lines course through the tip of his nose. His skin is dark and rubbery. He wears half-glasses and looks at me over the rims.

"No, sir. I don't know what that paper is."

"I've received this letter," he says. He picks it up again and debates whether to give it to me or not. He decides against it. Then he waves it once in front of me. I see that it says "Brooks-Bollo" and something else across the top.

"I'm not in the habit of receiving letters like this," he says.

"No, sir."

"Mark, would you please read him your copy of the letter."

"Yes, sir," Mark says, and he pulls a copy from his suit jacket and begins to read, and as he reads I can hear the white-cracker, hillbilly voice of some weatherbeaten wildcatter who's used to getting his way in the hardscrabble mountains of West Virginia, and who thinks he's been taken for granted by some fancy-dancer Park Avenue New York City law firm. The cracker's pissed, damn pissed, and he complains how they'd brought the business to this Westphall, Sellars place as a personal, though ill-advised, favor to the former CEO of Brooks-Bollo, and that although they have no major complaint about the work handed in by Messrs. Pomeroy and Stillman, it strikes them as more than a little curious as to why, after weeks of inquiries, questions, complaints, and demands, this fancy-dancer Park Avenue New York City law firm has been unable to provide the board of directors of Brooks-Bollo with a simple closing binder comprising the many and various documents evidencing their most recent transactions with Citibank, et al. And after that the letter begins to get nasty as Mr. Brooks or Mr. Bollo, or whoever it is, reprimands Mr. Westphall himself, saying that if the leader of the organization took a little more interest in the workings of his own firm, perhaps clients such as Brooks-Bollo wouldn't be driven to such drastic ends as the drafting, execution, and transmission of letters such as this.

Mark finishes the letter and the room is silent. Mr. Westphall stares at me. His eyes don't waver, though they flinched once at Mark's recitation of a particularly ripe passage of hillbilly invective. The phone rings, and everyone breathes a sigh until Lois picks it up and speaks in hushed tones. She says that this is not a particularly good time to interrupt an execution.

"So what am I supposed to do about a letter like this?" Mr. Westphall asks.

I sit there. I don't know what to say.

"I'm not in the habit of receiving letters like this," he says again.

He looks at Mark. "Can you explain any of this?" he asks.

"I gave him the assignment over four weeks ago," he says. "All I know is that the documents are still in boxes in his office and that he's lost a letter agreement."

"Well?" Mr. Westphall asks me. I just sit there. Sure there's a story, but am I allowed to tell it? I remember the nuns and Jesus and Pontius Pilate. I remember the question I asked the nun. I remember that they killed Him anyway.

"I'm asking you a question," he says.

"Mark gave me the assignment about four weeks ago. There were some disagreements over the index, and I didn't lose a letter agreement."

"Disagreements over an index," he says. He's exasperated by all of this. This is too much. This has gone too far. He turns to Phil. Phil's his fix-it person. Mr. Westphall asks him to get to the bottom of this thing. He says that the closing binder is to be done by five o'clock that afternoon or "there's going to be hell to pay." He actually says: "There's going to be hell to pay."

Mark jumps up. He says it'll be done. He says he'll do it himself. Phil looks at all of us like we're crazy.

"Are these disagreements taken care of?" Mr. Westphall asks.

"Yes, sir," I say.

"And you say you didn't lose a document."

"No, sir. I didn't lose a thing."

"Then why is there all this trouble?" he asks, turning from Lois to Phil and back again.

Mark Stillman is almost out the door. He says it'll be taken care of. Mr. Westphall goes on to other things. They ignore me. I've been dismissed without a word. I get up to leave, and they talk about a revenue projection from a certain group in the tax department. Mr. Westphall tells Lois to confirm his luncheon with Garmont downtown. Lois checks her steno pad. And I'm outside the door.

I go to my office, but I can't get into it because it's crowded with Heidi and Jim and Beulah. They're standing there, picking up boxes and placing them in the hallway. Jim starts to carry them to Mark Stillman's office. Beulah tells me to take a very long lunch.

The curious thing is how everything stays the same: The traffic is jammed up on the cross streets; the crowds continue to walk with speed and purpose; the restaurants are crowded; waitresses in hamburger joints still take orders with that sense of urgency and displeasure. The city just goes on, unfazed like nature, rolling over whatever's happened within its five-borough boundary, absorbing, consuming all experience and digesting it as if it were nothing.

I never thought it would go this far. I didn't think Mark would risk his own reputation by allowing the problem to reach Mr. Westphall's desk. But the client was really pissed. And somebody wrote that letter.

I walk around the East Side and then head up Fifth Avenue. I stop by St. Patrick's. I go in and sit in the back. A priest is saying Mass, and up front people are standing and kneeling at the right time. I think about asking for help, but I feel like a hypocrite because of the years when I rode high and full of myself with the easy burden of potential and never said thank you.

The priest walks to the front of the altar, and the crowd gets up to take Communion. I watch them as they go up, the old women with the lace covering their foreheads, the businessmen, the young women, the homeless, the simple, and the meek. They take the wafer, stand a moment, place it between their lips, and then return to their seats. I wish that I could do that—just go up there and take it and believe in it and feel better for it. But there's always something holding me back. Something dark and cynical, something like honesty, but something self-righteous, too. I don't like priests, though I've only got one good reason to dislike one priest. And I don't like Catholics, though I wonder if it's not because I don't like myself. But now there's trouble, and this is the place I come to. Now there's trouble, and this is where I look for comfort. Now there's trouble, and it's dark as the priest gives his final blessing and leaves the altar. I watch the small crowd disperse. I smell the sweet smell of wax burning. I remember the smell of incense and the sound of bells, and I wish I could leave everything behind in this pew like a prayer scrawled on paper to the patron of those without hope.

I leave the cathedral and walk down Fifth Avenue and then over to Grand Central Station. I stop in a bar and order a screwdriver. I figure there's vitamins in the orange juice. It goes down like orange juice, so I order another and leave. It's only midday, but already the crowds have gathered and are passing through the place. This city is too much. A person has to be very resilient or very young or very healthy to take it.

I walk up Park Avenue. I stay with the flow of the uptown pedestrian traffic. I look at the faces when I pass them. I wonder who else has problems. I think how everybody's got problems. That's what I tell myself. I'd like to sit down and talk with them about it. I'd like to get some perspective on all of this.

I pass St. Bart's, where the Episcopalians do their own thing with bread and wine and Northern European reticence, a church of high American taste, light on the guilt,

heavy on the contributions. They run a club for young sin-
gles to meet and to breed for the upper crust. They have
nicknames like Chubb or Dex. The ministers would have
been fops if they hadn't become ministers. They've got accents, and the members of their flock acquire accents. The
Irish look on them longingly, and people like Ray and Joe
Monti look on them with unadulterated lust. Sometimes I
figure religions need more guilt. It's the ballast that keeps
the rituals honest and the social groups a little less satisfied
with themselves.

I reach the Seagram Building and cross the plaza with the
fountains. Larry Ackerman's on the other side of the revolving door as I pass through. I figure I'll follow him round the
door and talk with him, but from the way he waves and hurries off, I can see he'd rather not.

I go up in the elevator and past the receptionist to my office.
Beulah's out to lunch. My office looks clean. There's nothing
on the desk except a Xerox copy of a three-page letter agreement. Across the top it says Klein-Shorndorff. I stare at it. I
read it. I turn it over. I stare at it again. Then I pick it up and
walk to Mark Stillman's office. Susan's not there. She's taken
another personal day.

I enter Mark's office. He's sitting there with the closing
binder. It's stacked in three volumes in front of him.

"Here it is," he says. "It wasn't such a difficult assignment."

I can hardly talk.

"Where'd this come from?" I ask, holding the copy of the
Letter Agreement.

"I found the original in one of these boxes," he says, and
he points to the empty boxes piled along the back wall. "You
lost it, and I found it," he says, shaking his head with a look
of utter disdain. He picks up the phone and calls Heidi and

tells her to get Jim, and to make arrangements for overnight delivery to Brooks-Bollo in West Virginia. He sets the phone back down. He looks at me.

"Anything else?" he asks.

"You son of a bitch," I say, and we both know what's gone on here, and we both know it's too late for me to do a thing about it.

I leave his office and return to my own. I start making phone calls. It's not that I want to talk to anybody. It's just a nervous reaction to what's gone on. I call Mary and she's too busy to talk. I call Ray but he's out to lunch. I call Eddy at Jeanne's but there's no answer except for Jeanne's answering machine with the crazy sitar music in the background. Finally I reach Jeanne at the music studio.

"What's the matter?" she asks, and I start to tell her. Then I stop and ask her to meet me on the West Side in an hour.

"I don't know if I can," she says.

"Try," I say, "and bring Eddy if you know where he is."

"He's in New Jersey on an interview," she says. I ask her again. She says she'll do what she can, and we make it for late that afternoon.

When I was in law school I lived in a basement apartment on the West Side. It was inexpensive, and it was overrun with cockroaches. I did everything to get rid of them. But nothing worked. It was just one room with a bathroom off the back. Only a bookshelf separated the kitchenette from where I slept, and it was only two steps across a floor with dirty wood to the easy chair and the table I used for everything. At night I'd watch the shadows the people made as they walked by the windows. One night there was somebody standing there with his arms stretched out. I could see him clearly and I think I yelled with fear, though when I woke the next morning I wasn't sure if it had happened or if it had been a dream. I never stayed in the place any longer than I had to, and I spent all of my time in the school library. I didn't drink much then, and I was serious about things. My living conditions weren't the best, and I had no money, but I was younger then and full of energy and happy. I knew it was just the beginning of everything else and that the hard times wouldn't last forever and that everything would only get better.

Every night I bought my supper at this diner at the corner, where the waiters knew me and always told the chef to "make it nice" when I ordered my meal. After supper I'd walk across Lincoln Center on my way to the library. If I got there at the right time I'd watch the limousines pull up with the rich people, and I'd look at them, and I'd tell myself that the shortest route to Lincoln Center was to continue on to the library and to learn everything I was supposed to learn for the next day. I told myself that, no matter how difficult I found it, it was my job to succeed in school and then in the working world, and, after that, I'd have the means to drive about in limousines, to wear tuxedos on weeknights, to carry myself with that certain sense of accomplishment and pride reserved for those who make it to the top and have the good sense to stay there. That's what I told myself, and so I walked through the crowds and across the plaza, sometimes standing for a minute or two by the fountain, admiring the Marc Chagalls that hang in the windows there.

I'm sitting at the bar at O'Neal's and I'm looking out over the plaza at Lincoln Center. The Wednesday matinee performance has just gotten out. The plaza is full and crowded with traffic. The Marc Chagalls hang in the distance. They're brilliant things. I remember reading something about him, how he didn't know what light was until he moved to Paris, where the light changed him forever, and it was in Paris that he made his people fly over Russian villages, head over heels, upside down.

I've called Jeanne three times, but she can't get away, so I sit here by myself drinking slowly, trying to figure everything out. I watch some of the students walk across the plaza. They carry briefcases. Law students always carry briefcases. It's like part of their training. They're getting ready, trying on that piece of the armor before it's actually necessary.

About an hour ago there were some students standing by the fountain. They were arguing over something, each trying to convince the other how right they were, that what they'd heard or read meant something different from what the others had heard or read. I was tempted to join them, to tell them to stop, to tell them they were wasting their time, to tell them that what they think is important really isn't important at all. I wanted to tell them to be very careful about things they're not even concerned about, things like jokes and wisecracks and things like saying the wrong thing at the wrong time.

There are a couple of soap stars at the end of the bar. But I'm Mr. Cool; I'm Mr. New York. I don't even acknowledge them except for the little smile that says I know who they are, and that because I'm Mr. Cool, because I'm Mr. New York, I'm not going to trouble them with anything more than that.

The limousines begin to arrive, and men with silver hair escort women with silver hair across the plaza. There are many young people, too, hair slicked back, hair frosted and all of that. I shouldn't be sitting here. This is getting me nowhere. Sitting at this bar is not the shortest route to becoming one of them. Sitting at this bar is the shortest route to someplace else.

Jeanne doesn't show. Eddy doesn't show, either. They're busy now with their own lives. I have the bad habit of expecting too much from people. I want them to be witnesses.

The soap stars left hours ago. The place is full of patrons who are waiting for the curtains to go up, waiting for things to begin. They've got tickets. Things will begin for them whether they're ready or not. I'm not rushed like they are, but, then again, I don't get to see the show.

The bartender comes by and takes my order. He asks me my name. He says that a woman named Jeanne called to say that she couldn't make it, that she was stuck at work for the night.

"She asked me to give you this," he says.

"What's that?"

"It's a message," he says. "She made me write it down so I'd be sure to get it right," and he hands it to me. It's a sheet of notepaper with the bar's logo across the top. I read it and fold it up and put it in my pocket. I thank the bartender. I leave a good tip and then I leave. Later in the cab I pull it out again. I don't know whether to be mad or upset or flattered or what. I unfold it and read it. It doesn't make a lot of sense. I hold it up to the window and read it again. The streetlights catch every other word. It says: "Jesus Christ was the oldest soul of all."

I arrive at Susan's new apartment. There's no doorman, so I ring up, and she's surprised to hear from me. She hesitates awhile. Then she says it's all right for me to come up.

Her new apartment is small, and boxes are lined up everywhere. There's a bed and a TV and a table and a few other essentials, but she's living out of boxes.

She closes the door behind me. She's holding some clothes on a hanger. She throws them on the bed in the far alcove. Then she rummages through some more boxes and pulls out some other things. She's packing. She's going someplace.

"I missed you at work today," I say.

"You did?" she says, as if it's a pleasant thing to hear,

though she really doesn't want to hear it. There's a feeling of being rushed here. She's busy. I don't have her attention, though she's trying to make it look like I do.

"Yeah. I really needed to talk to somebody this afternoon."

"Oh?" she says, and she checks her nail after she catches it on a staple in the flap of the box near the foot of the bed.

"Mr. Westphall grilled me today," I say.

"Oh?" she says again, curious, but only politely curious.

"Yeah. And Mark was there, and Phil Wessen. They just about finished me off today."

"That Mark," she says, and she stands up straight and looks at the wall at the head of the bed. All of this is a major distraction for her because she wants to pack.

"How was the kayaking?" I ask.

"Great," she says, but it's one of those false "greats" where the voice rises just barely and then drops off and fades away.

"What's the matter?" I ask.

"Nothing," she says, and she turns quickly and spies some shoes near the closet. She hurries to pick them up.

"Nothing?" I say.

"I'm really in a hurry," she says. "Bill's coming by in about an hour and we're headed off for the weekend."

"Wait a minute," I say. "Bill who?"

"Bill Vierps," she says.

"Bill Vierps," I say.

"That's what I said," she says, and she blows by me with two gray sweaters and starts to fold their arms in so she can double them up and place them in the suitcase on the bed.

"You and Bill Vierps," I say.

"Yes," she says. "Me and Bill Vierps," and she sounds a little annoyed.

"Are you two, you know, like, going together?"

"Just for a long weekend," she says. "He's booked us into a

bed-and-breakfast on the Island. He says we'll be roughing it, though."

"Bill Vierps," I say.

"Yes."

"Roughing it," I say.

"Well."

I sit there and watch her. She says nothing. I say nothing. There's really nothing to say. I get up to leave, and as soon as I do she returns to her normal self.

"I'm sorry," she says, "but it seemed to be the way you wanted it. I mean . . . I don't know."

"It's all right," I say.

"Can I get you anything?" she asks. "Some soda or something to drink?"

"No," I say. "I think I'm all right," and I feel like I'm upside down, head over heels, walking across the sky, over a village, where the light is different and strange.

This happened when you were a kid:

It was the long weekend in mid-October, and you were home for the holiday. Earlier that afternoon, some kids from the neighborhood had knocked on the door and asked if they could play football in the field behind the tea-man's barn. You said "sure," because you knew your father didn't care about the untended field anymore, at least not in the way he had when you'd lived at home and when things were different for your parents.

After that you made the sandwiches your father liked with the cold meat from Sabia's and the French bread from Deloo's, and you took your seats in the den and turned on the TV to watch the football game. The TV was a bulky, oversize thing with a medium-size screen, and the colors were dull beneath an overwash of aqua and pink.

"I think you need a new TV," you said, and your father shrugged off the suggestion as if it had missed the point of something he'd just been thinking about.

"What's this about a new TV," Father Curry said, as he entered the den for the first time that week, taking your father's hand and shaking it, moving to the chair on the other side of the room as if he'd been there for hours, as if he belonged there, as if you or your father wanted him there.

"TV's fine," your father said, acknowledging the priest's

entrance in mid-thought, while Father Curry stood there at almost-attention, offering you two fingers of a halfhearted wave before he settled into the brown chair, the second-best chair in the room.

Despite the Irish burned to his bones and raised like the ashes of redeemed roses in a blue field of translucent skin, your father was not queer for priests like the other Knights of Columbus who fell all over themselves whenever a good father entered the room. Therefore, Father Curry was always and unceremoniously relegated to the second-best chair in the room, because your father was not about to offer the little man his chair, which was more comfortable and, at that moment, afforded the better view of the TV and the lanky wide receiver who'd just outrun a defensive back from South Carolina, known to be possessed of the tensile strength of spun steel.

It might have come as a surprise to you that your father didn't like priests in general, but it came as no surprise that your father didn't like Father Curry, even though he had to let him into the house every Sunday afternoon because your invalid mother had to have her Communion, and your father wouldn't deny her what she half-expected on the rare day when she knew what day it was.

The Giants called a time-out, and you got up to get a beer. As you left the room you heard the priest begin to talk, and you knew his monologue would probably go on forever because Father Curry was a talking machine. Talk was his substance, the thing he was made of. It flowed out of him, extending him, making him larger than he was, more substantial, more important; and it was the illusion he created, having long since failed to see himself in any light made less perfect than the grandiloquence of his mirrored self. Even when he allowed himself the rare moment of silence to catch his breath, the sound of his voice continued as an after-shadow of something once present and soon to return. And so, in a small room kept extra hot because your father took blood thinners, Father Curry held forth in full blow, a white powder puff of a man, glistening with the sheen of too much talc that creased the folds of his neck with short lines of white sweat.

When you returned the priest nodded, not to acknowledge you, but to remind himself to speak more quickly, so that your entrance wouldn't disturb the seamless sound of his voice, and with the studied reproach of a face highly skilled in the efficacy of certain expressions, he warned you that in his presence conversation was tantamount to impertinence. Then he started another diatribe about vocations and the high standards of the diocese, and all but directed you to take your seat on the couch and be still.

You watched the TV and the players in the brilliant jerseys who ran over a synthetic green field in the Midwest, where it was bright and still hot like summer. When some of the players gathered around one of their own who wasn't getting up, their hands effeminately cocked against their hips, a few with their helmets off, the sun glistening in the sweat running down their faces, you knew something was wrong, although the cracking sound that had stopped an entire stadium had made no impression on the priest.

"So I told him," Father Curry continued, "no matter what the shortage, we don't need priests that badly that we have to put up with nonsense. And of course I knew him, knew his older brother, too, the football player, probably played the same time as your brother."

"Pardon me, Father?" you said.

"I said his older brother probably played football the same time as your brother. Though he wasn't a kid, either, not the oldest, but not a kid. There was another one, from

New Jersey or New Orleans, I don't remember which; he was almost thirty-nine, which always makes me wonder what they think they're going to find if they haven't found it by then."

"I knew Tommy McGraw," you say.

"But that's just me," the priest went on, "and with all the distractions, maybe it takes longer today. But we don't keep everybody, and the first time I saw him I knew he drank too much, didn't even try to hide it, and I could see it was a problem. Used to be they'd just ship them off to Kingston, where they'd drink themselves to death with the natives to keep their rooms clean, though they've changed that and made it a school where they don't allow it except on holidays, you know, to keep it under control, though there's no way to keep it under control. If they've got a mind to drink, they'll drink."

Father Curry took a moment to rearrange himself. His legs were short, and the tips of his shoes barely touched the floor. He caught his breath, and the stadium erupted with applause as they carted off the player on a stretcher. He was the cornerback from South Carolina. Somebody had almost snapped him in two, but only his legs had given way. One arm dangled, and his limp fingers almost scraped the field. His other arm gave a short wave to the fans, but it fell so quickly it was hard to tell if he was all right or not.

Either Father Curry hadn't seen it or didn't care, because he just continued on about some whiskey-priest who'd scandalized some community outside of Bridgeport. The name of the city registered, but that was about all because you'd stopped listening and you were pretty sure your father had stopped listening, too. The Giants were losing, and you paid no more attention to the priest's voice than one pays to the barely audible, high-pitched hum that interrupts radios for wars and hard weather. You just let the sound roll along the edges and faces of objects, waiting until all reflections washed back upon themselves and disappeared.

Years ago you'd been told that Father Curry was a cousin or "something like a cousin" to your mother, and since that time Father Curry had been a fixture at the house, your own pet priest who performed the annual baptism or occasional wedding or funeral. Your mother had always paid him with bottles of Scotch and invitations to dinners and family gatherings, where he was treated with the suspicious and curious respect adults accord magicians; and, sometimes, when he was being particularly priestly, and the family was being particularly pious, with the vestiges of that awe in which children hold circus performers. It was the arrangement your mother wanted, not because she was particularly religious (at least not like her sister, Maureen), but because she entertained notions of a certain respectability that neither your father's salary nor the lingering stories of your brother's athletic abilities could afford. In short, your mother felt that being close to a priest might lend a certain something to the family.

The Giants scored, and the small roar from the visitors' seats subsided when the sportscasters raised the volume of their microphones and spread their coffee-colored voices over the noise. You measured the arc of the applause as it barely swept through the stadium, and you remembered the applause you'd heard on Friday nights at Fuessenich Park, when everyone in town had paid to watch your brother play football. The autumn nights were perfect then, and even during the excitement of the games a cold breeze and the crisp air would unexpectedly strike you with its beauty, and you'd think how perfect life could be despite everything that was mean and dark and poor in your hometown.

You didn't like your hometown. You'd called it a mean-spirited town separated by a river and a mean streak, because that's how it had been for you living there. You had longed for the day when you could move away from it, as you had when you first left for college. You weren't a hometown hero like your brother, and you figured that if you could get away on your own you'd be something else—maybe not a hero, but "something else." Those were your thoughts, and you clung to them the way people with small hopes cling to things. Your father didn't know that these were your thoughts, and even if he had, it wouldn't have made much difference between you, because there never seemed to be enough between you to mark your arrivals or your departures as being anything more unusual than the comings and goings of someone he knew from a distance and not very well.

Your father was the product of that strain of ascetic Irish made reticent by hardship and guilt. He was one of those angry men who practiced silence not for its meditative qualities but as a weapon to confuse and sometimes to control. Although he'd told you some things over the years, he'd done so only after time and distance had drained the stories of all emotion so that he could recount them in a quiet, unaffected voice, purged of his parents' brogue. His stories described life as it was without the unpredictable and sometimes lively feelings attendant to hopes for life as it could be. You recognized each session with your father as a marker of your growth, but the occasions for such talk were few and far between, because your father didn't speak unless it was absolutely necessary—and, in truth, it was never absolutely necessary.

Father Curry excused himself, with the kind of self-deprecating remark a person who's long been unconcerned with his audience offers on his departure, having grown suddenly concerned at the point of his departure, not with his audience, but with what they might say about him after he's gone. You touched your father's arm as you got up to follow him. Your father didn't look away from the TV screen. He just said: "When he's done, get him out of here," and you walked through the front rooms with the furniture from your grandmother's house and caught up to the priest ascending the stairs and listened to his labored breathing and, with each step, the scrape of polyester.

At the top of the stairs the priest turned and entered your mother's bedroom. The dusk light of November threw gray ash over the linens and the bedspread like a vapor of quietude in which the not-living, not-dying woman lay in a suspended state of forgetfulness and terminal fatigue, lying like a husk of leaves gathered under a blanket, shriveled, drawn up to herself, as if to collect herself to herself in order to keep intact whatever identity remained after an illness that had sculpted the frayed edges of herself from herself, like wind ever diminishing the circumference of leaves gathered for burning in a field.

In the alcove of bay windows her sister, your aunt Maureen, read her Latin missal from the old church. When Father Curry entered the room, she stood and took small steps on the toes of her oversize shoes, frowning and shaking her head in the sad half-sounds of sorrow. She pointed to what was little more than an object for dying, huddled and crumpled under covers. Then she returned to her chair, where she lowered her head and closed her eyes.

You watched from the doorway and felt resistance to your entering. Your aunt and the priest had made this their temple, their chapel, their mausoleum, and they orchestrated its rituals with inordinate care, as if grieving were an acquired skill or talent given to the few who are sensitive enough to appreciate the shadows of life as they wane to the great mystery of death.

In truth, Aunt Maureen and Father Curry couldn't stand one another, but as allies in a struggle for a common goal, they'd substituted process for personality, and the ritual they exercised with clipped and precise care, the artifice of something mimicking compassion, was the substance of their conspiracy in the joint effort of sweet suffering.

Your aunt relished the opportunity to pray in a semi-public way, as if the words she muttered in silence over the respirations of your mother's failed body were her way of chastising a world which had never stopped for her, a world which was beyond her, a world which had never appreciated her. In a world which had lost control, she deemed her prayers to be the sweetest revenge, and her sister's dying bed afforded her the perfect stage from which to hurl quiet admonitions in English and Latin at those who seemed to move so effortlessly through life. She prayed that they and their world would soon be engulfed in the wrath of a particularly angry Christ, if for no other reason than such an end was a proper and just end for all of those who had somehow conspired to make her life a miserable affair of endurance.

You knew that your aunt had never liked your mother, believing her sister to be a frivolous woman too concerned with money and social affairs. But now, in her final illness, your mother was more valuable to your aunt than merely being a person against whom Aunt Maureen could measure her outsized holiness. Now your mother provided her sister with the perfect sacrificial object for whom she could prepare altars of linens and quilts, perfumed with the scent of flowers, made holy by repetitive prayers to Jesus' mother.

As for Father Curry, he drew strength and identity from it all, eager to exaggerate the rituals attendant to the vigil, as if he knew certain secrets which the Lord had imparted to him regarding innocent suffering. Although he'd considered your mother to be a useful friend (knowing, as she had known, that any serious examination of the family lines would show that her Currys had been Careys from Waterford, and that both had indulged the charade of blood and common ancestry for their mutual benefit), he, too, no longer concerned himself with the person under the covers but only with the vessel of shallow breath who was about to die and with her death provide him with some focus, purpose, even authority.

You hung back. You were twenty-one and a law student, but you were still a kid, waiting at the door as they played their roles scripted for the portrayal of dark, purgative emotions. But the whimpering sadness of your aunt and the priest's offer of solace seemed to be nothing more than the well-rehearsed, cool displays of a self-conscious and measured response.

When your aunt saw you in the doorway she stiffened in her chair, because your presence might ruin everything. You might actually feel something; you might show some genuine concern, and that concern, that feeling, might cause you to say the wrong thing, to move too quickly, to conduct yourself without the proper solemnity. So she didn't acknowledge you. Instead she watched the priest as he took a purple stole from his pocket, unfolded it, kissed it, and draped it around his neck. Then from a small gold ciborium that opened like a large pillbox, he took one white wafer of unleavened wheat, the size of a quarter, made the sign of the cross, and placed the wafer between the lips of the barely conscious woman. After he finished, Aunt Maureen joined him by the bedside. Again they talked in whispers. You watched her as she raised her hand to her forehead, and you wondered why some acts appear genuine and others appear false. You questioned whether there might be something real and compassionate in their sadness. You wondered if you'd judged them too harshly, and you were about to say something kind, but they ignored you as they left the room. At the head of the stairs the priest placed a finger to his lips. He said: "There now," to comfort the woman who pretended to be sad.

You felt awkward and hurt, and your feelings for your mother became confused with everything else until the commingled emotions unsteadied you as you entered the room and walked to the bed hoping, even suspecting, that the figure under the sheets would miraculously appear healthy again. You hoped that from across the room her appearance had been a mistake of the eye caused by the interplay of light and shadows, and that at some point as you approached her lying there you would see that she was really quite fine, resting comfortably, essentially healthy, but a little tired. You hoped that she'd look at you and recognize you, and that her eyes would be warm and her voice would be warm and she'd be happy to see you and want to comfort you, as you wanted to comfort her. So, as you approached her bed, your hopes for her well-being almost distracted you from the impact of the sight of the woman who lay before you. And then you saw her without any illusions, and no thought, however kind or hopeful, could diminish the impact of the eyes that stared without movement or life at nothing.

You remembered the day when her eyes had died to any light within her, the day when they were wild with the pain of betrayal as Father Curry had tried to walk her to the car for the trip to the home. On that day in the early summer, although she'd lost most sense and memory and strength, she knew what they were about to do and that it was something your father had promised he'd never do, having given in to Father Curry, who was all for carting her off to the nursing home, saying: "It's the best thing."

On that day the sun was too hot, and the doctor had spoken with your father, and your father had listened as the bad news multiplied like another disease—a disease of the spirit, which, having spread over everything, invaded the tissue of his will until he was tired and changed, passive to the onrush of the most fundamental things. And it was in the grip of this disease that your father, with the sun crowding his forehead and driving his eyebrows hard together over the bridge of his nose, had let the priest break his (your father's) promise and usher your mother from the steps of the porch down the walkway to the car. And it was on that day in the early summer, somewhere between the bend on the sidewalk where Augie and Vinny DiLorenzo had mispoured the concrete twenty years before that your mother more than felt, more than knew, that something was wrong—more than knew that the world that shone about her, in the unforgiving shafts of sun on the hot land that wasn't made cool even by the oaks in the front yards along the street, was wrong—more than knew that the short man with the roll of gut bulging in the black shirt over the black belt looped around his black polyester pants was someone she'd never really known, someone distant, alien, and strange as he bore down upon her, sensing her resistance, barely able to restrain the pressure with which he wished to dispose of her in the car, speaking soft words of encouragement, forcing himself to adopt the gentle pressure of persuasion used by military men as they direct traffic and move crowds. "Everything will be all right," he said as she looked from his face to the car and back to your father, who with his two-day stubbly white beard just stood there. Then she spun around, her eyes dark and hollow with the sense of being violated by this stranger who was taking her from her home and her bed, and, with the cotton house-coat flashing open in the sun, uncovering her shiny and blue-veined legs, she raised her arm with the strength that comes to drowning men when they'll take their rescuer down with them, looked at her husband, and closed her eyes that had died already with the clarity of betrayal. She moved away from the priest with determined yet faltering steps. She opened her mouth and made to scream, and it was then, at the moment when the air had not been broken by a sound that would have killed you, that you, who'd watched it all like the quiet and observant son you'd always been, stepped between her and the priest, took her by the arm, and led her back to the house, up the stairs to her bed, where she lay for weeks breathing shallow, paper-dry breaths that barely moved the shadows along the white cotton quilt that rested against her bony old body like a shroud.

RESUME PLAY, MR. McENROE

The first thing I do is look for Lester Bartok. I figure, OK, I'll never make partner at this place, but I can work for a guy who doesn't stay awake nights thinking up ways to terrorize me. It's mid-morning and the place is pretty quiet. Brooks-Bollo is history, and I'm as anonymous as I was in September before it all began.

I head down to sixteen and approach the corner office where Marty sits. It's dark. He and Mark Stillman are out of town, negotiating one more deal. I turn the corner and head to the back of the building, past the conference room and Larry Ackerman's office. I figure I'll tell Lester about the meeting with Mr. Westphall. I hope he'll be able to put it into perspective. I'll ask some questions about France. I'll talk about Paris and what I know about it from the books Hemingway wrote.

I reach his office and the lights are off. His secretary's taking directions from the blonde with the English schoolboy glasses. They talk a little business, and then the secretary tells the blonde about some concert she went to on the Island with Tony. Tony sounds like a tough guy, and the secretary brags about the way Tony handled some locals. The blonde listens. She's very polite, a vestige of her breeding, but she really couldn't care less. Finally Lester's secretary looks at me, and it's like this big problem for her to talk to me. I ask her where Mr. Bartok is. She says: "He's gone."

"Gone?"

"That's right," and she goes back to her typing. She's busting my balls; she doesn't want to tell me another thing.

"Do you know when he'll be back?"

"Don't know," she says. "Could be a week, could be two weeks."

The English schoolboy blonde then tells me that Lester's gone to France.

"A vacation?" I ask.

"He takes one every six months or so," the blonde says, "and he was due."

"He was due, all right," Lester's secretary says, and I look at her big hair, all teased up and stretched out as if each strand had been scraped naked of its electrons, all of it left to stand there like a screaming tiara.

"Can I help you?" the blonde asks.

"No, thanks," I say.

I head back down the corridor. I look for Larry Ackerman, but he's also out of the office. It's a bad day for making connections.

I return to my office. I have to walk by Mr. Westphall's office and I dread that, but as I approach the corner where he sits, I see that the lights are off, and he's someplace else. Phil Wessen's standing in the corridor, though, entertaining the secretaries as he swings his tennis racket. I'm tempted to ask him about the arcane origin of words, but I think better of it and try to slip quietly by him. He's talking about some temper tantrum McEnroe threw at Wimbledon, and he talks about it as if he were actually there. One of the secretaries says: "I think he's cute," meaning McEnroe.

Phil sees me walk by.

"There he is," he says, and I turn with that stupid smile I put on without thinking. He fakes this over-the-head serve with this imaginary tennis ball, and I stop and look at the tip of my shoe and drag it slowly across the carpet and point to where I've darkened the carpet fiber.

"Out," I say.

"C'mon, that was in," he says, and I say, "Resume play, Mr. McEnroe," and he doesn't know whether he should take the setup and throw a phony tantrum or not. He doesn't. He just laughs a good natural laugh and follows me to my office.

"How are you today?" he asks.

"Honestly?" I ask.

"Not if it's depressing," he says.

"Then I'm fine," I say.

"Let's go for some coffee," he says.

"Why not," I say.

"Bring your briefcase," he says.

"What for?" I ask.

"I might want you to take some notes," he says. "Just bring it. I'll explain."

We head outside, and I figure this is a definite plus because he seems like a normal guy, and he's got Mr. Westphall's ear. I can tell him the real story, the story behind the story, and he'll listen, and he'll be sympathetic, and when the time's right, he'll tell Mr. Westphall what really happened; and, no, I'll probably never make partner, but I can work for two years, get a good recommendation, and move on to some-place else.

The air is cold and the sky is overcast. We walk a block or two. There are Halloween party favors in the windows of the stores. There are masks and costumes hanging in the win-dows of a five-and-dime on Lexington. The president stands next to the Wolf Man. The masks sag in like the features are melting, and both look grotesque.

"When's Halloween?" he asks.

"Tonight," I say.

"Damn," he says.

"What's the matter?" I ask.

"I'll have to take my kids around the building."

"Oh," I say, and I think: Yeah, that is a big problem.

We find a small restaurant that's still serving breakfast, and we take a booth near the back. The waitress hands us menus before we sit down. I stuff my trench coat and briefcase in the corner of the seat.

Phil orders coffee for both of us and says we need a minute or two. I'm not hungry, but I figure I'll get a buttered roll. Phil says he just wants coffee for now.

"I can't believe what I saw yesterday," he says.

"It's pretty unbelievable," I say.

"All of that over one closing binder."

"Yeah," I say.

"So what really happened?" he asks, and I figure this is my only chance to get the story back to Mr. Westphall, so I tell Phil Wessen everything, and I spare nothing, not even the parts about Susan and the breakup with her husband and the laugh heard round the world.

"And if you ask me," I say, "I'm sure that he had the Letter Agreement the whole time, locked up in his office someplace, just waiting for it all to blow up, though I don't think he expected it to go as far as the letter to Mr. Westphall."

Phil sits there. Now he's heard it all, and it's like he can't believe it. I think that I've convinced him of my innocence in the whole thing, and I feel pretty good about telling the story. I think maybe Westphall, Sellars does have a heart.

"Thanks," I say. "I appreciate that you listened to me."

"I'm sorry," he says. "It just makes this all the more difficult."

"What's that," I say.

"Do you remember the orientation session we had for the first-year associates? It was back in September."

"I'm afraid I missed that," I say. "There was this problem with the subway, and . . ."

"Yeah, sure, well, the firm made it clear then that we have this ninety-day policy."

"A what policy?"

"It's a ninety-day policy," he says. "It's like a ninety-day free-look provision. It means that if for any reason during the first ninety days the firm feels that things aren't working out with an associate, we can . . . you know . . ."

He hesitates. Nothing registers. I'm trying to remember what this ninety-day policy has to do with anything. I'm trying to figure out what he's saying, and I'm staring at my spoon as I draw it over the table, making a small line of coffee that will stain the table.

"So what we've decided, meaning what the partnership has decided, is to exercise our rights under the policy effective today, right now."

"What are you saying?"

"What I'm saying is that the firm is letting you go."

"I'm fired?"

"You're fired."

"No," I say.

"Yes," he says. "I've got this for you." He pulls an envelope from his suit jacket. He hands it to me. "There's a month's severance there, which is better than standard. Your personal effects will be boxed and delivered to your apartment this afternoon. You're not to return to the office, though."

"Wait a minute," I say. I say, "Lester Bartok and I are going to work together. He told me so before he left."

"I'm sorry," Phil says, "but this is something the partnership has already voted on."

I look at the envelope with my name on it.

"There's information in there about medical coverage and whatever else. Lois has set it all out for you."

He gets up to leave. He places money on the table for the coffee. He starts to leave. Then he stops. He debates whether to say something else. He decides against it, and he leaves.

I sit there. The waitress comes by and picks up the money. She asks if I need anything. I tell her no. I tell her that I'm all set.

LOST SOULS PARTY

I'm bothering people at the bar at the Lemon Lime. There's this one couple there, and I'm standing there with my head over her shoulder, talking to this guy with my who-the-fuck-do-you-think-you-are voice, because he's wearing a stupid tuxedo and red low-top sneakers, and with his shiny well-scrubbed face and hair slicked back, he's acting like he's some kind of big-town swell from someplace obnoxious, and I'm not going to take it from anybody tonight.

The bartender's watching me, but it's Halloween and he's got all kinds of wackos at the bar, dressed up in tuxedos and other weird little outfits, so I'm just a blip on the whole wacko scene.

Tonight I'm getting real drunk, that kind of drunk where I don't give a fuck about anything, that kind of drunk where I feel like I'm continually entering new rooms and closing doors behind me, doors that lock as soon as they close so there's no going back no matter what.

The kid in the tuxedo puts his arm around his girl and escorts her off to a booth in the back, and I see another couple sitting there. He's got silver hair, and he looks like a younger version of a guy who wrote a book about how not to get screwed on Wall Street, and I walk up to them, and they ignore me, and she's got her back to me, and I put my head over her shoulder, and I'm saying, "Who the fuck do you people think you are, sitting there?" And it's a stupid question, and it's like I'm just begging for somebody to take my head off and put me out of my misery, but it doesn't happen. He just sits there, and he ignores me, and nobody spends the energy to acknowledge what I'm doing, and I'm like the Invisible Man screaming from the margins, and I say something about all these frivolous bastards with their hair in this fucking Babylon, when the bartender stops by and asks them if everything's all right. They say nothing, and I just slink off to the back, and when I get there there's this whole crowd of them standing around, and they're all these swells with their breeder-dates, talking their useless we're-too-rich-to-work talk, and all the guys are wearing these red sneakers as if it's a class concession to the charm of the holiday. They're all waiting to go upstairs to the ballroom. It's one of their theme parties. There's a sign there that says "Lost Souls Party," because these swells all want to be Scott or Zelda, and I'm about to get on a table and tell them that they wouldn't know a lost soul if they tripped over one. Then there's this stupid bullet-headed guy with his average girl, and it's obvious that he's still got all that lip-sputtering righteous Johnny-Marine anger of macho men from conventional bars, and he's decided to take my head off. So I walk right up to him with my little hands of stone, and I say to this dumb country fuck who's about a foot taller and many pounds heavier than me: "Just who the fuck are you, Gomer?" and I wait for the explosion that's going to split my jaw and paralyze my arms. But it doesn't happen, because somebody grabs me from behind and pulls me away. It's Eddy, and he's wearing one of those tuxedos and the red sneakers, and he says something like, "Let's get out of here," as he tries to smooth it with the huge guy, who's so pissed he wants to break some furniture.

Eddy drags me to a booth in the back, where he's sitting with Jeanne and Mary and Ray. Ray's got a tuxedo on, too, and Mary's got this super-expensive gown on, and Jeanne's got one of her long Earth Mother dresses on, and Eddy says:

"What is the matter with you?" and he's pissed because this confirms what Ray and Mary have been saying about me. There's nothing I can say, because I don't want to tell anybody what's wrong; and I'm so drunk, I'm staggering, and there's nothing funny about this.

They're all going to the Lost Souls Party, and none of it makes sense. I know that I've lost them, and Mary tells me the "good news," which is that her father has given Eddy a job at his firm on Wall Street. There's a bottle of champagne stuck in a bucket there. Ray says how great everything is, and he ignores me like I'm some kind of leper he knew in a previous life before things went bad on the big wheel. Only Jeanne is really concerned, and she looks at me with her Lady of Sorrows look, and I just look away with my head moving faster than my eyes so that they have to swim across my field of vision in order to catch up with everything else.

It's like something should be said here. It's like they should say something, or I should say something to wrap it all up. Somebody should just admit the fact that life can go wrong for some people, but there isn't anything to say, because it's all so obvious and evident as we sit there.

The room begins to clear out. The others are beginning to make their way up the spiral staircase to the ballroom, where the bass has begun to throb and shudder its sound down the walls. Ray asks whether they should take the champagne, but Mary's in a hurry. She says no. She says there's plenty more where that came from. Only Eddy stays a step or two behind, looking a little embarrassed and apologetic about it all.

"Are you going to be all right?" he asks, and before I can answer, two muscle-men bouncers are standing behind me. One says, "That's him," and they grab me under the arms, and because I'm a coward I just go limp, and I don't care what happens to me. They're going to throw me out, and some of the people in the tuxedos and the gowns look on, and the big beefy asshole who dropped the dime on me starts applauding and howling to the moon like some cracker from a white-trash neighborhood. Eddy tries to intervene. He says he'll take responsibility for getting me out of the place if they'll just take their hands off me. They say OK, because Eddy's got a tux on, and they don't know how well he's connected. So Eddy walks me to the door, and the bouncers walk behind us, and there's this applause from the whole room as I leave. Then I'm standing outside on the street, and Eddy's standing at the doorway. He's not coming with me. He's got a new job and a tux and a party to go to. He says: "Call me," like the way people say it when they hope you don't remember, and it doesn't matter, because even if I do remember enough time will have passed and enough things will have happened that he'll have all kinds of new excuses to put me off. Outside there are people walking the streets, and they're wearing costumes and masks, and everybody feels the need to frighten everybody else, so I start the long walk home, talking to myself for the sake of the company on the scariest night of the year.

THOSE KOLIKS WERE ALWAYS CRAZY

I lean over and pick out the little clear space on the mirror. I shake the plastic head of the razor under the water. The floor is cold. It's cold outside. It's hard to heat these old houses.

It's been three days. The first day wasn't bad because I was so hungover. But the second day was bad. I figure today will be bad, too. I still have the headache, and I sweat all the time, even when I'm cold. Last night I just felt nervous about everything. It was a long ride, and I wasn't used to the rental car. When I reached Hartford I was tempted to stop off at a place and have a couple to ease myself down. But I didn't. I'm serious about this.

My father was surprised to see me. It took a little dancing to get around what I was doing, showing up the way I did, late at night. I don't want to tell him the hard things. I don't want to tell him where I'm going. I told him about business meetings upstate and how I took a detour on the way back. I told him things were OK.

I open the door to the bathroom and listen as he calls from the foot of the stairs. There's the smell of breakfast and coffee. He asks me what I want. I tell him coffee and some juice. I don't know what my stomach can take these days. It's always full with something.

———

I finish shaving and pull a comb through my hair. I'll be bald before I'm thirty. I look at my eyes. They're clear, but they look tired. My nose looks red and sore. It is sore. I'm young, but I've changed.

I go to my room. There's the bookshelf with the books I read when I was a kid. There's a trophy with the little gold swimmer. There's a ribbon and a painting by Andrew Wyeth. The desk is there, too. I did a lot of homework at that desk. I was a good student. I was even good in physics, and that surprised everybody.

I put on a suit and a new tie. I've got to look good. I've got to pull this thing off.

I walk down the back stairs and I'm about to enter the kitchen. I can hear my father talking with his sister. They just returned from the cemetery. Every morning Aunt Meg stops by and picks him up and they drive to church and then to the cemetery. It's a ritual.

My aunt Meg is a good person. She takes care of my father now. She loves him, and it's a good thing. He needs someone to look after him. He hasn't been the same for years.

My aunt is saying that Gerry Kolik told his former wife, Sheila, that he didn't care what any court order said, he'd take the kids so far away she wouldn't ever be able to find them. My aunt Meg has a rich and textured voice. She used to smoke cigarettes, but she gave them up when she started to worry about getting cancer. When I enter the kitchen she places her cup down. She turns to me; her voice rises. She's pleased to see me.

"Passing through on business," she says, and she asks me the name of the law firm where I work. She says her daughter called her weeks ago looking for my number. She says it must be exciting working in New York on Park Avenue. She says it's the very place for a young man to be. Then she asks me about the nightlife there, and she says it mustn't be any trouble for a young man like me to be out there on the town breaking all the young girls' hearts. She says she wishes she were young again. She says that growing old can be a cruel joke.

I kiss Aunt Meg, and I sip the orange juice in the tall glass. My father asks me again if I want something to eat. He says it's a long trip back to the city. He says a meal would do me good. I say no. I say that I never eat breakfast anymore. I tell him I'll have to leave soon because there's a big deal going on in the office, and Mr. Bartok is depending on me to be there.

My father turns to the stove and flips the eggs in the large skillet. Then he turns the bacon. The sound of the bacon crackles in the kitchen, and the sound of my aunt's voice crackles with the sound of the bacon. She asks me more questions about New York. She asks me to describe Park Avenue. She asks if there really are small pine trees planted up and down the center of the street. She says she hasn't been to New York since she and her husband went there over thirty years ago. "I couldn't believe how crowded a place could be," she says, and then she tells me how impressive it was and how she'd like to go back sometime for a visit.

"It's OK," I say, "but it's like every place: It's good and it's bad," and I try to steer the conversation to topics other than New York City.

My aunt says she's certain that Gerry Kolik has taken the twins to New York City, because there are so many people there he'd figure that he'd never get caught. She says that Gerry Kolik always thought he was a New York kind of person with the flashy car he drove and the fancy suits he wore.

"The people around here never could understand what Sheila saw in him," she says, and she says how Sheila was such a pretty girl.

"Those Koliks were always crazy," my father says, and he sets my aunt's plate down in front of her.

"You knew her," my father says.

"Who's that?" I ask.

"Sheila Donovan," he says.

"Yeah. I think I remember her," I say.

My father takes his plate and sits at the head of the table. He starts to tell my aunt some more about Westphall, Sellars, things I've told him on the phone when I'd call him on Saturday afternoons to see how he was doing.

My aunt asks me about my apartment, and my father tells her that I live in a place where an actress from one of the soap operas lives. I remember I'd told him that because I thought it might impress him. My aunt finds it all real interesting, and she says how everybody is proud of me for having made it to the big time with my law job in New York City.

"Like I said," I say, "it's like everything else: It's got its good points, and it's got its bad points, too."

They finish their breakfast. Then my aunt says that Father McCormick gave a very nice little sermon about storing up treasures in heaven. She says how happy she is with the church since the bishop moved Father Curry to someplace else.

"That fat little man almost ruined the parish," she says, and my father says nothing. They drink their coffee and pass the paper between them. This is something they do every morning. My father reads the sports pages. He likes to read about the football team at the high school. He says they beat Naugatuck for the first time since my brother played. I say that's something. My aunt looks at her part of the paper, and she reads the headline about the late-season hurricane that devastated some islands off the coast of South Carolina.

"Those poor people," she says, and she goes on about what it would be like to have to leave your place and know that a hurricane is coming.

"I saw it on the news," she says, "the night before it hit. They were gathering their things and getting off the island, and they knew that when they went back there'd be nothing there. How does a person deal with something like that, having to leave the place where you live?"

My father says nothing, and I finish my juice and stir the spoon in the mug of hot coffee. My father watches me and pushes the sugar and the cream across the table. I tell him that I drink it black now, and he just looks at me.

"We'll have to change those flowers," he says, and he's talking about the headstone at the cemetery. "Maureen said she was going to do it, but she didn't do it."

"You can't rely on her," Aunt Meg says, and my father nods.

"They must have some nice arrangements for this time of year," he says. He looks at me. "Your mother always liked this time of year, leading up to the holidays."

I excuse myself. I tell them I have to make a phone call. I stumble slightly as I leave, catching myself on the corner of the table. After I leave the kitchen I hear my aunt say that I was never a "graceful" boy, and my father says that my brother was certainly the athlete in the family. My aunt says, "That one," and laughs.

I walk through the front rooms and up the stairs to my father's bedroom. It's November, and the light is dull outside, and the room is dark. I pick up the phone on the night table in the alcove. His books are there. The blue one is called the "Big Book." The other one is this small black book. It says *One Day at a Time* across the cover. He reads these books, and he stays sober.

I dial the number, and the digits make their short tones. My cousin answers. She's been waiting for my call.

"So, how's it going?" she asks.

I tell her things are OK. I tell her that her mother is downstairs with my father. I tell her that they just returned from church and their daily trip to the cemetery. I tell her that they don't know a thing about what's happened or about what I plan to do.

"Greg checked with the hospital," she says. "It's called Serenity Hall. It's the one they send the policemen to."

"OK."

"So how long are you planning on staying?" she asks.

"How long is the program?"

"Two weeks inpatient," she says.

"Then I guess two weeks," I say.

"It'll be all right," she says.

"Maybe," I say.

"I guess it's final with the job?"

"It's final."

"What about that partner you talked about?"

"He's out of the country," I say. "And he's got his own problems."

"Oh," she says, and there's nothing left to say. I feel this fatigue that makes me want to sit down and think things over, take a long rest and start over again.

"We'll talk about all of this later," she says. She tells me to be careful driving, and she gives me the directions again.

I leave my father's room. I walk by the doorway to my mother's room. There's nothing there anymore. Just the bed and a chair and a bureau. Everything is draped in white. The room is on the south side of the house. It catches all of the light.

Down the hallway, I sit in my room, and I stare at the bag sitting on the bed. I pack the few things I brought with me. I wonder if there's anybody else I should call. But there isn't.

Everybody's busy, and it's not the thing busy people want to hear about. I've left a lot of busy people back in New York.

I look in the mirror again. I turn off the overhead light. The copper chain swings in a small arc and scratches the green plastic shade. I listen to the wind brush against the window by the bed. I pick up my bag and my coat and start down the stairs.

My aunt says she thinks it was Gerry Kolik's gambling that made Sheila divorce him in the first place. "I never did understand why she married him," she says, and then she looks up, and she sees me standing there.

"Leaving so soon?" she asks.

"It is Sunday," my father says.

"I know," I say, "but we work on Sundays, too. That's what the phone call was all about."

"No rest for success," my aunt says, and she tells me to take it easy. She tells me not to get ahead so quickly that I don't take some time to enjoy myself along the way.

I tell her not to worry, and I kiss her, and I pick up my bag.

"Are you sure you don't want any breakfast?" my father asks, and I wish he weren't so concerned. It'd be easier if he just let me go. It wouldn't hurt so bad, if he just let me go.

I tell him no. I tell him I'm fine.

"We shouldn't stand in the way of our young lawyer," my aunt says, and my father turns to her and stands up and walks with me to the car. There's a chill from the night air that settles in this valley and doesn't burn off until noon. I can see his breath, and I tell him not to catch a cold. He shrugs his shoulders as if to say don't worry about that. I put my arms around him, and I hold him. He's smaller than he was. He's lost some weight, and I hold him hard. Enough time has passed that we can do this now.

He asks me if everything is all right.

I say, "Everything's fine, Dad." Then he tells me to be careful, and I walk to the car.

I turn and wave to him and to my aunt, who's standing on the back porch. They wave good-bye. My father smiles, but he looks old and tired.

I start the car and drive to the center of town. I turn west toward Goshen and the New York State Thruway. It's a couple of hundred miles to Syracuse.

As the morning passes I dare to feel better. The headache is gone, and I'm not as nervous as I was. Some of the other pains have gone, too. I put on the radio real low—just a sound to keep me company. I try to breathe more easily, and I try to forget certain things. I look beyond the road to the brown hills and the almost-bare trees standing in the hard light of the low sun. I listen to the imaginary call of birds perched on the branches of trees. I measure the shadows that stain the dark road, and I feel the brush of cold air as the car is quietly peeled by the winds that must have blown all the way from Canada.

ACKNOWLEDGMENTS

I want to thank Adam Chromy, my agent, and John Flicker, my editor, for their faith, support, good taste, intelligence and wisdom, without which this book would still be a manuscript hidden away somewhere.

ABOUT THE AUTHOR

Attorney, artist, and screenplay writer, Michael Hogan lives in Lakewood, Ohio. This is his first book.